# The Canyon of Bones

# The Canyon of Bones

## RICHARD S. WHEELER

A TOM DOHERTY ASSOCIATES BOOK / NEW YORK

This is a work of fiction. All of the characters, organizations, and events portrayed in this novel are either products of the author's imagination or are used fictitiously.

THE CANYON OF BONES

Copyright © 2007 by Richard S. Wheeler

This book is printed on acid-free paper.

A Forge Book
Published by Tom Doherty Associates, LLC
175 Fifth Avenue
New York, NY 10010

www.tor.com

Forge® is a registered trademark of Tom Doherty Associates, LLC.

Library of Congress Cataloging-in-Publication Data

Wheeler, Richard S.
    The canyon of bones  /  Richard S. Wheeler.
        p.   cm.
    "A Tom Doherty Associates Book."
    ISBN-13: 978-0-765-31324-9
    ISBN-10: 0-765-31324-3
    I. Title.
    PS3573.H4345C26   2007
    813'.54—dc22

                                                                    2006102846

Printed in the United States of America

0   9   8   7   6   5   4   3   2

For Win and Meredith Blevins

# The Canyon of Bones

# One

It was time to take another wife. Barnaby Skye had been thinking about it for a long time, and knew he could not put it off. White streaked his hair and the trimmed beard he wore these days. His youth was gone.

He wanted a child, a boy if God would give him one. All these years he had hoped. But Victoria was barren or maybe he was, who could say? He had no child and thus was the poorest of men.

A man without a child does not see far into the future or care about it; he can live only in the past or present, as Skye was doing more and more. It was as if life had become sunsets rather than sunrises, memories rather than dreams.

He loved to awaken early, even before first light, and slip outside his lodge into the sweet morning air. Then he would stretch, enjoy his own well-rested body, and walk to a nearby hill to greet the day and to pray in his own way.

Now he stood on a ridge, the Absaroka village still slumbering in half-light below him, while he absorbed the blue dawn and the quickening light that began to give color to a gray world. On clear days, such as this one, dawns started out blue, a thin line of blue across the eastern horizon, promising the return of the sun and the stirring of life.

Those were the best moments. Victoria would still be asleep, warm under the thick buffalo robes in winter or a light two-point Hudson's Bay blanket in softer seasons. All the years of their marriage she had been his companion, adventuring where he did, sharing his joys and perils. He loved her.

And now he was aware of the passage of time. The life he had chosen had taken its toll on his body. One could not live as the nomadic Absarokas did without experiencing bitter cold and torpid heat, starvation, poor diet, thirst, and always the danger of war or pestilence. Ancient injuries, some of them going back to the days of his youth when he was a British seaman, would lurk in his body, awaiting the chance to hurt again. And his long thick nose, battered and broken by brawls, was as sensitive to hurt as baby's flesh.

The Crows, as they were called by white trappers, were blessed with a land that usually offered abundant food and hides from the thick herds of buffalo roaming the prairies; that offered strong wiry ponies descended from Spanish Barb stock released by the conquistadors. There were cool mountain valleys to comfort them in summers, sun-warmed river flats to pull the sting out of winter, alpine meadows rioting with spring wildflowers, tumbling mountain waterfalls, and bald eagles riding updrafts, to make a poet of each Crow.

It was a good land if the Crow people could keep it. When Skye thought of the changes that were disrupting the world just over the horizons, he wondered what the future would bring for these cheerful people. Off to the south a vast migration of Yanks heading for the Oregon country and California had decimated grass and wildlife and woodlands for miles to either side of the trail. Riverboats plied their way up the treacherous Missouri, discharging adventurers as well as goods deep in this land where the tribes had been sovereign for as long as their memory knew.

But so far, the life of the Absarokas hadn't changed much. It followed the stately passage of the seasons, and Victoria's people were just as they always were. Her band, the Kicked-in-the-Bellies, drifted from cool mountain valleys in summer to hunting on the plains in the fall to protected river flats in the winter. Its hunters had little trouble making meat; its gatherers had little trouble harvesting buffalo berries, chokecherries, wild onions, various roots and vegetables.

This late summer day, the Crow people would begin their trek southward for their annual encampment with the Shoshones to trade and gossip, and to cement the alliance that helped both peoples to resist the dangerous Sioux and Blackfeet and their allies, the Cheyenne and Gros Ventres or Atsina, and sometimes the Arapaho.

These were festive days. The band would load its possessions on travois, and then meander south past the Pryor Mountains, south past the Big Horn Mountains, then through an arid land along the great river called the Big Horn, to rendezvous with the Shoshones. There they would make sweet the days of late summer, enjoy the cool eves, flirt, smoke the red-stone pipes, and dream. This year the place would be on the extreme west edge of the Big Horn Valley, where pine forests guarded the land of geysers far above. It was a good place.

It would take Victoria only a little while to load the two travois. He and Victoria had a small buffalo-hide lodge and few possessions. He might be a headman, a war leader for her people, but he was not rich the way most Crow chiefs and chieftains were. They had many wives to make them wealthy.

A good hunter could keep a dozen women busy cooking meat, making pemmican for winter, and scraping and tanning hides that could be traded at the various posts for all sorts of treasures, such as guns and powder and lead, beads, knives, awls, calico, and great kettles. Some headmen had hundreds of horses that could be traded for valuable things. Skye had only a few horses. Jawbone, his strange, ugly blue roan medicine horse, was chief among them. There were a few more, two riding horses and two travois horses, and a few half-broken mustang colts for the future.

His family was too small. Victoria was forced to do everything, and had no one to share the heavy load of daily toil. Neither did she have any children or sisters or grandmothers in her household to share the day with, to gossip with, to talk about herbs and medicines with, to discuss ailments with, to sew with, to make moccasins with, to dig roots with, to pound berries into fat and shredded meat with. It grieved her, having no other wife to share the toil of this household. It wore her down. Other senior wives among her people were luckier. There were younger wives to share the work. They were like servants, responding to the bid and call of the older or first wife, the sits-beside-him wife. It was a matter of status. It was the right of the first wife to have the company and service of young wives.

Which is why Victoria, as much as she loved Skye, was often moody and even angry, and spent much of her time away from his small and sterile lodge, preferring the society of other women.

But there was something else. No self-respecting headman among the Absaroka people would think of having just one wife. A man's authority was measured by his wives. His wealth was measured in wives. His status as an important man among the people was metered by wives. Even a young and modest youth who had counted coup once or twice, and dreamed of being a great leader of his people, managed a couple of wives. And a chief often had six or eight, and sometimes even more, and had fat lodges, with extra poles to hold up all that buffalo hide, to house his menagerie. And those fat lodges teemed with children too. A chief might have half a dozen, plus two or three pregnant wives to increase his family.

It had taken Skye a long time to realize that Victoria was ashamed of him, for he had but one wife, a small lodge, no children, and few horses. Yes, he was esteemed as a hunter and his Hawken had contributed much meat to the band as well as defending it against horse thieves, Blackfeet raiders, and the ominous and ever-present Sioux.

How often Victoria had hinted, and finally begged for a larger lodge. Far from dreading the presence of another wife or considering one a potential rival, she had pleaded for one or two or a dozen. And there it had stopped. Something in Barnaby Skye had faithfully adhered to the European way of looking at marriage: one man and one woman, bound sacredly together always. He had her and he loved her; why seek anyone else?

He had always been hesitant. How could he split love in two? How could he bring another woman into his lodge and love and nurture her as he had tried to love and nurture Victoria? How could he divide himself in such fashion? How could he spend his nights in the arms of one and not the other? How could he even embrace one while the other lay inert in her robes, well aware of those intimacies that would fill the lodge with soft noises? How did the Absaroka people manage such things, except by indifference, and a sense of wedlock that had more to do with convenience and child-bearing than love? In this tribe the women formed their own nation and society; the men formed another, and little did the separate nations care about one another. Find a gathering, a party, a smoke, a feast, and it would usually be all women or all men.

He had not sought anyone else. At least until now. This dawn he was afflicted with two desolating thoughts. One was that he had wounded Victoria, not heeding her wishes and hopes and dreams. And yet she had faithfully abided in his lodge all these years, even as his own hair was graying and his life was beginning to enter its last chapters. The other, felt just as keenly, was a sense of loss. He would leave no child behind him. He would be a dead end. With him, the race of Skyes would stop. He was a sole son and if he brought no child into the world, the sun would set.

It was an odd and sad moment. Had he grown up in London, secure in its ways, he would have an English wife and family now. But his life had taken a hard and in some ways cruel turn long ago, and here he was, swiftly becoming too old to rear a child, teach a boy how to read and think and reason, how to shoot and live in nature, how to respect women and elders and all helpless things. How to give a boy a name, or a girl a name, and make that name a part of his past and a part of the child's inheritance.

Now he stood on the brow of the hill watching the skyline turn gold, watching the earth turn into the sun, watching the smoke of cook fires rise from the fifty lodges below him. He scarcely knew who or what he prayed to; the old Anglican God he had always known, or some other great spirit, maybe the same great spirit, but one he saw simply as a Father of all things. He lifted his arms to the bright heaven.

A wife, a child, a gift not just to himself but to Victoria. If it was not too late.

*two*

good day! Many Quill Woman loved to travel. Now she busied herself preparing to move out. Skye had brought in the horses from the herd and they stood quietly near the lodge.

She unpinned the lodge cover, which was held tight by willow sticks threaded through eyelets, and watched the lodge slowly slide to the ground until only the seven poles remained standing. This was a small lodge, truly a hunting lodge, and it grieved her to be so poor.

Her friends always took pity on her because Skye had no other wives and she was alone. It took more than one woman to erect or lower a lodge. Yellow Paint and Scolding Bird appeared at once, and helped her drag the heavy eight-hide lodge cover free, fold it, and stow it on a travois anchored to the packsaddle of one of the ponies.

"It's very sad," said Yellow Paint.

"Maybe someday he will bless you," Scolding Bird added.

"Sonofabitch," said Many Quill Woman, her favorite English expression she had learned long ago from the days when

Skye was with the trappers. The other women had heard this phrase many times, always expressed tartly when she was feeling testy, and laughed. They drifted back to their own lodges, for there was much work to do and the Absaroka women did almost all of it. Men hunted and made war and played games and made love and smoked and listened to elders and sought spirit helpers. Women worked.

Many Quill Woman, whom Skye called Victoria after the great woman chief of his English people, lifted three lodgepoles from the skeleton, set them on earth, and then toppled the four-pole pyramid that formed the core structure of the lodge. It was her lodge, not Skye's. Women owned the lodges. She unwound the thong that bound the four poles, stored it in a parfleche, and then anchored the long, slim lodgepoles to the packsaddle of another pony, a yawning mare that wasn't good for much else.

Skye wasn't very ambitious, she thought. She heaped their remaining robes and blankets and other possessions on the second travois. Some great men of the people required eight or ten travois and many wives to move. It was odd: the people respected Skye as a hunter and warrior, whose Hawken kept enemies at bay and brought meat to them all. But how could any Absaroka respect a man who had only one overworked wife? And hardly any horses? Something was wrong with him. She still loved him, and would always be beside him, but something was plainly wrong with Skye. And not just Skye. All white men.

They all had just one wife except those ones who were heading for the big salty lake. One woman. It made no sense. How could they get along with only one woman? Many Quill Woman pitied those poor white women, living all alone, doing all the work. That was a great mystery. For years after she and Skye had become mates, she never saw a white woman.

Where did the trappers hide them? Back East, they said, but why? Why were white women hidden back there?

Then finally she saw one or two who had come west with the missionaries, and knew immediately that white women were so frail and pale that they couldn't stand living away from special shelters the white men called houses. That was it. They were all so weak and sick that they couldn't function.

It certainly made no sense, but white people made no sense at all and she had given up trying to understand them. For years, he had tried to help her with her chores but she had always shooed him away. Nothing could be more shameful than having a man who did women's work. He kept trying to pack things in the parfleches, help lower the lodge cover, pack everything on travois, clean up after meals, while the whole band watched and shook their heads and women came privately to Many Quill Woman and expressed their pity, and hoped she could overcome the shame of it. A man who did that wasn't a man.

So she had angrily chased Skye away and snapped at him whenever he tried to do woman things, such as gathering firewood.

"All I want to do is help you. Make your life easier," he explained.

"Dammit all to hell, Skye, get out."

So he did, greatly puzzled by it. She knew he was trying to be kind to her, loving to her, but he had no idea what a scandal it was among her people. It took a long time, many winters, before she cured him of such bad habits.

She saw him grooming Jawbone and admired him anyway even if she didn't understand him. He was combing the great blue roan medicine horse, while Jawbone snapped his teeth and switched his tail in warning. Never was an uglier horse born; never was a more noble and fierce horse set upon the breast of the earth. Jawbone had narrow-set eyes, flopping ears, an overshot jaw that gave the beast his name, and a nose as formidable as Skye's own awesome beak, which rose from his skull like the prow of a ship, dominating his entire face. There was something strange and fearsome about it all; as if from the beginning of the world, Jawbone and Skye had been destined to come together.

The Kicked-in-the-Bellies were soon ready. Children perched in baskets on travois along with the very old. A great mass of horses had been gathered and young herders were ready to drive them. Women had at last loaded their heavy lodges on groaning travois. Many were festively dressed in fine quilled doeskins, but a few had gotten themselves up in bright calicos from the trading posts. Even the young warriors had taken the time to put on their finery.

The great exodus began without a visible signal from anyone. It simply began its course along the north bank of the Yellowstone, called the Elk River by these bronzed people. Soon it was stretched out a vast distance, but carefully guarded by outriders flanking it on both sides. Many Quill Woman's heart lifted at the sight of the imposing column; the People of the Black Bird were a great people, strong enough to keep the more numerous Lakota and Siksika away.

Skye was among those who guarded this great procession. His favorite place was far forward, where he hunted for surprises and ambushes. That was a dangerous place but he preferred it, and the war chiefs of the Absaroka preferred to see him there. Victoria sometimes saw his shining black beaver hat far ahead. He was like the antennae of an insect, sweeping and feeling the country for danger.

Sometimes he left game in plain sight, a deer or elk he had

killed. These were immediately given to the poorest and weakest among the Absarokas. When that happened Many Quill Woman was very proud of her man. His presence was blessing the People.

At night they slept out; in these warm days of late summer, there was no need to erect a lodge unless bad weather threatened, which it never did. At that time Skye would settle beside her in the robes, never forgetting to catch her hand and hold it or to draw her tight for a little while, his love unspoken but profound. Jawbone stood over them like some demented sentinel, letting no one close, not even the People.

They crossed the mighty Yellowstone at a place where the water ripped over gravel, and even the channel was hardly more than ankle deep this time of year. The travois poles dug trenches in the river bottom, but the stream never reached up to the heavy loads securely tied to the poles with thong or braided elkhide ropes.

Skye rarely spoke to her in these times, when his duty was to protect the People day and night. Oddly, she missed his company even though she was surrounded by chattering friends, young mothers with children to look after, boys playing tricks or showing off writhing garter snakes. Secretly, she wished she could ride beside Skye in the vanguard far ahead, before the great caravan had sent every bird winging away, and every rabbit and fox diving for cover.

For three days they passed through starkly arid land, a small desert caught in the rain-shadow of the mighty Beartooth Range to the west, a part of the great Absaroka Mountains named after her own people, but then the majestic mountains seemed to pull back, and they descended into grasslands, and finally into the valley of the Shoshone River. This was still an arid country, but not far upstream the river tumbled out of the noble mountains, and there, in a lush green valley surrounded by timbered slopes, the Absarokas and Shoshones would have their annual rendezvous.

It was easy to see from the marks of exodus that Chief Washakie's Shoshones had arrived ahead of the Absarokas. That only made the trip more exciting. It had been a safe and blessed journey; no child had drowned, no horse had fallen or broken a leg; no thieves had filtered through the night to steal the wealth of her people, whose abundant horse herds were legend among a dozen envious neighboring peoples.

Now she saw her spirit helper, the Magpie, dancing from limb to limb in the riverside cottonwoods. Many Quill Woman had long ago dreamed the vision dream and found this big, raucous, bold bird, white and iridescent black, her helper and guide. She always knew when she saw her friend the Magpie that times would be good or that help was present if times were not good. But now times were good, and here was a whole flock of her birds making loud protest against this invasion. The magpies were like her people, bold and noisy and sometimes reckless, just for the fun of living close to danger.

They paused close to the campground, taking time to don their headdresses, gaud themselves and their ponies with paint, and prepare for a grand entry, in which the Shoshones would howl their delight and cheer the People as they paraded home.

Only Skye did not get into finery. He always wore whatever finery he possessed, which was simply his black top hat and a handsome bear-claw necklace over his chest. And yet, for reasons Many Quill Woman could not fathom, whenever the Absarokas were all dressed in their best it was Skye, on his spirit horse, who always drew the most attention, and those who admired him the most were the ladies. She sighed. Skye was unaware of what great waves and ripples he caused among the women of the northern plains. He only had eyes for her.

# three

With a whoop the Crows paraded onto the meadow, joyously greeted by the Shoshones. Skye enjoyed the parade. A great column of Victoria's people, all dressed in their finery, wended past the Shoshones. The women flaunted their beaded and quilled doeskin dresses and had gaudy ribbons tied in their braids. The warriors paraded their war honors, their rifles and bows, their colorful lances with a feather for each coup. The chiefs and headmen wore their bonnets, which glowed in the afternoon sun.

Children raced on foot beside the column, the boys in breechclouts, if anything, and the girls in little skirts. The Shoshone hosts were just as brightly gauded for a celebration, all smiles as the allied peoples greeted one another. This would be a festive time, a time of horse races, contests of strength and skill at arms, the exchange of mighty gifts, and also a time when the headmen from both tribes would gather together, smoke, summon the spirits, and cement the old alliance.

Skye spotted the young and noted chief of the eastern

Shoshones, Washakie, standing before his great lodge awaiting the arrivals. His gaze was less festive; it was one that as-
sessed the military strength of these allies, the coup sticks, the
lances, the number of rifles or muskets, the number of youths
who were ready to fight.

Skye had not met Washakie and was eager to do so. The
man had grievances against the horde of Yanks flowing along
the Oregon Road to the south, but so far had contained his restless people and had chosen diplomacy instead. But the whites
neither heeded Washakie nor were his people compensated for
the loss of game, grass, and firewood. Even less were they compensated for insults, wounds, shots fired at the Shoshones, and
the fouling of watering holes. Skye thought he might add disease to that long, hard list; the Yanks brought all manner of
plagues westward upon vulnerable native peoples.

The Shoshones had raised their lodges along the western
edge of the verdant meadow here, close to firewood and out
of the wind; they had left the center open, knowing the Absarokas would camp on the eastern side, also close to dense
forest with an abundance of deadwood in it for fires. The open
meadows in the middle would soon harbor dances and drumming, bonfires and feasts, games of skill, races, and a great
marketplace where the women, in particular, traded with one
another.

There were few Shoshone speakers among Victoria's people, and few Absaroka speakers among Washakie's, yet the
peoples got along with a sort of lingua franca, some sign language, and some good guesswork.

Then Skye spotted something else: a white man's wall
tent, a wagon, some draft horses, and several white men. Were
they traders? Skye, instantly curious, could find no evidence
of it; no array of gaudy goods laid out, no shining axes and

rifles, no virgin blankets or stacks of pots or cotton sacks filled with beans or coffee or sugar.

He would know soon enough. For now, there were formalities. The Absaroka headmen paused before Washakie, whose own headmen had clustered around them, and there were greetings. The Big Robber, chief of all the Kicked-in-the-Bellies, descended from his pony, embraced Washakie, and then greeted each of the Shoshone leaders. Skye dismounted and did the same, knowing they were as curious about him as he was about them.

For the time being the white men stood discreetly aside, aware that they needed to heed the protocols of this moment. Two appeared to be bearded teamsters or servants; the third, dressed in polished brown boots, a white shirt with a gaudy red silk scarf at the neck, a gray tweed jacket with leather arm patches, and a black, wide-brimmed felt hat, watched cheerfully.

The wagon intrigued Skye. It was well made, sturdy, and light. It was drawn, apparently, by the two homely Belgians, Skye thought, grazing quietly close to the wall tent.

Red Turkey Wattle always selected the exact campsite because his visions offered protection against disease and disaster. Now the old shaman led the parade to a sheltered strand, slightly higher than the rest of the meadow, where the soil was sandy and a rain would vanish into the porous ground. Here he paused, nodded to the four winds, lifted his arms, and then the Crows swiftly erected their camp.

Skye let Victoria select the spot for his lodge. Whenever he interfered, she glared at him, as she was doing now. She would brook no meddling from a white man when it came to something so sacred as a campsite. He knew better than to help her, and indeed her fierce glances were intended to ward him off. Sometimes when they were off alone, she welcomed his help; they would share the toil of making camp, cooking, keeping warm. But when they were among her people, every-thing was different.

He slid off Jawbone, feeling the ache in his legs as he landed on the meadow. He wasn't so young now that he could leap on and off horses without pain. Jawbone would graze here; the village herders were afraid of him because he'd whirl and kick at them if they approached, so the ugly horse was given leave to wander the village, poke his snout into lodges, and generally offend as many ancients as he could. Sometimes an old warrior, wizened and angry, would threaten to slash Jawbone's throat, but the whole band knew the horse had great medicine, and the old shaman, Red Turkey Wattle, had said that this was the greatest of all horses and must be hon-ored. And no one ever disputed the wisdom of the grand old man.

Skye unsaddled Jawbone and curried him with a bristle brush, while Jawbone shivered and snapped his big yellow teeth and threatened murder.

"Cut it out," Skye muttered.

Jawbone responded by plowing his snout into Skye's belly, a moment of bonding, and then trotted off, snatching at green grass whenever his hunger overcame his curiosity. The blue roan never drifted more than a hundred yards or so from Skye.

Even as Skye busied himself, Victoria wrapped four lodge-poles with thong and erected a pyramid with great skill. Then she laid the remaining poles into the niches, and spread robes over the floor of the lodge. Later, she and the neighboring ladies would help each other to draw the lodge covers upward and pin them in place with green willow sticks poked through eyelets, like buttons.

Skye stretched. This was a glorious late-summer after-noon, not too hot, and the nights promised to be deliciously cool. He lifted the old top hat to let the zephyrs flow through his graying hair, and then began a cheerful tour of the camp. It wasn't that he was looking for another wife, exactly, but somehow his prospects were bleak. Not Missus Crow Dog, no, married and fat and happy. No, not Missus Black Bear, skinny and nervous and unhappy and hard on her little boys. No, not lithe Beaver Nose, youngest child of old Walks to the Sun; too young, too giggly, too . . . Skye suddenly felt he was not decorous, and recovered his dignity and paced on.

This marriage proposition was not easy. You didn't just up and marry the first nubile lady you saw. At least not if you were a born and bred Londoner. You needed to be a little choosy.

He meandered past Missus Sheep Horns, who was pulling up the lodge cover, along with her friend Missus Black Wolf. Skye knew all about Missus Sheep Horns, who was not satis-fied with her husband and was a great flirt. Once, during a war season when the village needed constant protection from the Sioux, Skye was doing picket duty, mostly by watching the countryside from a sun-warmed ridge, when she appeared, smiled, sat down beside him, and made her intentions clear at once. He demurred, having only eyes for Victoria, but not with-out a struggle. She was a most attractive lady. "Missus Sheep Horns," he had said. "I must keep an eye out for the Sioux."

She had taken offense, got her revenge by telling every woman in sight that Skye wasn't much of a man. That got back to Victoria, who reported it to Skye, who tried to ignore it but couldn't, and never quite lived it down.

That was Crow sport. Trysts were as common as eating a supper. Divorces were the daily entertainment. Which, come to think of it, was reason enough not to marry a Crow woman. He laughed at himself: all he needed to do was join the fun and quit worrying, and everything would be quite fine, and he might have twenty wives, severally and serially, before he departed from this world. Why was he so reluctant?

Romantic, that's what he was. Damned romantic.

Still, the notion that he might find a Shoshone woman swelled up in his head, though he hadn't considered it because he couldn't talk their tongue. But love has its own language and maybe they didn't need to talk. A few smiles would do.

Yonder, across the meadow, there might be a hundred eligible ladies of the Shoshone persuasion. And what better time to go courting than during this great summer festival, this moment of amity between tribes, this period of fun and races and contests?

He saw The Big Robber's women erecting the chief's lodge, but the chief was already padding across the meadow to pay his respects to Washakie. Fires were blooming, pine smoke drifted on the breeze. Tonight there would be the first of many feasts, and maybe some dancing and drumming too. Who knows? These things happened almost unplanned, in some mysterious fashion that Skye never understood.

Then he found himself drifting toward the wagon and the white men. Curiosity drove him; that, more than wife-hunting, was much on his mind. These gents were a long way from anywhere; far from the road to Oregon; far from the river road along the Missouri. Far from any known wagon trail.

He headed that way, at once discovering that they kept an orderly camp. The light wagon was obviously in good repair even though they had crossed rivers and gulches with it, roped it down steep slopes, cleared trails for it through brush and trees. For no ordinary wagon could get here; Skye could scarcely imagine how they managed it, or to what purpose.

The gents were lounging in canvas camp chairs. One stood when Skye arrived, the obvious owner of this outfit, nattily dressed, his face chiseled, his blue eyes bright, his smile genuine.

"Ah, you're Mister Skye," the man said.

It no longer surprised Skye that his name was known even in remote corners. The man continued. "It's a pleasure, sir. I'm Graves Duplessis Mercer, at your service."

A three-piece name. A rich man. But why?

*four*

nd some familiar tones in the man's voice.

"Are you British?" Skye asked.

"My father was a captain in the Royal Marines; my mother a Frenchwoman. I grew up in Paris and know France better than my home country. I live in London. And you, Mister Skye, are a Londoner, I've heard."

"Long ago," Skye said. He wondered for a moment whether to reveal more to this son of a naval officer. And decided to put it all before them: "I was a pressed seaman and jumped ship at Fort Vancouver in 1826."

Mercer laughed heartily. "I would have too. Having volunteered for His Majesty's service by press gang, you decided to volunteer your resignation!"

Skye smiled. Maybe the bloke wasn't going to be a pain in the butt after all.

"I've heard a little about you; in fact, Mister Skye, I've been making inquiries. Now, take that Mister that prefixes your name. The story I have is that you require it. Is that the case?"

"It is, sir."

"And why is that?"

"In England, a man without a Mister before his name is a man beneath notice. I ask to be addressed as Mister here in North America, where a man can advance on his merits."

"A capital answer, Mister Skye. I should introduce you to my assistants, Mister Corporal, and Mister Winding. Floyd Corporal and Silas Winding. They're teamsters and hunters from Missouri and both have guided wagon trains out to Oregon, and know the ropes."

Skye shook hands with both. Winding, in particular, interested him. Beneath that gray slouch hat was a pair of wary hazel eyes set in a face weathered to the color of a roasted chestnut. The man looked entirely capable of dealing with wilderness, and indeed, this pair had somehow gotten a wagon and its gold-colored horses through streams, across gulches, over boulders, up precipices, around brush and cactus and forest, to this remote Eden.

"Never been called a Mister before," Winding said.

"Well, Mister Skye here has set a good precedent," Mercer replied. "I'll follow suit! From now on, you're Mister Winding, if you can stand it."

Winding spat, pulled some tobacco from his pocket, and placed a pinch under his tongue. Then he smiled. "It don't rightly fit but I'll weather it," he said.

Around them, the Crows and Shoshones were swiftly erecting their encampment while children gathered into flocks and raced like starlings hither and yon. The Big Robber and Washakie had settled on some thick robes to enjoy a diplomatic smoke, each of them flanked by headmen and shamans.

Skye itched to learn the nature of Mercer's business but constrained his impulses. If the Briton wanted to talk of it, he would.

But Mercer had a disconcerting way of plunging into the middle of things. "You're wondering why I'm here, Mister Skye. Now, I'm quite happy to tell you. I'm an adventurer. I make my living at it. All of Europe starves for knowledge of the far corners of this great world. A man who can feed them stories about Madagascar or Timbuktu or Pitcairn Island or Antarctica is able to make a pretty penny, nay a pretty pound, by scribbling away."

"You're a writer, then?"

"Oh, you might call me that. I fancy myself a good and exact chronicler, recording the world with a steady scientific eye. But I'm really a rambler. I go where no one else has gone and write about it. I examine strange people, exotic tribes, bizarre practices, and write of them. I keep a detailed journal, a daily log, in duplicate and in weatherproof containers, in which I record everything. I explore not just the terrain, describing what has never been witnessed by white men, but also the natives. That's why I'm here. These two tribes are unknown in Europe, and here I am to tell the readers of the *London Times* or the *Guardian* what I witness. And the darker and more fantastic, the better. But I also organize my journals into book form. What I see is not for all eyes, of course, and these volumes have an eager readership; people can't get enough of them. I do have a bit of trouble with censors but that only increases the sales. If I didn't have a spot of trouble, the books would hardly fly out of the stalls the way they do."

"A journalist, then," Skye said.

"Ah, you might say it. But it's the least of my vocations."

"What are your larger ones?"

"Explorer, cartographer, ethnologist, geographer, biologist, zoologist, artist, linguist—I have several European tongues, French, Flemish, Dutch, German, Spanish, Portuguese, and a reading knowledge of several others, and by the time I'm done here, I'll have a few thousand words of Shoshone and Absaroka in my notes, and I'll be able to speak to any of these people. Now what I don't have, Mister Skye, is their finger language, sign-talk, and I shall be approaching you for lessons, and especially the nuances."

Skye found himself studying this wunderkind, curious about the rest: Did he live alone? Alienated from his roots? What of his family? Was he a perpetual boy, living each day for its excitement? Was there a woman anywhere in this life or did he live entirely in this male world he created? How were these exotic articles and books received on the continent? But Skye chose not to be nosy and simply welcomed this remarkable man.

"Actually, Mister Skye, I've been hearing of you for weeks. We came out the Oregon Road, of course, but turned off and headed north, roughly paralleling the Big Horn Mountains. A grand continent, sir. A vast, mysterious land, utterly beyond the grasp of Europeans, who live in little pockets across the Atlantic."

Skye was aware of the sheer energy radiating from this man; it was as if Mercer were a live volcano, brimming with unfathomable powers and exuding energies that would shape not only his own destiny, but those of everyone he touched. It almost made Skye weary just to be in the presence of such force.

The meadow was now lined with colorful lodges, buffalo-hide cones with smoke-blackened tops. Some of their owners had rolled up the lower skirts, letting the playful zephyrs flow freely through their homes, rather like a housewife opening a casement window to air a room.

"See how they make a village out of a meadow, Mister Skye. And in the space of an hour too."

"I've always marveled at it, sir."

"That's why I'm here! I will catch every detail! And after this, we'll head for the geysers bubbling up on that plateau in the mountains I've been hearing about. The headwaters of the Missouri, I believe."

"Not exactly, sir. The Indians call it the roof of the world. Some of its waters flow to the Pacific; some of the waters drain into the Yellowstone River and then the Missouri. Some of the waters drain into the Madison River, which forms one of the three branches that form the Missouri. But the true headwaters, the farthest reaches of that river, are up the Jefferson, far to the west."

"Ah! You have set me straight. We shall go there. Maybe after we explore the Crows and Shoshones and the geysers, we'll tilt west to the Jefferson, named by the Yankees Lewis and Clark, I remember. Yes, go right on up to the last valley, the final creek, that dumps its waters into the tributaries that carry it to the Missouri, the Mississippi, and at last to New Orleans."

"You have a good grasp of the continent, Mister Mercer."

"How could I write if I didn't, eh? Well, I'll put it on my list."

"List?"

"Things to do. I've a list. It must run to fifty items now. And I'm pleased to have made your acquaintance, Mister Skye. I was hoping to meet you. I need your assistance on a variety of matters, and thought we might work out some sort of accommodation."

Skye was never averse to earning a little cash, so he nodded.

"Ethnography is what absorbs me just now. The Absarokas, the Shoshones, most interesting tribes. Religion and all that. I am thinking that you might enlighten me about the Absaroka. I believe you're married into the tribe and know its ways?"

"I am."

"Well, I want to blot it all up, see it, experience it. The shamans, they interest me. I would like to sit in, if I might."

"It isn't something to sit in on, Mister Mercer. The seers have opened themselves to their spirit guides and listen in their own way, and offer thanksgivings. They may or may not share these insights with anyone else. Sometimes a gift is required."

"Yes, yes, of course. But surely there are things about these people to explore. Things you might be willing to share; anecdotes, things you've seen, all that."

Skye sensed that Mercer was driving toward some goal but so far, it wasn't very plain. "I imagine you'll find plenty of material, sir, just by observation."

Mercer leaned forward. "What especially interests me, Mister Skye, is the secret rituals, the nighttime cults, the things that would affront European sensibilities. It's time for Europe to see how the rest of the world lives and thinks. Why, some of the things I witnessed on previous trips to Africa I was forced to describe in Latin in order to pass muster with the royal censors. You get the idea, eh?"

Skye nodded, wondering about the man.

"Actually, I would like to invite you over for some gin and bitters when the sun is over the yardarm. I always carry plenty on my expeditions to ward off the malaria. I've a few canvas camp chairs, and then, over a tonic or two, we can see how this rustic world works.

"I do my research, Mister Skye. In St. Louis I talked to several men of the mountains, inquiring what to look for. To a man, they told me that the Crows are the most lascivious of all the tribes. So I came here! Where better to get a great story?"

Skye listened, startled.

"Why, fidelity is unheard of," Mercer continued. "And a maiden can scarcely get firewood in the forest without being waylaid by half a dozen swains. And even grandmothers tell stories that would make a sailor blush. It's true, isn't it? I want to see it firsthand, record it, lock it in my journal for future use. That's what I'm after. And that's where you come in. You know these people. You can introduce me. You can take me to their rituals, help me befriend them. Tell me where these bacchanals take place. That's where you can earn a pretty penny, eh?"

All the ship's bells were clanging in Skye's head.

*five*

lmost before Skye could respond to Mercer's probing, the man was off in a new
direction.

"Mister Skye, they told me that the Yellowstone tumbles
over two great waterfalls up there; magnificent falls, scarcely
seen by white men. Show me a falls like that, let me measure it
and sketch it and I'll have a story. Take me where white men
have not been. Take me into that forbidding land of shadows
and forests and monster bears where no European has ever set
foot, and I'll turn it into something. I'm told there's a geyser
up there that blows a hundred feet into the air, and goes off
once an hour, and a man could set a clock by it. That and the
falls and grizzlies ten feet tall and hot springs where a man
can take the best bath he's ever had."

"That can all be done on horseback. It's not wagon country."

"Of course not! I'm sure I could scarcely get a pack mule in
there. This wagon, sir, is simply a home base, a portable station
where we might resupply. It's been keenly outfitted. I took

counsel from a dozen men in St. Louis, friends of yours such as Davey Mitchell, Broken-Hand Fitzpatrick, the Chouteau family, eh? Preparation, that's the key to everything. They all advised me."

"You were in good hands, then."

"Ah, Mister Skye. My list! You should see my list! There's a medicine wheel in the mountains north of here. Very mysterious. I must see it. I hear it's the work of ancient ones and has something to do with astronomy. Maybe like Stonehenge, fitted out to reveal the equinoxes or the solstices. The newspapers love items like that. I can sell it to the *Times* for a pretty penny. And I'm told there's a shy tribe called Sheepeaters up there, now you see them, now you don't. Like the African pygmies or bushmen. They're watching you even if you're not watching them. There's a few stories I'm after. Interview a Sheepeater and I'll sell to half the papers in Europe."

"I've never met one and I'm not sure they exist, Mister Mercer."

"Ah, hoodoo! Vanishing tribes! That's all the better. Well, we'll just look into it. Especially the hoodoo. Find me a tribe with some hoodoo, and I can make a book out of it. Did you know there's some tribes off to the south that make a religion out of the visions they get from eating a certain bean called peyote? Takes a bean-eater right into a different world. The very thought of it would give bishops and archbishops dyspepsia. Yes, sir, I've researched it. Too far south for this trip, but on my list. I should like to sample this bean and see for myself whether I see God, or a reasonable facsimile."

Skye nodded. He was growing dizzy from this man's waltz of mind. He glanced around him, seeing only the peaceful progress the Shoshones and Crows were making toward a festive summer encampment on a cool meadow.

"Yes, Navajos," Skye said. "Some others too."

"Mister Skye, I could sell a dozen stories about polygamy. It's rife here on this continent. The Mormons are on my list. We might just slip down there when the season is colder, and I'll record my impressions, talk to the wives. I'm told that each wife has a separate house, so the husband has separate families. That's how they do it. But in your tribe and other tribes, the chiefs and headmen have several wives and they all live in one lodge. Now that's a cozy affair I want to explore. Suppose one night the chief chooses one wife for his nuptial pleasures. What then? Does he send the others out in the cold, and summon them when he's done? I'm going to find the answer to it. It might ruffle a few peacock feathers along the Thames, but I'll weather it. Answers, sir. I'll get answers to everything. Maybe someday I'll do a paper for the Royal Society."

"Yes, well, you have a world to explore," Skye said, hoping to escape. The idea of escorting this man was growing less and less attractive.

"And that reminds me, Mister Skye, that exploring is at the heart of it. It's all science. All fact. All recording what I find and publishing it for the benefit of the civilized world. You know, Mister Skye, that I am going to be nominated for fellowship in the Royal Society? The greatest honor of all, its fellows selected so carefully that each of them is at the forefront of the frontiers of knowledge. They are the princes of science."

"An honor when it comes, sir."

"Ah, I'll elucidate for you. The Royal Society of London for the Promotion of Natural Knowledge is the most prestigious of its kind on earth. Think of it, Mister Skye. Francis Bacon! Christopher Wren! Edmond Halley! Isaac Newton! Being published in the *Proceedings,* or better still, *Philosophical*

*Transactions*. The papers I write pay the freight, but the goal in this bosom, sir, is to put the whole world, as observed by me, between the covers of those journals."

The odd thing was, Skye thought this bundle of energy would probably do just that if he survived. A man like that could walk into trouble faster than any ordinary mortal and scarcely know he was getting into danger.

"Now, Mister Skye, I do have one small favor to ask. Chief Washakie brought me, but I have yet to meet the headmen among the Crows, and I would take it kindly if you would introduce me."

"I can do that, sir. And how shall I introduce you?"

"What do you mean?"

"How would you like to be known to them? They don't grasp the idea of explorers. This whole world is perfectly familiar to them and so are the customs of their own people and all the others with which they have contact. They can even tell you a great deal about the religions of their neighbors."

"Well, that's a good question, Mister Skye. What would you advise?"

"I would suggest to them that you are a storyteller, sir. That you want to see everything so that you can tell true stories to your own people. That you keep a journal, just as they keep their histories painted onto a sacred buffalo robe. They call it the winter count, and each year is named and remembered. One year, when there was a great meteor shower that awed us all, they remember as the winter of the falling stars. That's what I propose."

Mercer smiled, revealing even white teeth in the chiseled, lively face. "Good, sir. Maybe they'll put down this year as the winter of the storyteller."

Skye smiled. The man was not without a certain conceit.

"Very well, then." He eyed the teamsters. "By all means, join us," he said.

Skye hiked across the meadow, feeling the thick grass tug at his steps. Or was it just a sudden weariness or reluctance? He wasn't sure he wanted to introduce this amazing man to anyone.

But the headmen saw Skye coming and waited in their circle to welcome him and the other Europeans. Skye paused. It was necessary that he be summoned or invited before he proceeded. The Big Robber examined Skye's entourage, and addressed Skye: "You have brought strangers to us?"

"I wish to make them known to you so that the People will know who is among us."

"That is good. Bring them forth."

Skye brought them to the edge of the circle of the elders and chiefs, and in the Absaroka tongue introduced each man.

"Mister Mercer comes from across the big water, where I come from, and is a storyteller. He makes it his business to see this world, which he has not seen, and meet your people, learn their ways, and then tell these stories to his people. He records what he learns. He is eager to learn of your people."

"And we will be eager to hear his stories. Welcome them. Let them live among us. Tell them to come and tell us stories this night. We will listen. You will translate."

Skye turned to Mercer and his teamsters. "They welcome you. They give you the freedom of the village. They ask that you come this evening and tell them stories."

"I will do that. I will tell them about Africans, or Asians, or crossing the waters in a sailing ship, or a dozen other things. I take it you'll translate?"

"I will."

"We're in your hands, Mister Skye."

With the introductions concluded, Skye returned to Mercer's camp and then excused himself. The truth of it was that in the space of an hour, Mercer had worn him out. Skye could think only of a nap, a rest, an escape from that crackling energy that had engulfed him from the moment he approached the explorer.

He wandered across the meadow intent on rest. Jawbone spotted him, cantered up, and started to butt Skye.

"Avast!"

Jawbone snorted. Someday this free-ranging horse would get himself into serious trouble with these people, Skye thought. But the animal simply would not stay in the herd.

Skye plodded to Victoria's lodge and stumbled inside. Jawbone poked his nose in, checked to see what was what, and retreated. Skye tumbled into the robes, utterly drained and not knowing why. It was not yet evening. Nothing had happened other than an encounter with a man who radiated energy, yet seemed to draw energy out of Skye. What was it about Graves Mercer? Skye couldn't say. Mercer was one of those men who walked along the knife edge of life and yet was rarely in trouble. But there was always a first time, and maybe Mercer's plunge into this world would be a first time.

Skye felt almost drugged, and lay gratefully on the robes until Victoria slipped in, squinted at him, knelt beside him, and pressed a hand to his forehead.

"Dammit, are you sick?"

"No, just worn-out."

"That ain't like you."

"I just am, that's all."

"I saw you with those strangers."

"An Englishman named Graves Mercer. He has two Missouri teamsters for his wagon."

"And big horses. There's fifty Shoshone looking at them."

"Draft horses. For hauling and plowing."

She eyed Skye. "You better tell me what's wrong with you. What's wrong with them. It's them, isn't it. Something wore you out. Who are these men?"

"He's an explorer. He thinks no one's seen this world."

"Typical white man," she retorted. "You rest. I'll go tell him a few lies."

Skye thought that maybe by God she would.

# *six*

*V*ictoria was worried. In all the time she had
known Skye, she had never seen him take to
his robes after meeting someone. He wasn't
sick. At least he said he wasn't. She had been beside him when
he was fevered, injured, or exhausted. And when he was deso-
lated or angry or starved or thirsty. But he had never been like
this, lying in his robes and staring at the sky through the
smoke hole.

The visitors had returned to their wagon after meeting
the chiefs, so she headed there. Some sort of ritual was under
way: one of them was bringing a bucket of icy river water
while the big boss was setting out glass tumblers. It surprised
her. One didn't see much glass. Half the people in this camp
had never seen it. The big boss was lean, tanned, in a clean
shirt, clean britches, and clean boots. He wore a wide-brimmed
gray felt hat.

She thought some English would do: "Whatcha got there,
eh?"

The big boss turned, surprised. "You speak our tongue?"

"Sure, pretty goddamn good too."

"Ah! You're Missus Skye. Your reputation precedes you."

"What the hell does that mean?"

"It means that the men we talked to about this trip in St. Louis made mention of you. You're salty, they told me."

"All I did was hang around trappers a few years. What's wrong with that, eh?"

"I'm sure that would do it. Come join us, Missus Skye. I'm Graves Duplessis Mercer. These gents are my helpers, Mister Winding and Mister Corporal, from Missouri in the States. They take care of my horses and the wagon. Come join us for an evening libation and by all means summon Mister Skye."

"He ain't feeling so good."

"I'm sorry to hear it. He promised to drop in for gin and bitters."

"What's that, eh?"

"Spirits and a decoction of cinchona, guaranteed to ward off malaria."

She didn't know what the hell that was all about but she liked the spirits part of it. "Serve her up, eh?"

Mercer waved her toward a camp chair and she settled in it.

Mister Corporal swiftly poured some spirits from a cask into a glass tumbler and added some of what they called bitters, whatever the hell that was. He handed it to her, she sipped, and sipped again, aghast at the flavor. It was plainly the most vile flavor she had ever experienced. She sipped again and the bitterness swilled down her throat.

"That's one hell of a drink," she said. "It must give you great powers. The worse the taste, the bigger the powers. Does it make you fly? Do you see visions?"

Mercer grinned, baring even white teeth so perfect it made her ache. No one on earth had teeth like that except for this man. She had heard that all the English had rotten teeth but here was one with teeth that came from heaven.

"It's gin, the favorite spirits of Englishmen," he said.

"I'm going to get drunk," she said. "I'm going to drink this stuff until I roll on the grass. This heals the sick. This makes the lame walk. This cures fevers. It wakes up the dead."

"Ah, Missus Skye, you are true to form. Now I want you to tell us about your people. I try to learn everything there is to know about a place and the people in it."

"What do you want to know?"

Mercer thought and sipped and thought. "Are there any other tribes here, people hidden away somewhere? People the world doesn't know about?"

"Hell yes, there's the Little People."

"You don't say! Who are they?"

"Only the Absaroka see them. Sometimes they help us, sometimes they play tricks on us like the coyotes."

"Ah, yes, but where are they?"

"Everywhere," she said grandly with a sweep of the arm. She sipped more of that awful stuff, coughed, and smiled. "They could be right here and you'd never see them."

"What do they look like, Missus Skye?"

"About so tall," she said, pointing to her knee.

"Truly they must be taller than that."

"Hell no. They're always hiding."

"This is a joke, isn't it?"

"Ask any Absaroka! Ask The Big Robber, he's the chief. Ask Red Turkey Wattle, he's the man who sees the Other People."

"A good story, Missus Skye. I'll make note of it. What do the Little People do to help you?"

"Hell, anything. Chase bears away, bring water, warn us about trouble, lead us to berries."

"Do they look like Indians?"

"They look like people from under the earth."

"Devils?"

"How should I know. I never saw one."

"Maybe I'll meet someone who's seen one. Now, are there any other strange things here?"

"Damn right. The One With Big Feet Who Walks in Snow."

Mercer stared. "More, please. This is valuable."

"Ain't nobody seen him. But he's a big person, with bare feet twice the size of any of us. Big long steps, up on the snow, any winter."

"Big Foot! Now we're getting somewhere. He is well known and I've been looking for Big Foot for years. He's been seen in Russia, Canada, Siberia, and now here."

"What the hell is Russia?"

"A great northern nation across the waters. This Big Foot has a name. Yeti. Do you suppose there's a tribe of Big Foot?"

"Damn right. Thousands, all over the mountains."

"What does the Big Foot look like?"

"Lots of hair, twice the size of us, big feet, carries a club. Very dangerous, very shy."

"Could you lead me to his footprints?"

"Naw, you just find them when you're not looking."

"Where?"

She sipped. "This stuff, it ain't gonna kill me, will it?"

"It's good. We drink it to ward off the intermittent fever."

"Who knows where? When you're not looking, that's when you'll see the footprints. It'll lift the hair on the back of your neck. You see this footprint, and it's a person, and you peer around, and look into the pines and there's no one there, and something passes through you and you know you shouldn't see this."

"Could you draw the footprints for me with my pencil?"

"I can hardly put quills down straight. Skye's shirts, they look like I got ten thumbs. How about more of this stuff, eh?"

She polished off the dregs and handed the glass to Mister Corporal. This was fun. She would get some booze out of it.

"Are there caves here?"

"That's where the Little People live."

"Big people who make tracks in the snow, and little people in caves. Very interesting. These are Crow, ah, Absaroka stories?"

Victoria was feeling a little resentful. He had to be told everything three times.

"Lots of caves. That's where the Old Ones lived. They made pictures on the walls. These were First People. We don't go in there. Don't disturb the spirits. That is their place, not ours."

"I'd like to see them. Are there any around here?"

"Naw, not here. Long ways away. But there's something not far from here you'd like to see. Big bones in the rocks. Big animals got turned into stone. Some bones south of here, some more up on the big river. The one you call the Missouri. Biggest sonsofbitches you ever saw."

"Fossils. Yes, indeed. In England we have many. Seashells, things like that. Little creatures caught in stone from long ago. No, I don't need to see anything like that."

She shrugged. "You don't want to see a big bone, eh?"

He smiled. "Actually, no. Or let me put it this way: it's low on my list of things to look at. Now, tell me about what the Absaroka do at night. Are there secret meetings out in the woods? What do you do on the night of the full moon?"

"You sure are keeping your eyes shut, ain't ya. This here

bone, it's sticking out of rock. It's bigger around than I am and taller than I am. Lots of others around there too."

"I'm sure there's no bones like that. Not even an elephant has bones like that. It's just the way the rock weathered."

"Well, dammit, that's that. I tell you about something around here and you say it ain't so."

He smiled, revealing all those even white teeth. "Forgive me. Tell me about the big bone."

"There's a mess of other bones. This is from a giant bird. Everyone says it's the bones of the big bird."

"How big?"

She stared, finally pointed at a tall pine. "Big as that."

His eyes twinkled. "You love to tell stories, I can tell."

She stood up angrily and dashed the drink in the ground. "I don't want your gin. I don't want nothing to do with you."

He absorbed that. "My most earnest apologies, Missus Skye. Maybe there are such bones. Maybe you'd show them to me."

"Maybe I will, maybe I won't. I don't want you messing with them anyway. Big spirits in there."

"Let me refresh your drink, Missus Skye. In truth, I greatly desire your company because you can translate for me."

"Fill her up, damn good spirits," she said, and sat down again.

## *seven*

Good stuff. The more Victoria sipped the gin and bitters, the better she liked it. Clean, tart taste, cool drink, just right. These British knew how to live. Wooee!

She sipped and eyed her host. This was good, sitting in a canvas chair with this Englishman. A drink for a story or two. The more stories, the more drinks. Hey hey, things couldn't be better.

Where the hell was Skye? He was hiding. She had never seen him hide before. Not in all the winters they had been together had she seen him hide from anyone. But now he was in the lodge with the robes pulled over his head hiding from this man. That was strange. She would tease him tonight. Make him ashamed of himself.

It worried her. He never missed out on a drink. Something was wrong.

Mercer was enjoying himself too. Sometimes his gaze drifted to the encampment. He seemed not to want to miss a thing. If some boys knotted into a gang somewhere, his gaze followed them. He sipped, totally relaxed, plainly happy to be there.

"Missus Skye," he said. "I consider this a most fortunate meeting. I want to learn all about your people. This is fortunate for me because you speak English. So I hope you won't mind if I ply you with all sorts of questions."

"Then you write it all down?"

"I do. I write it down and publish it."

"I've seen books," she said. "Damn, I wish I could get the meaning out of them."

"Well, I want to record everything about your people."

"Such as?"

"Your rituals, your religion, your demons. When someone dies where does his spirit go? Up to the stars? Down into the ground? Up to the sun?"

"They start their spirit journey by greeting the elders, and then they head east until they get to St. Louis, and then they turn into mosquitoes and bite white men."

He laughed. "Very good, Missus Skye. Now we're getting somewhere. Are there secret meetings in the night? All boys, all girls? All women? All warriors? All virgins? Do you sacrifice prisoners to the gods? Do you sacrifice animals? Do you drive a stake through the heart? Do you drive demons out of your village? Do you bury the old and the sick alive? What do you do with the sick? Do you have herbs and potions? Does a medicine man drive out the evil? What do you do with crazy people? How do you torture enemies?"

"Sonofabitch, you sure ask questions!" She eyed him. "Best damn questions anyone ever asked."

"Is one animal favored over another? Do you eat the flesh

of other people? You know, to give you power over them? What do you do with criminals? Banish them? Kill them? Do you have fertility rites? Do men trade wives?"

Victoria sipped her drink. He noticed and smiled. "Have another," he said.

She thrust her half-emptied glass at Winding, who promptly refilled it and handed it to her. That gin was good stuff, oh ho ho! It was making her feel better and better. Damn, how could she answer all those questions?

Then she knew. She sipped, smiled, and sipped again.

"At the beginning of time there was a big raven. Its wings filled the whole sky. It had been born on a mountaintop and pretty soon it was bigger than the mountain. Then it flew here, casting a shadow so big that the world was dark under it, and it decided this was the place for the raven people to be. It settled on another mountaintop and opened its beak and began spilling out raven people . . ."

Now Mercer was scribbling busily, catching everything she said. Good. This should be worth a few more drinks.

"Out they came, many raven people, and they named themselves the People of the Raven, or Absaroka."

"Good," he said.

"They all had black hair, but then one had white hair, and the people knew they had to kill the white-haired one so they cast him into the sun."

"Good, good, Missus Skye. The origins myth."

"What the hell is that?"

"The creation story. All groups have one."

"Well, all right. But the white one didn't die. It became the moon, so at night we see the white one, and know it was cast out of our midst."

"Is the moon evil? Do you gather at night to look at it?"

"Oh, you bet. That's when we do the forbidden things. The nights of the big moon."

He perked right up at that, staring at her with a devouring look. Good. This was fun.

He waited, pencil poised, but she simply sipped. Let him wait. Besides, she didn't know where to go next.

"That's when we sacrifice a baby," she said. "Each full moon, the people give a baby to the pale god, deep in the night when the moon is big and fat."

"Sacrifice! You don't say! How is the victim selected?"

"Not a victim, dammit, an honor. The holiest, most sacred honor. The shamans select the one, and make a bundle and place the bundle before that lodge."

"And then the parents know their baby will be honored?"

"Hell yes."

She had him running now. She finished her drink and edged the empty glass forward. Promptly, Winding filled it with more gin and bitters.

"This is done by the Wolf Society," she said. "That's a secret society of young warriors. It's their task. If a young man really wants honors he will go steal a Siksika baby."

"Siksika?"

"Blackfoot. The Piegans, the Kainah, the Bloods. They are the enemies of our people. A Wolf warrior must go all alone to the land of the Siksika, carry his wolf skin with him so he can wear it, and then wait to capture a baby. He lurks close to the Siksika camp, singing his song to the Wolf so he might succeed, and then when a mother is not looking, he creeps out, snatches the baby, and runs away with it into the forest. This is very difficult. Many of the Wolf Society die; the Blackfeet catch him and take their baby back and kill the Absaroka boy."

"This is remarkable. How often does this happen?" Mercer asked.

"Not often. An Absaroka boy must have a vision, then pledge that he will take a Blackfoot baby, and then do it. After that, there's a ceremony on a big moon night. All the men in the society count coups. Then the baby is left for the wolves to eat. But if a coyote eats it, that's bad luck. Watch out for coyotes. They're bad luck."

Mercer stared, slightly at a loss, and then wrote. The sun had set. A sweet cool evening breeze, scented with pine, drifted down from the slopes.

She was in fine fettle, and hurried on. The next one might be worth two or three drinks. "Now I'll answer another question. The Absaroka have the Wife-Trading Night."

"You do? Then it's true. I heard about this in St. Louis."

"It's true. It's the longest day of the year, when Sun doesn't go to bed but lingers on, and rises early. That's the night when everyone is happy. Wives are honored. It is the Night of the Wives. That's another Absaroka name for it."

"Tell me, what happens?"

"Oh, I shouldn't talk about it. It is sacred, very sacred."

"Please tell me. I'll not mention it or say where I heard it."

"You sure? We don't talk much. It's great honor. Every wife, she wants to try it."

He scribbled furiously, and then the lead snapped. He dug in his pockets, extracted a tiny folding knife, and whittled a new point on his pencil.

"Now I'm ready, Missus Skye. You were saying?"

"Ah, yes, the longest day, the light lingers, and husbands make big deals with friends, and give them their wives for the night, and because it's light everyone knows, everyone knows who goes to which lodge, eh? Sometimes when a wife is plain, the husband, he gives his friend a gift too? An elk skin, maybe. Then the plain wife gets to enjoy the honors too."

"Ah . . . I see."

Mercer looked like he was about to choke.

"You all right?" she asked.

"Fine, fine. Tell me more. Does this happen just once each year, on what we call Midsummer's Eve?"

"Hell no," she said. "It happens all the time."

Mercer was turning an odd red color. "Remarkable. I shall want every detail."

But then the drumming began. She glanced at the meadow, and sure enough, a crowd was collecting at a bonfire, even as old men gathered into a drumming circle and began their plaintive songs to the demanding beat of the drums.

"I must go look," he said. "We'll continue this little talk tomorrow, Missus Skye."

She smiled. She was in a smiling mood. If there was anything the People loved, it was a good joke.

She drifted to her lodge, ready to confess what she had done and celebrate with him, but Skye was gone.

## eight

Skye drifted from the lodge after darkness cloaked the valley. The drummers had begun, their heartbeat drumming throbbed through the camp. A crowd had collected around them to listen to songs of triumph, great events, war, and power.

He was in no mood for that and wished the tribes had some other and quieter way to spend a summer's eve. He had no relish for the company of the explorer, Mercer, either. In fact, he was using the darkness to dodge the man. He had nothing against the energetic Briton who had welcomed him cordially, and yet he did not want further commerce with the man. Somehow, Mercer was an intruder, and few of the Absaroka or Shoshone people grasped that he was noting everything there was to know about them.

It was one of those moments he often experienced, when he felt caught between the European world of his youth and the world of his adopted nation, the Crows; a moment when he was not really comfortable in either.

He did not dislike Mercer, yet he found himself avoiding

the explorer and knew he would continue to do so, no matter that they shared a tongue and a world across the sea and the prospect of a few gin and bitters was enticing. He used the thickening dark to drift from camp, reaching darkness and quietness after he reached the Shoshone River. He treasured the quietness of the woods. A three-quarter moon, fat and yellow, was rising in the east and paving the path with glistening light. That was good. It bid fair to be a sweet summer's eve.

Soon the drumming was only a distant throb and then the sound vanished altogether and he was alone. He found a game trail leading upward through forested foothills, and took it, letting the white moonlight filtering through the pines be his lamp. Juniper-laden air eddied down the hill, perfuming the world. The pungence of the juniper, or cedar, evoked the biblical in him and made this place the Holy Land. The malaise he felt in camp left him and he was at peace. He climbed a sharp rise and found an open ridge, its rocky spine lit by moonlight, a place of peace.

And there was a woman. Yes, no mistake, a jet-haired woman sitting on the rock, her back pressed into a shoulder of rock, her gaze rapt. She saw him at once, a swift startled gesture, and he paused. He did not want to frighten her.

"I am Mister Skye. I will go. This is your place," he said in Absaroka, but she did not respond.

He thought she might be Shoshone, but who could say? He made the friend sign, palm forward, the peace sign. She did not move. He felt himself to be the intruder, and turned to leave.

She said something he could not translate but her voice was soft and warm, and she patted the rocky table next to her. He accepted the invitation and discovered a young woman, slim and beautiful, perhaps half his age. She had the strong cheekbones of her people, and almond eyes, and even in the white and glistening moonlight he caught her interest in him. Her survey was as complete as his own and lingered at his gray beard and the beaver top hat. She smiled and spoke again and he could grasp nothing except her meaning: come sit with me and enjoy this sacred place, lit by Mother Moon.

He did, easing himself to the sun-warmed rock beside her. They sat well above the valley of the summer camp, but could not see it here in this quiet basin, and were alone.

"I'm Mister Skye," he said in English, "and I live with the Absaroka people."

"I know," she said, "and your name is familiar to me. We all know it."

He wondered how he understood her. She said it in Shoshone. Maybe he knew more of it than he had realized. He liked her voice, resonant of woodwinds and wind chimes.

"I am called Blue Dawn," she said. "I am twenty winters, and have turned aside many suitors because I wanted to."

He thought about that a moment, her words meaningful to him, as if a wizard were translating somewhere in his soul.

He nodded. Neither she nor he spoke. It was as if they had already tested the limits by which two people of different tongues could understand each other. She had not used the finger language though she no doubt understood it.

Some night bird glided nearby, hunting the rocky ridge for a meal. A small cloud hid the moon, so he could barely see her for a while.

He thought of things to say to her and then spoke: "I wonder who you are. I wonder why you are here, apart from your people. I wonder how you chanced to hike up this side trail to this ridge."

She smiled, almost as if she understood him. It was almost eerie. But of course she didn't.

"I wonder what your dreams are: each of us has dreams, but yours have taken you away from the drumming, and your people, to this place. It is a quiet place but not a lonely one. It is a place to dream, or seek help from the spirits, or try to find a way through troubles."

She was watching him, so intent that he imagined she was understanding his every word.

"But I think you are not troubled," he continued, imagining she understood. "I think you are seeking something, maybe something the moon can give. I am too. I am wondering what to do. It's my wife . . ."

She smiled. Could it possibly be? Yes, she was smiling.

"I know," she said. He was startled. Had he really heard it? Of course not.

This was getting altogether too odd for his taste. He emptied his mind of everything and settled beside her, letting the sacred scent of junipers drift past him. But now he was imagining what she was saying, maybe because he knew a little Shoshone: it was as if she was talking and by some magic he was receiving every word.

"My spirit helper is the Unknown God," she was saying. "He was made known to me by a white man, a priest of his people, named Father De Smet. Ever since then I have sought this Unknown God who abides beyond the beyond."

Skye couldn't believe he was thinking such things. Once he got back to the camp he would inquire about her. What was her name? Had the great Jesuit, Father De Smet, ever visited her people? Surely this was nothing but fevered imagination at work.

Still, she smiled at him and reached across the rock to touch his hand with hers.

"You want a wife," she said in her tongue. But he caught the meaning.

"No, not I, I'm married, I . . ."

He stared helplessly at her, his mind refusing to accept this mysterious talking, translating without a translator.

"It is known among us. Many Quill Woman has told all the People that you are looking for a young wife."

She sat there quietly, her gaze dreamy, the moonlight flooding her face and revealing friendship in it. She really hadn't said anything intelligible. He must be imagining all of this. There had been only the deep silence of the wilds, the occasional whir of a night flyer, the fat moon slowly crawling upward into a smaller whiter ball, and peace. Not just peace, but a sweet and savory peace.

Now he spoke aloud: "I came here to dodge the white man, the Englishman with the wagons and two helpers. He's a good enough chap. I have nothing against him. But I am not at ease around him."

She listened, her eyes uncomprehending.

"I don't really know what the matter is. We just don't mix. He's a storyteller, I guess that's as clear as I can make it. He's adventuring to the distant corners of the world, looking for strange things. Strange to him, anyway, but not strange to you or me. And he writes all these things down each evening, and then he goes back to England, the country of my birth, and tells them what he has seen. It might be volcanoes or geysers one story; it might be your people or my wife's people too. It might be strange animals, rare birds, who knows? But he tells the stories, and many people know the stories."

She stared. Good. For a while there he swore he was out of his senses, thinking she and he were mysteriously conversing.

They watched swift silver-rimmed clouds play tag with the moon. Sometimes he discovered her gazing at him and sometimes their gazes locked. She didn't smile or seem flustered by it. She was accepting and enjoying this silent encounter. He felt drawn to her, as if she was offering him a circle of sweetness if he would step inside of its circumference.

Who was she? And why did this encounter play out here?

She said something he could not understand, and rose. She was going to leave.

"Would you like my company?" he asked in English.

She nodded, responding to words she didn't know. She smiled, touched his arm, and they started down to the summer camp. She walked ahead of him, lithe and sure of foot, until they reached the river and then they followed it to the moonlit meadows. The camp had fallen into slumber.

She paused at a place where her path would fork from his, looked up at him and smiled. He placed his hands upon her shoulders and drew her close, yet not touching. It was a gesture as ancient and universal as man and woman. She said something, placed his bearded cheeks between her hands, and pressed them gently. That was all.

She left him, walking toward the Shoshone lodges. A dog found her, raced up, recognized her, and trotted along beside her as she fell farther and farther from Skye's sight, until at last she vanished into silver moonlight.

A strange, sweet eve, he thought. He made his way to his lodge, found his way into its blackness, and tugged at his moccasins.

"Dammit, Skye, tell me about her," Victoria said.

An awkward feeling engulfed him, but it passed.

"I don't know her name but she'd make a good wife," he said. "If you want me to."

"Shoshone," she said. "No Absaroka wants a white man with smelly feet."

She laughed, found him, and opened her arms to him as he settled beside her.

# nine

With the first hint of dawn, Skye slipped out of the lodge and into the chill. He always loved this hushed moment in the day, just before the world stirred. In that he was unlike his wife's people, who would sleep to noon if it suited them. For the Absarokas this was still the middle of the night.

Skye surveyed the camp. No cook fires burned either among the Crow lodges or the Shoshones. There was probably no one awake except the horse herders, whose task was to be alert for trouble at all times. It was an honor for a boy to be chosen as a herder. Great was the responsibility, and great was the trust, and it meant that manhood was not far off.

The sun was cutting a ribbon of blue on the eastern horizon, and soon the gray and night-shadowed world would take color into itself. Skye headed for the river, to perform his ablutions, and then he thought he would climb a slope and watch the sun come up.

But at the Shoshone River he found he was not alone: a woman stood silently, watching him. When he drew closer, he was amazed. It was the young Shoshone he had spent time with at twilight. How could it be?

"Good day, Mister Skye," she said. In clear English. "I wait for you."

English? How could that be?

"Wait for me?" he replied, utterly flummoxed.

She nodded. "I know all that you do. You leave the robes before anyone else. You like to see the day begin. I do too."

He could scarcely fathom it. "But last night you didn't speak English."

"Last night I chose to listen. If you want to know someone, say nothing, and listen and watch."

"How do you know English?"

"My father is called Pompey. My grandmother is named Bird Woman, Sacajawea in my tongue. I learned your tongue from my father and grandmother. They were very careful to teach me many words, saying it would be good for me to know this tongue. Your people are making the world that will come."

"And you?"

"Blue Dawn. Like this." She waved toward the sunrise.

"Then you understood all my babbling."

She nodded.

"And you know me but I don't know you."

She smiled. The widening light in the east lit her face. "I know you. Come. I will make a meal for us."

He had the odd sensation of being drawn into something ordained or planned that he was the last person to know about. She smiled. He thought she was the most striking woman he had ever seen, straight and lithe and proud, with a long-limbed body that arched like a drawn bow.

"We will eat up on the meadow," she said, leading him in

the direction of their rendezvous last evening. "I have made everything ready."

He drew his top hat from his head, more and more uncertain about all this. Too strange. Back out. "That's a most thoughtful invitation, but I can't accept. I ought not to be accepting invitations from a lady I scarcely know."

She smiled, her black eyes flashing in the quickening light.

"Come," she said.

He surrendered and followed her as she trotted ahead of him, her doeskin skirts dancing about her calves as she climbed the steep side trail toward the plateau. She moved so fast that it winded him to follow, but when they did reach the high meadow he was glad he came. The whole eastern sky, with a handful of pancake clouds, had turned rosy, and the alpine meadow was gilded in silvery light. It was their private Eden, a place of beginnings.

But he could not fathom what inspired all this. Why she had arisen before light, prepared this place, and waited for him to appear.

She reached the very ledge of gray granite where they had sat only hours before, sitting in what he supposed was a babble of languages. But now she had a fire already burning. She added some deadwood and placed a small black iron kettle over her fire.

"This is all just fine but I'm a little confused," he said.

"Oh, there is no reason to be. Time to be the wife. I decided to marry you."

"Marry me? You decided . . ." This was progressing all too fast.

She smiled, this time shyly. "It is so. It is the word of Many Quill Woman that comes to us. Her man seeks another wife. I think that I am this one. I have always known it. Long ago, when I was little, I saw you."

Skye stared mutely. He could not think of a thing to say. Not one word. She stirred the contents of her small black kettle. Orange flame licked its bottom and a thin gray veil of wood smoke lifted up and drifted across this alpine park.

Now her demeanor was not so certain. "I will be a good wife for Mister Skye," she said in a small voice.

This was taking more getting used to than Skye was prepared for. He saw doubt in her face, the beginnings of self-rebuke, and swiftly caught her hand.

"Blue Dawn . . ." He wanted to accept, but that seemed odd. He wanted to propose, but it was too late.

She smiled, clamped her fingers over his.

"I've never been proposed to," he said.

"I waited for you," she said. "I knew you would come."

"Everything is upside down."

She frowned. "What is upside down?"

He laughed. "It's when the sky is under our feet."

She stared, a slow smile building at the corners of those young lips.

"I will get used to you," she said. "I will try to be a good woman. A very good woman for you. I will work hard. I will be to you whatever you like me to be. Your beard will tickle my face."

"Where I come from, men propose to women. And they get to know each other first."

She smiled. "I pity the women where you come from."

"It's sacred, you know. It's for a lifetime. You don't rush into it."

"A lifetime! I wouldn't want to live with your people."

"Your father must have told you about all that."

"I didn't believe it. How could people be so savage?"

"But it's civilized."

"Savage. How can a man and woman stand one another for an entire life?" She waved her horn spoon at him. The contents of the pot were beginning to bubble.

"I am glad my father did not take me with him," she added.

"Where is he?"

"In some place called Europe across the sea. He said it's old and cold and I wouldn't like it. So I am glad I stayed here to marry you."

"I haven't said yes yet. I want to get used to this."

"We can wait until tonight if you want."

"Wait until tonight!"

"If you insist. Or, we don't have to wait at all." She stood straight, smiled at him, and waited. "Are you my man?"

He was feeling half crazy. It wasn't yet six in the morning, and apparently he was betrothed. "I want to get the permission of your parents first," he said, hoping that would delay matters for a few months.

She shrugged. "My father, he is far away. My mother," she paused. "She is not here. She is dead. I am with my brother and my cousins. You call them cousins. I call them kin, little brothers, little sisters. You can ask him."

Skye was feeling out of sorts. There she was, desirable, her lithe young body moving under those doeskin skirts, inviting him, provoking him. How could he be an honorable man? How could he do what's right? How could he be proper?

"Well?" she asked.

He lifted his top hat and settled it. "You have to meet my wife first. She has to approve."

She was grinning fiendishly. Victoria had the same grin.

Did all Indian women possess that grin in their arsenal? "I already did," she said.

"You met her? You met Victoria?"

"She sure swears, doesn't she?"

Skye began to shrink down inside of his buckskins. This was getting dangerous. Maybe he could bolt for his lodge, leave her stirring her stew.

She touched his arm. "You have a good woman," she said. "She told me about you. She said I should tell you to marry, because you never would. She said you'd be very strange about it at first but you would like the idea. She said I should be called Mary. I think that is a pretty name. You need to name me with one of the names your people give to women. So she said I would be Mary."

"She did, did she?" Skye squirreled his top hat around in his hands. He squinted at her. "She told you that? She set this up?"

"What does set up mean?"

"I don't know what it means," he replied, feeling huffy.

She smiled. "Victoria said you'd be angry, and very strange, and then you would be very happy."

"She said that too?"

Mary nodded.

"Am I Mary now?"

"How should I know? All I do is get moved around like a chess pawn."

"What is that?"

He sighed. She was smiling sweetly. "Let's eat some of that good stew," he said.

# ten

lue Dawn ladled some of the broth into a wooden bowl and handed it to Skye.

He sampled it. The meat was odd. Maybe dog. But he bravely spooned it into himself and smiled back at her.

"A fine breakfast, yes. Very good," he said. "You'll make someone a fine wife when that person comes along."

"Badger," she said.

"It's badger?"

"My people believe that badger meat makes lust in a man. Give a man some badger if you want to make a baby. They are hard to catch. They have mighty arms to claw a badger hole. I paid two boys to catch one for me."

Skye, always ruddy, suddenly suspected he was ruddier than usual. He chose silence as the best of all responses, and slurped up more of the badger stew.

"Good! Eat it up! We will have a big time."

He thought that maybe eating the badger stew so heartily was a mistake.

"My people don't think there's anything special about badger meat," he said, squinting at her. "It's just meat. Nothing to it."

She smiled wickedly. She and Victoria had the same lustful smile. He thought it would shock all the prissy girls in pinafores in England. But this wasn't England.

"You should finish it," she said. "Then I'll be happy."

"Ah, I think I've had enough badger."

He was feeling more and more snared, and the more he fought the web of cord being wound around him, the tighter it got. She took his half-empty bowl, swiftly ate the contents, and then packed it.

"It works for women too. I asked our prophet, whose name in your tongue is Glow Bug, and he said the meat of the badger is a great, ah, what's your word? Benefactor. A great benefactor. It makes a man and a woman . . ." She laughed winsomely.

Skye thought, it is not yet seven in the morning and already the rest of this day is laid out for me. And I knew nothing of it.

"Don't worry, Mister Skye. When you are old and your belly is cold, I will catch badgers and feed them to you day after day, moon after moon, yes?"

"When I am old I will want to sit in a chair and smoke my pipe and look back on good things."

"Yes! I will do just the same. But we need to find good things to look back upon."

Her bright eyes brimmed with merriment. He sneaked a look at her. He didn't want her to know he was getting interested so he devoured her with small glances from the corner of his eyes, while he pretended to watch a circling crow. She was serenely putting her breakfast gear into the little sack, humming a sweet tune as she worked.

Then she was done.

"Do you want me yet?" she asked.

"I think I should meet your parents first. When Jean Baptiste returns from Europe."

"The badger meat isn't working yet. But it will. Badger never quits. I can feel Badger in me. Pretty soon Badger will take hold of you and shake you."

She was giggling.

Skye ached for some tea. Or even some of the Yank coffee, though he really wanted tea. Some good Oolong would quiet him, let him think. Maybe some tobacco would do it. He wanted a pipe and a smoke. Yes, let the leaf quiet him.

"I will walk with you back to the village," he said, mustering his tattered dignity.

She nodded enthusiastically. "Tonight, then. That will give us a whole day to think about it."

"Ah, no, I'm going to go hunting."

She thought that was pretty amusing. "Badger says no, we're going to get married."

She was so fetching he didn't really mind the idea. Maybe it would work out. Obviously, he had been trapped. Victoria had done it. She had woven this snare and cast it over him as if he were a raccoon. It amazed him, being the object of a great conspiracy between the Crows and Snakes, the intent of which was to overwhelm all his European civility, his pride in being a sensitive and gentle man, his pleasure in being addressed as Mister.

The sun was well up now, casting cheerful golden light across this silent plateau hidden from the camp below. She had collected her things, put out the little fire, and now stood hesitantly, uncertain at last about all this.

The look in her face touched him. It was solemn, almost

fearful, as if everything had failed and she would regret this hour for the rest of her days.

He took her hand, peered into those eyes that brimmed with unbidden tears, drew her close, felt her lithe body pressed tight to his own, and then he kissed her. She received his kiss quietly, and slid her arms about his neck, and kissed back, fierce and honeyed.

It sealed everything. If this was the future, then he would welcome the future. This would be good. If this indeed was what Victoria had created by design, then he would welcome it with a full heart. Love? Who could say? Love was something that came out of the south winds, and it would come whenever it blew into his heart. She was beautiful, and felt good in his arms, and held him eagerly as he held her.

"Yes," he said.

"Choose the path and I will walk with you," she said.

"I would like to do this according to the custom of your people," he said.

"I hoped you would."

"What is the first step? How do I make my intentions known?"

"I am in the lodge of my brother. You would bring him a gift."

"A pony? I have several."

She nodded, pleasure suffusing her face.

"Your brother and you are the children of Jean Baptiste Charbonneau. That is good. Two bloods in you will make the life we share easier. You will know my ways better, and I will understand your ways better."

She touched his beard. "It scratches," she said. "Who of the Shoshones has a hairy face?"

"The better to tickle you," he said.

She laughed and clasped his hand as they started toward the village.

"I will bring a horse to your brother. What is his name?"

"In your tongue, The Runner."

"The Runner will take my horse and then what?"

"My people will bring you gifts. The men will smoke with you. The women will spend this day dressing me in beautiful things. White doeskin, fringed skirts, quills, beads, and maybe ribbons in my hair."

"Then?"

"Then, when I am dressed, maybe late in the day when Sun is ready to hide, they will bring me to your lodge. And you will see me."

She gazed anxiously at him.

"See you?"

"You could turn your back and I would be led away."

"Why would I do that?"

"It would mean that I do not please you."

"You already please me . . . Blue Dawn."

"It is Mary. Your older wife is very wise. She says I must be Mary."

"Mary of the Shoshones. Why?"

"It is her wisdom. I will not ask why. I am very pleased with this new name. I like the name. It is a holy name among the white men, is it not?"

"It is."

"Then I am honored. Maybe your first wife knows this and thinks this sacred name is good for me to have."

"Then, when you are brought to me, what next?"

She smiled sweetly. "Then we go into your lodge!"

"And then what?"

"And then your senior wife, sits-beside-him wife, she blesses us."

"How does she do that?"

"Who knows? We'll find out, yes?"

Skye walked with her down the steep trail through scrub trees and grassy parks until they reached the river. He felt oddly unsure of foot, as if the ground might cave in or he might step through thin ice, or a hidden branch of a tree might lash him when he least expected it.

Two wives. This day he would take a second wife. It all seemed so strange, so fraught with peril, he could scarcely imagine it. But it was unfolding now at its own speed, in its own way, almost as if he were a spectator, and this were the work of others. But he knew it wasn't so. He might have been hesitant, might have worried about many things, but he was a willing participant now. He hadn't merely acquiesced; he had embraced this, and her, and the new world into which he was plunging this sweet summer's day.

He and Mary walked quietly into the bustling village, where children caromed here and there, and youths congregated, and the women, ever-busy, were turning the work of the day into gossip and entertainment, and the sunlight lay golden.

His six horses stood at his lodge, groomed and haltered, their tails switching at flies.

Suddenly he laughed.

"Victoria was very certain how this would end," he said.

Mary laughed too.

"Which horse should I give to The Runner?" he asked.

"The best one," she said.

# eleven

She stood there, smiling. He realized suddenly just how beautiful she was. She was glowing. Her glossy jet hair was parted at the center, and hung in braids over her breast. Her flesh, a golden amalgam of two races, glowed in the sunlight. Her figure was slim and ripe. But it was the humor in her eyes that bewitched him. She truly liked him; it was written all over her face.

Around them, the people of the combined villages were enjoying the festive day. Children congregated in odd little knots; young men were already at their archery contests. The maidens were collecting into little groups to share their secrets.

Jawbone eyed Skye suspiciously.

"No, I'm keeping you," Skye said. "Lucky you."

The horse snorted, lowered his head, and threatened anyone to come close.

Skye eyed his best buffalo runner, a line-back dun that had fire in its belly and loved the chase. He would give that to The Runner.

Victoria suddenly emerged from the lodge, eyed Skye and Mary, hands on hips, and began cackling. It was the famous granny cackle of the Crows, lecherous and insinuating.

"Hah, badger meat did it!" she said, and wheezed.

Skye stopped untying the line-back dun. Was this a conspiracy? Had all this been plotted by this powerful woman?

"I told her nothing else would work," Victoria said. "I told her Skye is a desperate case. It would take Big Medicine to make Skye look at another woman. I told her don't go to the damn shamans; their medicine ain't good with white men. She's gotta pull a badger out of his hole and feed you some meat, and if that don't do it, the whole thing's hopeless."

"Hopeless is it? What do you mean, hopeless?" Skye shouted. He didn't know what else to say. He couldn't think of a damned thing to say. "You think I can't, ah, court a woman on my own? That I need some help? That I'm, ah, not a man?"

Victoria was looking pretty smirky and so was Mary. His bride-to-be was smiling blandly, saying nothing, and looking sweeter than ever.

Skye lifted his top hat and smashed it down upon his locks. "Maybe I'll just quit this camp and go off by myself," he yelled.

But his fingers betrayed him. He had loosened the picket line of the dun, and was holding the freed lead rope in his hand.

"Wait," said Victoria. She ducked into their lodge and emerged with the very thing Skye prized most, his bear-claw necklace. "Take that to The Runner too," she said.

"I won't!"

He fingered the necklace. It had been made of grizzly claws, and invested Skye with great powers, the very powers of the most fearsome of all animals. Each claw was six or seven inches long, and had been strung on a thong, through

76

holes in their roots, with trader's beads in between. Defiantly he slid the bear-claw necklace over his neck and tied it in place.

"Dammit, Skye, she's worth it," Victoria said.

Skye was stricken. He looked at Mary, who stared solemnly at him, at the handsome necklace adorning his chest. Yes, she was worth anything he possessed.

"Let's go," Skye snapped. "Show me what lodge."

Quietly, Mary led him across the grassy meadow that separated the two villages, past staring people, all of whom seemed to know what this ritual was about. They entered the Shoshone camp. The lodges rose in a crescent, their lodge doors all facing east as was the custom. A crowd collected and followed, at a respectful distance, with small nods and small smiles directed toward the young woman they knew as Blue Dawn.

Skye soon found himself before a large lodge, artfully decorated with black and brown drawings of successful hunts. Then, suddenly, Mary paused, looked up at him, her face brimming with tenderness. No one emerged from the lodge, but Skye had expected that. The time of meetings and introductions would come. He tied his line-back dun to a stake nearby. Then, while she watched, he undid his treasured bear-claw necklace, fingering those giant polished claws, each one looking like ebony, and then retied the necklace around the neck of the dun. He noticed Jawbone surveying all this from a distance. A silent crowd of Shoshones had gathered. Courting was not done in private, it seemed. There it was; his best running horse, his most treasured medicine item. He turned to her. The look in her face was so loving, so proud, that he would gladly have given everything he possessed at that moment.

"It is time for you to leave me," she said.

He nodded. He didn't want to leave. He was in the middle of something, and he didn't want to wait. But he left. He would know in a glance whether his gifts had been accepted. If they were, his dun would be led away to the herd; if not, it would be returned to him.

She stood before him, while the Shoshones watched their every gesture. Then she nodded, smiled, and slipped into the lodge. He watched as she vanished through the oval door, watched as the door flap fell closed, and then he was there on a grassy field in the middle of morning with twenty or thirty of Mary's people standing politely close by. He nodded, lifted his hat, and hiked back.

Jawbone, in an indignant mood, butted him.

"Avast!" Skye rumbled.

It was odd. He had been nothing but a puppet in this drama. No, that wasn't quite right. Victoria had simply led him through the customs of the two people. The decisions were still all his.

Jawbone veered close and rubbed shoulders with Skye. He reached over the ugly horse's mane and held on.

"We're adding to the family," Skye said. "You'll be a gentleman. You're going to watch over her and protect her. You're going to keep her safe. I will be paying lots of attention to her, and you'll accept that. She's going to be my wife. My wife, understand?"

Jawbone turned his head, eyed Skye, and then walked with his head close to the ground, in abject surrender. Skye didn't like it.

When he reached the Crow camp, he found himself trapped. There, hovering about his lodge, was the one person he would rather not see: Graves Duplessis Mercer, who was practically hopping about.

"Ah! Found you!" he said. "Is it true? You're taking another wife?"

"It might be true; I'm waiting to know."

"Waiting! What's there to wait for?"

"Whether I am acceptable to her family."

"Acceptable! Why wouldn't you be acceptable? You're an Englishman, aren't you?"

"That may be the problem," Skye said.

"I don't understand it. Most of the maidens of the whole world pine for an Englishman."

Skye laughed. The explorer hadn't seen as much of the world as he supposed.

"You old dog! Two wives!"

Skye didn't like the direction of that, so he nodded curtly and kept on toward his lodge.

"Two wives, Skye. But any Englishman can handle six. I suppose you'll keep adding to the menagerie, eh?"

Skye didn't want to confess that this was actually Victoria's idea; that he had been deeply content with one wife; that this was virtually an arranged marriage, worked out in mysterious ways among friendly peoples.

"Now how does this work, Skye. Separate lodges?"

Skye stopped. "It's Mister Skye, sir, and that topic is closed."

"But it's all for science, Mister Skye. I shall write a piece about this. It'll singe fingers at the *London Times*. Two wives! One so gorgeous I had to rub my eyes! You old rascal. Leave it to the English! Now if a Yank tried that, he'd be rebuffed. It's in our blood, you know."

Skye stared stonily.

Mercer subsided. "Mister Skye, I've given offense. I'm truly sorry. It's all a bit exotic to me, and my mind tends to run with the things I see, so far from home. I want to wish you a most blessed nuptial day, and I hope your household is blessed with happiness."

Skye accepted the apology. That was the thing about Mercer. New things, exotic things, were all the same to him. Absaroka marriage custom excited no more curiosity than geysers or giant bones in the earth. The odd thing was, Skye rather liked the man, and enjoyed all his boyish enthusiasms.

"Thank you. My household will be improved. I hope you will be on hand when the moment arrives."

"Capital, capital! I'll have a fine journal entry today. Now what happens tomorrow? How long does this little summer festival go on?"

"Oh, who knows, sir. Until there's no more grass for the ponies. Until the trading and marrying and cementing of alliances are done."

"But a day? A week? The year's well advanced and I have a whole world to conquer, and I rather have plans that involve you, if you're interested."

"I'm not."

"Well, think about it. I would like a guide. I'll pay you handsomely. I earn plenty from my journals and books, and will reward the right man. I'd like someone to take us up to the geysers. And take us to the giant bones. And take us to any other peculiar places. Or show us lost tribes, pygmies, things like that, that might be hidden back in the wilderness somewhere. Is there not a strange rock formation called a medicine wheel, that invokes the sun or solstice? I'm here to record it all, sir. And do it before the snow flies. Maybe end up at Fort Benton, eh?"

"I don't think I'm the man, Mister Mercer."

"A hundred pounds. That'd fetch a man a few things, wouldn't it? Credit any way you want it."

A hundred pounds was a lot of money. Five hundred Yank dollars, more or less.

"That's not for me to decide today, sir," Skye said, suspecting that it was already decided.

## twelve

kye was as nervous as a groom about to walk the aisle of Westminster Cathedral. He twitched and paced. He sighed. He threatened to bolt and never be seen in these parts again.

Victoria sat him down and pulled out a tiny German steel scissor.

"I'm going to trim your beard," she said, and gently began shaping it into a disciplined round form. He submitted peacefully, enjoying the attention.

"White men have too damned much hair," she grumbled. "We see the first white men, we didn't call them white men, we called them hairy men. The hairy men are coming!"

"Are you sure you want me . . ."

"Don't wiggle your head or you'll be cut. Maybe you should be cut. Maybe that's what I'll do."

Skye submitted at once. "Where will you be? What are you doing tonight?" he asked.

"You'll see."

"I need an answer."

"I will be in our lodge."

Skye sank into himself. This was going to be a very difficult night. He didn't know how or when he would ever see another dawn. What would happen in a lodge with his older wife and his new one?

She finished the trim, turned his head this way and that, and proclaimed herself satisfied.

"Now what?" he asked.

"Wash. Your feet smell like a swamp, as usual."

"You don't have to insult me."

"I love swamps."

"Victoria . . . I . . ."

"You don't have to say anything."

He didn't feel particularly guilty. Victoria was the spider who had spun this web; she'd been after him for years to find another wife. But . . . yes, he did feel guilty. Blue Dawn, who would become Mary soon, evoked lust in him. He ached to make love to her. And that was too much for him to cope with.

"I just want you to know I'll always love you," he said.

Victoria broke into that granny smirk so famous among Crow women. It was a lewd, winking smirk. He had seen it thousands of times. Crow grannies could make a soldier blush.

"If you give one thought to me tonight, I'll be mad at you," she said.

At this point he wasn't capable of giving one thought to anything; not her, not Mary, not himself.

He headed for the river, pulled off his moccasins, laved his feet carefully, and the rest of himself as best he could. When he returned, she had laid out his best skins, golden fringed buckskin shirt, with geometric red and black Crow quillwork. And a new pair of moccasins he hadn't known about. The quillwork on them matched his shirt.

She brushed his beaver top hat, cleaned away some mud, popped out some dents, and restored it to him.

"What do they wear where you come from?" she asked.

"A black swallowtail suit. Or gray. Or nothing fancy if a man is humble."

"England is a scandal," she said. "Utterly savage."

Handsomely adorned, he stepped into the late-afternoon sun. An odd hush had settled over the meadow, an air of anticipation. Jawbone squealed and boomed down upon him.

"Whoa," Skye said.

The horse sniffed, bared its yellow teeth, and screeched.

"You get to be Best Man," Skye said. "You going to have a ring ready for me?"

Jawbone reared, pawed the air, settled to earth, and grunted.

It was odd thinking of marriage in white men's terms, brides, grooms, rings, attendants, churches. This was all so different it seemed not to be a union of a man and a woman.

"Ah, there you are, Mister Skye, looking capital, capital," said Mercer.

The man had gotten himself up in his best, which wasn't half bad considering how far he was from a clothier or laundress. He had brushed his trousers, cleaned his boots, trimmed his hair, washed his face, clipped his own beard.

"Thank you. I'll never get used to this," Skye said.

"You old dog. I haven't decided whether to send it to the Manchester paper or the London. Manchester, I imagine. London's too cosmopolitan. A little spice works better out in the provinces, you know."

"Spice, Mister Mercer?"

"Spice, Mister Skye. It's a good thing you are marrying the most beautiful girl in this entire camp. I plan to make note of it."

Skye laughed. One could not escape Mercer.

Victoria herself emerged from the lodge, pulling away the flap from the oval door. He saw at once that she had adorned herself. Her hair was parted and shown bright in the sun. She wore her loveliest gingham, blue with a white pattern running through it, and she had blue-quilled moccasins to match. What would her role be? She wasn't exactly the mother of the bride.

She smiled at Skye, took his hand and squeezed, and then smiled at Mercer, who bowed gallantly.

By some mysterious clockwork known only to Indians, a party gathered over on the Shoshone side of the meadow, a dozen people perhaps, and Skye could see even across that verdant flat that they were festively dressed, and lots of bold reds, sky blues, and creamy buckskin colors filtered to his vision.

There were several women, fewer men. Back a way, much of the Shoshone village followed. So the cathedral would be filled; every pew!

Skye simply stood, not knowing whether to meet this oncoming party halfway. But Victoria simply smiled and waited. Leading the party were two slim people, a young man and a young woman, and Skye knew at once these were The Runner, and his sister, Blue Dawn, soon to become the second Missus Skye.

How handsome they were, their faces bronzed by a benevolent sun, their dress breathtaking. He wore fringed elk skins without a single bit of decor, but over his neck hung that bear-claw necklace, its long, lethal black claws curving down in an arc over his breast. Her dress was quite the opposite, for she had been festively attired in every way. Her jet hair was parted at the center and hung in shiny braids laced with scarlet ribbons, and with a white ribbon at the tip of each braid. A streak of vermilion was painted on her amber forehead. She wore a whitened doeskin dress, as soft as flour, and lining each sleeve were jingle-bells that sang merrily in the hush of the afternoon. High moccasins trimmed with red encased her feet. A blue girdle, or sash, caught her waist. It truly was a bridal costume, and her eyes danced with anticipation as she caught sight of Skye.

Behind were other handsomely dressed women, each bearing burdens Skye could not fathom.

They approached.

Jawbone screeched and whinnied. They paused a moment, but Skye smiled, assuring them.

He only had eyes for her. She only had eyes for him.

The Runner stopped before Skye. "Prithee, be thou Mister Skye?"

"Yes, and are you The Runner?"

"Verily, thou knowest my name. My Shoshone name. I am also, in thy blessed tongue, St. John. Thus did my pater christen he who standeth before thee."

"Ah, I see."

"I rejoice to speak in thy blessed tongue. My good father taught me words, and gave me the secret of reading, and left three books upon which I might whet my powers. Thy holy book, and one of a teller of tales, one Shakespeare, and other whose blessed name I don't fathom because his name was torn from the front. From these I have mastered thy tongue."

"You do very well, sir."

"It has taken much practice. But sirrah, thou hast spoken for my sister, and thus cometh I to present her to thee. Is she comely?"

"Ravishing."

The Runner frowned. "You would call her that?"

"Beautiful."

"Ah, that is a comfort. We bring thee emoluments and honors. See? Thou shalt have a quilled shirt, and thou shalt have a holy bundle to wear about thy neck, upon thy bosom, in which shall be the sacred things of the One-God black-robes, along with our holy things, a turtle stone and an eagle claw."

Skye accepted the small leather bundle, and lowered the necklace over his chest.

"Sonofabitch," said Victoria. "Big stuff!"

"And now, prithee, Mister Skye, dost thee wish to take hold of my sister and carry her away to thy abode?"

"Yes, sir."

"Then we rejoice and sing Hosannas. Take her. She is thine. Be thou blessed. Maketh her fruitful; fill the world with thy children. Seal with her the peace betwixt the Absaroka and the Shoshone, and thy own pale ones from across the seas."

He nodded to his sister, who walked forward to Skye, stood before him expectantly. Skye scarcely knew what was required, so he caught her hands in his, answered her smile with his own.

"To you I am wed; to you I pledge my love and life," he said.

That seemed to fulfill these people. A sudden relaxation swept through this large crowd.

"Well done, old sport," called Mercer. "She's a handful."

Skye found himself so joyous that nothing the explorer might say could possibly mar the moment.

The Runner stepped close, clasped Skye, and smiled. "It is blessed," he said.

And so the moment dissolved, until there was only Victoria, Mary, Jawbone, and himself.

"I guess we'd better go home," he said, uncertainly.

"No, I will go to our lodge. I will carry these things given to you," Victoria said. "You and Mary, you go that way, dammit." She pointed toward a distant lodge, one Skye hadn't noticed, far apart from the Crow village.

"It is a place the People have prepared for you and the Shoshone woman," she said. "It will be a good place."

## thirteen

The lonely lodge stood perhaps a thousand yards distant, and Skye hurried toward it in the thickening dusk. Mary was as eager as he, and matched his stride with her own. A fine, hot, wild passion was building in Skye, and he knew she was enjoying the moment as much as he.

It was a soft night. The lodge had been pitched beside some larches in a moist hollow, somewhat below the surrounding meadow. A jovial moon was climbing the rim of the world and tossing yellow light upon this Eden. The air felt balmy, somehow more moist than elsewhere in the camp.

He clasped her hand.

Jawbone meandered along behind, not quite abreast but not inclined to abandon his owner, either. The horse was envious. It amused Skye. Where else on earth was such a beast?

They reached the lodge, a small cone nestled in moist grass and screened by the trees, so that the village was invisible.

He handed her through the oval door and into the hushed dark, where only a little twilight filtering through the smoke hole lit their way. The floor was plush with robes.

He couldn't wait, and swept her into his arms, and she hugged him fiercely. But the whine at his ears troubled him. He slapped away a mosquito, and more, and again. The faint humming swelled to a night whine now, and he and she began swatting fiercely, surrounded by scores, and then maybe hundreds. They lit on his neck and hands. He swatted. He felt the sting of several.

She slapped at her neck and her calves.

He yanked the door flap aside and pulled her out, but the mosquitoes found them outside as well as in.

"Mary, head for that high ground. I'll get some robes and follow," he said.

"This is a bad place," she said.

He laughed. "It's a Crow joke. They love nothing better than a joke like this."

"Joke! This is a joke?" She slapped at two mosquitoes that had landed on her wrist.

"Go!" he said.

He dove into the lodge, plucked up two heavy robes, and plunged out, cussing at the cloud of whining bloodsuckers that were tormenting them.

He caught up with her as they raced up a long grade into air that was somehow dryer and scented with juniper from the slopes above. Eventually they were free of the swarming mosquitoes.

"This is a joke?"

"Yes, and probably Victoria's little surprise."

Mary was quiet, and then turned to him. "She is your sits-beside-him woman. Will she be kind to me?"

"You have to understand Absaroka humor," he said. "It is not meant to harm, but to frustrate. There's nothing a grandmother loves so much as a story about lovers frustrated by mosquitoes. Or anything else. It could be a snake or a skunk or a horse. It could be old coyote. When Coyote frustrates lovers, that's the biggest joke of all."

"Can we play a joke on her?"

Skye laughed. He liked that. "We'll think on it."

"We will make a joke!" she said, delighted at the prospect.

They climbed an arid hillside through thickening juniper brush, the resinous scent sweet to his nostrils. There was something clean and bracing in the scent.

"It is good, here," she said. "Find a place, Skye."

The request was so winsome, so tender, so eager that Skye felt half mad. Ahead, pale in moonlight, was a bluff. He headed that way. Behind, he heard Jawbone crashing through the dense juniper. The bluff proved to be a rocky outcrop, so he followed its base until they happened upon a bower, half cupped by overhanging rock, and surrounded on its lower side by a wall of juniper as high as a man's chest. There were no mosquitoes there, and no harsh wind and nothing but nature's own invitation to lovers. Swiftly he scraped away the debris of gravel and juniper sticks under the overhang until the clay was clean and the ground was sweet.

She stood quietly.

"This is good, Mister Skye," she said.

It was good.

"You are my man," she said.

"And you are my woman, Mary."

It was almost dawn before they tumbled into sleep. Then he dreamed sad dreams: everything a mistake. Victoria, hurt. Victoria, silent. He dreamed of pulling into himself, talking to no one. Going away, never coming back. Cold. He awakened in bright daylight. She was staring at him, sitting bare on her robes, her eyes soft.

"You did not sleep well," she said. "I think you maybe too tired, yes?" Her eyes were merry.

He nodded. She was beautiful, her golden flesh aglow in the morning sun. Yet he felt a sadness he could not define. It was not rational. He had spent the sweetest night of his life.

But the serenity of the morning swiftly stole through him, that and her sweetness as she settled beside him and pressed her lips to his. The kiss was honey at first, and then paprika, and then as fiery as chili peppers. He thought only of her, and she was thinking only of him. There was nothing else; no warm sun, no sweet morning, no resinous junipers guarding their bower. They captured each other and fell back onto the soft mat of the buffalo robes, and let the world return to their consciousness. A bee hummed past, hunting for blooms hidden under the juniper canopy.

Only hunger could have driven them from that place, and in time Skye was ravenous for a haunch of buffalo. He helped Mary collect the robes, and they wound their way down the foothills to the encampment and their peoples. The Shoshones smiled at them shyly; the Absarokas smiled slyly. Skye sensed he was facing yet another of those small hurdles that a multiple marriage might bring. How would Victoria be this bright morning? How would he feel toward her? Maybe it was all the nonsense of his European ways; maybe not. Maybe there were many men who would wonder whether they could divide their love among two or three wives.

And what else? How would Victoria treat Mary? How would the wives get along? What if one wife tried to ally Skye against the other wife? He suddenly realized he was borrowing trouble, thinking this way. He laughed, and plunged through the Crow camp toward his own lodge. Actually, it was Victoria's lodge. A Crow man rarely owned his lodge.

Victoria was kneeling beside an elk hide she was scraping; women's work never ended, even on festive occasions.

"Well, dammit, now I got someone to help me," she said. "I started this before the sun rose, while you were busy." She laughed suddenly, a small cheerful chuckle.

"I will work, grandmother," said Mary, hastily kneeling beside Victoria, and grabbing a bone scraper.

"The hell you will," Victoria said. She rose, fed kindling into the embers of a morning fire, and was soon rewarded with flames licking the black cook pot.

Mary rushed to help, but Victoria shooed her off.

Victoria stood, eyed the fire, and smiled at Skye. It was a loving smile. He hastened to her, drew her tight, and was rewarded with a hug. She welcomed his arms and he welcomed hers, and that was all that needed to be said or done. But Skye wondered how he would ever sort it all out. Mary was discreetly staring off toward her Shoshone camp.

Victoria plucked up Skye's arm and examined it minutely.

"I don't see any," she said.

"Any what?"

"Mosquito bites. I don't see none on her, either. I guess you were too busy to get bit." She cackled.

"Is the lodge still there?" he asked.

"Hell no," Victoria replied. She turned to stirring the stew, and let it go at that.

The wedding night sure had been public.

Suddenly it was fine. They would feast. He was ready to eat half a buffalo. Mary looked ready to eat the other half. This afternoon they would leisurely visit friends and family. There would be a good visit with The Runner. It amazed him: here were Shoshone siblings who could speak English after a fashion, a legacy of a father living in Europe.

Victoria poured the steaming stew into wooden bowls and bade them eat. This was a feast. Many a morning Skye had sawed off some cold venison or buffalo haunch or elk meat from a cooked roast, and eaten it. But the warmed meal was Victoria's way of celebrating the new day.

They ate greedily, and then Mary silently collected the bowls, let the camp curs lick them clean, and headed for the river to wash them. Skye watched her go, aware of the lovely body that shifted beneath Mary's skirts.

"You look worn-out, Skye. She wear you out, eh?" Victoria said. "Maybe she's too much for you, eh? Englishmen, they all wear out too fast."

Skye lifted his hat, settled it down on his locks, and roared. "Worn-out! Just try me and see how worn out this Englishman is!"

Victoria made bawdy noises, plainly pleased, and continued with her hide-scraping.

Skye stretched, fed and relaxed and comfortable as the sun pumped some warmth into the morning. Around him the summer's visit was winding down. Skye saw some of the women packing their kitchens into parfleches, while over in the Shoshone camp, the women were hooking travois to horses and loading heaps of robes and bundles onto them. The summer's fun was coming to a close.

That's when Graves Duplessis Mercer threw a shadow across Skye, and stared down at him.

"Well, you lucky dog, I don't suppose you're worth a thing today."

Skye nodded curtly.

"Camp's breaking up. I want to hire you. I need a guide.

It's now or never, Skye. There's things to see before the snow falls. You interested? A hundred pounds."

Skye found himself saying yes even before he could weigh the offer.

## fourteen

Skye waved the man to a log that served as a bench. Mercer always managed to look dashing and now was wearing a broad-brimmed felt hat, a canvas shirt, and short britches that bared hairy white calves.

"Let's talk about it," Skye said. "Where are you heading? What do you want to see?"

"The geysers near here. And the big bones your older wife was telling me about. I also want to meet strange tribes. I want to discover ones that have never seen a white man. There are some, you know. Down in the desert canyons. If you know of tribes that practice cannibalism, that's my meat."

He laughed at his own joke.

"And where are you headed? It's late in the year."

"Why, the Oregon country. After we're done here, I'll hook up with Hudson's Bay, take the first ship out. To the Pacific islands I hope, but I'll take China or Australia or whatever. I have journals to go to London. Need to find a ship sailing somewhere."

"You're too late to get to Oregon, Mister Mercer."

"Too late! How can I be too late?"

"It's August. You need to be on the Columbia a month from now."

"Well, we'll be there."

The man had little grasp of North American geography and even less grasp of its winter climate. He didn't realize how far he had strayed from the Yank road to Oregon, the only practical way over the continental divide, the only way to reach waters flowing west.

"If you were to head this day for the Oregon Road and then head west as fast as you can move with that wagon, you might barely make the Pacific coast before winter shuts you in."

"But, Mister Skye, it's summer. It's hot. I'm dressed in tropical clothing."

Skye was relentless. "You could do some sightseeing in this country, reach Fort Benton on the Missouri River in October, build or buy a flatboat, and reach St. Louis just ahead of bad weather."

"I should turn around? Return to St. Louis?"

"If you want to see the sights here, yes, turn around. If you want to hightail for Oregon, start now, this hour. Don't waste a minute."

Mercer sprang up and paced. He had a boyish quality but Skye sensed the man was harder and more resourceful than his demeanor suggested. Victoria, who had been listening, squinted darkly at Skye. He knew she didn't approve. But a hundred pounds would outfit Skye for years. It was worth the risk posed by this adventurer.

"Oh, pshaw, Mister Skye, I think I'll just do what I planned; see the geysers, see the bones. The weather will hold. You're looking at the luckiest Englishman on the planet. If I'd quit in the middle of half my projects, I'd be moldering as a printer's devil in London. Look at me! I've walked through jungles where bushmen waited with poisoned darts. I've watched Asian cultists lower a little girl into a pit of cobras. I've watched Pacific islanders give a goat to a phallic god. I've seen midnight fertility dances that I can't even write about. I've watched prisoners staked out upon a mound of meat-eating ants. I've watched African mutilation ceremonies that I would have to describe in Latin. I've walked into the bowels of an active volcano. I've weathered a Sahara sandstorm. I've watched cannibals eat their guests. I've swum rivers filled with man-eating fish. I have swum with sharks. I have sailed an outrigger canoe across the Indian Ocean. I have watched a blind man snare and eat giant frogs, and catch poisonous eels barehanded. I have ridden the backs of whales. Was I afraid? Never."

That did it. "Mister Mercer, I won't guide men who are never afraid," Skye said.

Mercer didn't even pause. "Why, I was just exaggerating, old boy. Showing off, you know." He smiled, revealing that row of dazzling white teeth so perfect Skye thought that maybe they'd been carved from ivory.

"I think you would find none of those things here, Mister Mercer. You're on the wrong continent."

"I'd give my eyeteeth for just a peek at a lost tribe, one that survives in some canyon somewhere. Or some ruins like those in Peru. Whole cities rotting away down there. They're common enough in Mexico. Do you suppose you could guide me there?"

"I would be as lost there as you, sir."

"Blast. I have to make a living. What is there to say about this dull place? Someday it will be villages and plowed fields.

And the Indians will all wear calico and leather shoes and get married by Methodist clergy."

"There's North American wildlife, Mister Mercer."

"No match for Africa. How does this compare with elephants and giraffes? Or Australia. Dingos, kangaroos, and all that. Pitiful. Who wants to read about bears? Mister Skye, what I want is strange people who live in strange ways. That's what sells penny dreadfuls in Liverpool."

"I'm fresh out of strange people, sir."

"There are some. Plural marriage. I've been thinking of wintering with the Mormons down in Deseret. That should be worth some ink, eh? How do they do it? A few stories from Deseret, and every lusty man in London will set sail. Ho, ho! That's the only interesting thing about North America. Every man on the continent has a spare wife or two stashed away."

Skye laughed. He thought it was time to get the horses and pull out. The Crows were loading their travois. "You'll do fine, Mister Mercer," he said, and stood.

"You win, Mister Skye. I surrender. You take us to the geysers, and then show us the big bones, and I'll head for Deseret for the winter. We'll just ride to the high country and take a few hot baths and then turn it over to Old Man Winter."

"There's a hundred miles of forest, canyons, cliffs, rocky creeks, walls of brush to get to the geysers. It would take a while."

"I have been all over the world. Whenever guides tell me I can't do something, I set out to do it."

"That's fine. I'll draw you a map. You can leave the wagon right here."

"That wagon's my supply depot. If I leave it here, I'll lose everything in it. I can't leave it here. It has to come with me. I want my men with me too. They're good men."

"If you want to stay with your wagon you'd better choose some other sights to see, Mister Mercer."

The explorer had an odd trapped look in his eyes. He wasn't used to being thwarted. "Where are the giant bones?"

Skye turned to Victoria.

"All over hell and back," she said.

"Madam, where is hell and back?"

She pointed southeast. "Some that way, on a ridge near the Medicine Bow Mountains. Near Fort Laramie." She pointed north. "Some that way, near Fort Benton." She pointed east. "Some that way in bad country. Lots of Sioux around there."

Mercer paced back and forth, weighing things, his lust for adventure frustrated by the impending winter and the terrain.

"The bones north of here, then. The ones near Fort Benton." Mercer smiled, that high-energy smile that always seemed to settle things in his mind.

"I'll talk to my men. You get ready to go."

Skye wasn't sure. "We need to address some things. A hundred pounds when? What are my duties? For how long? How will I be paid? Where will my services end? What exactly do you expect of me?"

Mercer seemed to be expecting the questions: "You will be paid at the conclusion of satisfactory service. I can give you a letter of credit good at any fur company post or Hudson's Bay. You will guide us and hunt for us, your women will provide meals and amenities, you'll show us natural wonders known to yourself or your women, you'll translate or use sign language; you'll keep us out of danger and warn me if any sort of trouble looms. You will work until winter prohibits further exploration, and then take us to Fort Benton and get us a flatboat."

Skye nodded. "I have some requirements of my own, sir.

In times of danger I will expect you to do exactly what I require, and without delay. If we should encounter some Blackfeet, there may be no time at all to debate. Is that suitable to you?"

"Oh, Mister Skye, those occasions are so rare they're hardly worth worrying ourselves."

"I must have that assurance."

"Oh, have it your way, Mister Skye. Let's be off, eh?"

Victoria was listening and frowning. Mary sat quietly on a robe. Victoria's eyes were filled with messages, which Skye swiftly understood.

"Something else, Mister Mercer. You will see things and places that are sacred to the people who live here. You respect what you see in any church; you will, I trust, respect what you see here. The bones we will take you to are the bones of the gods and must be treated as such."

"I enjoy writing about the local cults, old boy. The better the myths, the more I like them."

What was it about Mercer that worried Skye? No matter. He would deal with it.

"All right. We'll go to the big bones, and then Fort Benton."

Mercer nodded and headed for his wagon and men. Skye watched him as he addressed his teamsters. They sprang to life at once, collecting the draft horses, packing a mound of gear.

Skye turned to his ladies. "We've been engaged by Mister Mercer. It will earn us a lot of money; there will be good things for all of us at the trading posts." He turned to Mary. "We'll be going to see the giant bones in the rocks. If you wish to say good-bye to your brother and your people, now is the time."

"We will leave my people?"

"Yes. We'll go north with Victoria's people. The man is a storyteller, and is gathering stories to tell people where he comes from."

"Will you give me to him?"

There it was. "Why do you ask?"

"It is the way he looks at me."

"If he tries something like that, I will stop it. You are my wife."

She lit up. "Then it will be a trip to remember!"

"If he doesn't get us in trouble," Victoria said.

## fifteen

he Absarokas reached the glinting Yellowstone four days later. Mercer and his teamsters tagged along without difficulty as they traversed level and semi-arid ground with few creeks to ford. Skye rode Jawbone, keeping an eye on Mercer and his teamsters and the wagon as well as Mary and Victoria, who guided the travois-burdened horses. The wives fell smoothly into companionship. Skye was pleased. Victoria was less crabby than she had ever been, finding that her life had improved.

Mary had offered a tender good-bye to The Runner and her people, and had joined Skye's small household with no visible emotion. Somehow, it all was working and Skye's uneasiness had gradually dissolved. He was also more at ease with Mercer, who proved to be a good travel companion, undemanding and competent to deal with life far from anything resembling civilization as he knew it.

They traversed a grove of cottonwoods and reached the Yellowstone River at a place where it ran through a broad meadow, hemmed by distant bluffs. Even as the Absarokas pulled up on the south bank to water and rest their ponies, they were hailed by a lone traveler heading west, a white man in a gray slouch hat, leading two pack mules.

The Absarokas greeted him with curiosity and asked Skye to translate. Graves Mercer and his teamsters headed toward the stranger even as the Crows flocked around him. The meeting was all smiles and the stranger doffed his slouch hat time and again, his salute to these people.

The man actually was middle-aged with a trimmed gray beard, spectacles, watery blue eyes, brown canvas clothing, and laced boots.

"This is a surprise," he said. "Nutmeg here. Samuel Storrs Nutmeg at your service."

The man halted his pack mules and acknowledged the collecting crowd. The man's way of clipped and precise speaking awakened curiosity in Skye. Was he a Yank?

"I'm Mister Skye," he said. "My wives Mary and Victoria. This is Graves Duplessis Mercer and his assistants, Floyd Corporal and Silas Winding. And I shall introduce you to our headmen directly."

"Mister Skye, are you? I've been advised that you're the man to hire if one needs a guide. I made some inquiries."

"I seem to have acquired a reputation, deserved or not," Skye said. "And you, sir?"

"A Connecticut Yankee. New Haven, actually. I'm a professor," said Nutmeg. He turned to the explorer. "And you, Mister Mercer. I know your work."

"And I know yours, Professor. Yale College is it?"

"Indeed it is. What a stroke! A pair of wanderers out in the American desert."

Skye peered about, looking for evidence of a desert and

finding none. The meadow was mostly sun-cured tan grasses waving in the breezes.

"What brings you to this remote place?" Mercer asked the stranger.

"Science," the man replied. "I am doing a bit of exploration. Maybe you've read a paper or two of mine. Mostly academic journals, my own little sallies against orthodoxy. Took two years off, and spending my last dollar too. I'm heading for the geyser country. You know what's up there? Obsidian. The stuff has been traded all over the continent. There are regular work yards there, where it was flaked into arrowheads and spear points. It seems to be a prized item among the tribes. I've traced it to the Ohio River valley."

"Natural science! Why, that's why I'm here."

"I don't care to pigeonhole myself," Nutmeg said. "I'm the proverbial square peg. A bit of anthropology, a bit of paleontology, a bit of geology, a bit of zoology, and a dose of botany."

"You have no guide?"

Nutmeg smiled. "Maps and a compass. Two good mules. A field glass. Some interviews a few weeks ago with the mountain men in St. Louis. Some notes and sketches of landmarks. I can't afford a guide, Mister Mercer, not on my salary. So I ramble along quite on my own."

"Quite so. A brave man, sir. I congratulate you."

Skye intervened. "I'd like you to meet our headmen, Mister Nutmeg. They're waiting here, wishing to greet you."

"Very good," Nutmeg said.

Skye, translating, introduced the traveler to Chief Robber and the headmen as well as dozens of Absarokas, who welcomed him. Some of them wanted to know what this lone traveler did and Skye responded that he was a collector of plants and animals and stones. Very like the other one, Mercer.

And in turn, he translated for Nutmeg. "The Absarokas are heading east, downriver, into buffalo country. It'll soon be time for the fall hunt and the buffalo usually are thickest east of here. You are welcome to join them."

"Ah, a pity. I was hoping they might join me for a trip to the geysers but we seem to be heading in opposite directions."

"You're going to the headwaters of the Yellowstone? Where that geyser is that you can set a clock by?" Mercer asked, an edge to his questions.

"Why yes, it's now or never before the snow flies."

"My man here tells me it's not passable. Rushing rivers and all that."

"For a man with pack mules it is. I understand I'll have no problem if I do it on foot."

"My guide wouldn't take me there," Mercer said.

Skye kept silent. Mercer's statement was not complete or true, but Mercer neither finished nor corrected it.

"All I have to do is follow this splendid river right into the bosom of the geysers, and catch fat trout all the way," Nutmeg said. "Simple enough, eh? Easy way in and out. Why, I'm told once I'm up there I'll see steam rising from geysers everywhere I look. Imagine it. Steam hissing and spitting out of a hole in the rocks. The earth belching a column of hot water and thundering like a volcano. I'm going to take some temperatures, and test the waters for minerals. A little sulphur, I suppose. Who knows what else? I've a kit, you know, a regular laboratory. It's time someone did some work on the geysers."

"All alone. Don't you prefer company?"

Nutmeg paused, eyed Mercer, and slowly shook his head.

"I'm a bit of a loner, Mister Mercer. I take my time, go where my curiosity leads me."

"Well, those geysers aren't the only things in the whole area worth writing about."

Nutmeg smiled. "I should think there would be wonders everywhere. But who am I to say? This gentleman, Skye here, is the best man to steer you. That's what I learned in St. Louis."

Mercer responded with one of those toothy smiles.

The Absarokas were restless, impatient to move, unable to understand all of this palaver. After much consultation they headed downriver. Victoria watched her people go, her face a mask. The Indians forded the Yellowstone at a broad gravelly shallows, the horses splashing through hock-deep water, and continued down the north bank until at last they rounded a bend and vanished. Now there was only silence, bright sun, crows and magpies, and a sparkling river.

"Mister Skye, I've changed my mind," said Mercer. "I think I'll just tag along with Professor Nutmeg. He can teach me lots of things. We'll wagon most of the way. Look at this flat. The river's running through a wide valley, no trouble at all to take a wagon upstream."

Skye stared sharply. Professor Nutmeg had offered no such invitation. "I thought you wanted a look at the fossil bones, Mister Mercer."

"Bones? What bones? What are you talking about, man?" Mercer seemed much put out.

"Fossil bones, Mister Skye?" asked Nutmeg.

"My wife's people know of some, north of here in the Missouri breaks and a few other places. Mister Mercer wished to be taken there."

Mercer dismissed it all. "Oh, I expect they'll be just a few trilobites, ammonites, little stuff caught in a limestone bluff."

"Damn big bones," said Victoria. "Giants from the old days. My people are afraid of them. Their spirits live there, don't like no trouble."

"Madam, I don't believe it is possible to find large bones in fossil form. The geologic pressures are too great," Mercer said.

Nutmeg was absorbing all of this with acute interest. "That would be interesting, looking at fossil bones, Mister Skye. I daresay, some recent discoveries have excited the whole world of natural science. Bones of ancient creatures twenty feet high, giant lizards, so they seem. Obviously extinct."

"Nothing around here, Professor. Wrong strata. Too recent," Mercer said. "A look at the fossils is just a side trip. We're really having a hard look at some of the tribes. Customs, dances, all that. That's what I do, you know, write about people they've never heard of in London."

"Yes, and your pieces are widely read, Mister Mercer. They make their way across the Atlantic."

Skye registered all of this with some surprise. Rivalry. But most of all, secrecy. Nutmeg didn't want Mercer tagging along to the geyser country; Mercer didn't want Nutmeg to know about the bone fields Victoria was going to show to him. Mercer was being deceptive, but not Nutmeg. The professor was straightforward. It was Mercer who had scented a rival.

"Mister Mercer, I think you'll be happy to proceed to the fossil bones," Skye said. "I think you will be delighted by your discoveries. That's where you hired us to take you."

For a moment there was thunder in Mercer's face and then the dazzling smile and the pearly teeth.

"Why, Mister Skye, old fellow, we'll continue on our way. I really wouldn't want to risk a wagon up in the headwaters of the Yellowstone. The geysers interest me not in the slightest."

Skye had a whole new perspective on the man who had employed him. First Mercer wanted to tag along with the professor, a sudden change in plans. Then Mercer tried to conceal what he was up to, lying to Nutmeg about the size of the bones. Clearly, there were sides to Mercer that would inspire caution. Skye wondered if he would last for the agreed-on period, or get paid.

# *sixteen*

avigation was in Victoria's hands. She knew where the giant bones were; Skye had seen them once but couldn't recollect just where. All she told him was that they were not far from the confluence of the Musselshell and the Missouri Rivers.

She led them north across high plains laced with giant coulees, sandstone ridges, and gulches filled with cottonwood trees. To the north and west, distant mountain ranges poked through autumnal haze. It was not a welcoming land. It was a place that made a man feel lonely. Sometimes when the wind quit, Skye could hear utterly nothing. The silence ran so deep that it made a man itchy. It was a land to hurry through.

The party proceeded peaceably enough. The two teamsters knew intuitively where to steer the giant draft horses as they worked up and down long grades and across a roadless sea of grass. The horses stayed fat, devouring the rich fodder.

At night, his women rarely raised the lodge, choosing to bed in buffalo robes under a bowl of stars. This always occasioned stares from Mercer and the teamsters, who put up their wall tent each evening. Let them think whatever they wanted to think. Skye didn't care. The nights were as black as nights could be and how he and his wives lived would be veiled from the men.

Skye roamed wide on Jawbone, training the young horse to close on buffalo from downwind and then race close to give Skye the lethal shot he needed to down the nimble animal. The great herds drifted across the sky-girt lands in small bunches, as feed and water dictated. Meat was never far away for Skye's party. This was, in its way, a food pantry, but Mercer didn't see it that way.

"When will we get to the bones, Skye?" he asked after several days of steady progress.

"Long way, mate. A week, ten days."

"But, Skye, there's nothing here. This is the most boring land I've ever crossed."

"It's a quiet land, I'll grant you that. But look around you. It's big country. Have you ever seen country so large or the sky so high?"

"But where's the story, Skye? I make my living writing stories. I can't see a story anywhere. I'm wasting time."

Skye hardly knew how to respond. "There's a story in every rock, I imagine. You've seen the way the wind sculpts the sandstone. All those little wind caves make dens for catamounts, nests for birds, cubbyholes for coyotes."

Mercer didn't see it and grew more and more testy.

"Skye, if we were crossing the Sahara, there'd be a story every mile. Dunes as high as mountains. The Berbers! Bright blue eyes, Nordic faces. I'd swear they were Vikings except they have big noses, bigger than yours. Bedouins! Camel caravans! Ancient trade routes known only to those camel drivers. They smoke hashish. They eat sheep's eyeballs. They touch not a drop of spirits. They sometimes lose their trading goods to bandits, swift raiders on fine Arab horses that swirl out of the dust and cut them dead with scimitars. The whole Sahara is a thieves' den, Skye. Murders! Assassinations! Those caravans! The traders enter oases as if they were caliphs, and are welcomed by sloe-eyed women with flashing smiles behind their veils. Well, Skye, where's the story here? Am I on the wrong continent? I ought to have ten sensations a day to fill my journals!"

Skye nodded. A man looking for a sensation here might have a harder time of it. Skye couldn't help that.

The farther north they proceeded, the more he watched for Blackfeet. A war party could hide in any gulch and never be seen. So Skye roamed wide, examined the age of spoor, studied the world from ridges, and checked with his client now and then.

Mercer grew grouchy. "How long, Skye! This was a mistake! I should have known better than to come here! Can't you speed things up?"

"The pace is set by your teamsters, sir. It's the wagon that slows us. Mister Corporal and Mister Winding are making sure those draft horses don't fail you."

"I'll tell them to hurry it up. Those horses are fine, fit as a fiddle, fat. I tell you, this is a wasted time; I'll have to write off the whole business."

"You could study the buffalo, sir. Come with me while I hunt. They're a wise and majestic beast. They can't see well but they can smell. Only the fastest horse can outrun them. When they stampede, the whole earth vibrates."

"Who cares about the buffalo? Just big, dumb uglies, that's all. I don't like the sight of blood. Now if we were in Africa, I could write about lions and zebras and giraffes. There are places on this earth that evoke something mystical in the human breast. Africa is such a place. These endless plains are not."

"You might study the coyotes, Mister Mercer. Crafty fellows, mythic to all the tribes, tricksters, clever and devious, curious about everything."

"Nothing but a small wild dog, Skye. Now the Australian dingos are worth writing about. Predators, eat babies, brutal and cunning. The Aborigines have stories."

Skye sighed. He could not help a man determined to be discontent. Mercer yanked his horse away and rode off to be alone, while Skye stayed for the moment with his small party, his women, his horses, his burdened travois.

Victoria edged close. She had been listening. "I don't like that sonofabitch," she said.

"Oh, he's just restless. Some people truly see the land and its animals and people; others pass through a country and never see a thing. He's one of those, I imagine. But rather a pleasant bloke most of the time. We'll show him what we can, get our money, and have a good winter."

Then one day they reached the Musselshell River, a pallid stream dribbling along a shallow trench lined with willows and cottonwoods.

"What a poor excuse for a river, Skye. Where's the story here?"

"It's sometimes considered a boundary between the Absarokas and the Siksika," Skye said.

"Siksika?"

"Blackfeet. The most restless, proud, handsome, ruthless, dangerous, powerful tribe on the northern plains. They despise Yanks, but might be kinder to an Englishman. They'd butcher me because I'm married into the Crows; take my wives captive, kill your Missouri teamsters, and be content to steal everything you possess and let you hike for the nearest Hudson's Bay Company post."

"Which is where?"

"North of the medicine line. Canada."

"That's all the story here?"

"No; we are crossing the larder of a dozen tribes. This is where they come to eat. They fight over it."

"No story there, Skye."

Skye sighed. Victoria had selected a meadow under a sandstone bluff, well back from the water, where a prairie wind wouldn't topple the lodge. The bluff would also conceal the cook fire. It was a good spot, with natural defenses. Skye wondered whether Mercer grasped that the farther north they traveled, the more Skye sought to keep them safe. That was a story for Mercer if he wanted it. The incessant war between Crows and Blackfeet could fill ten journals if Mercer had wanted to learn about it. But the explorer had slid into a funk and Skye had no desire to tell stories to a man who lacked eyes and ears.

But this night was different. Mercer consulted his teamsters, dug into the wagon, and pulled out a small oaken cask.

"This stream mislabeled a river's got ice-cold water even if it's discolored. It'll give us yellow gin and bitters," he said. "But I suppose we might imbibe. Nothing else to do but stew ourselves to the gills. I've got enough to stew us for a month. I can stew us all the way to Fort Benton and then down the river. I'll stew us at breakfast, I'll stew us at dinner, I'll stew us on the prairies, I'll stew us in the mountains, I'll stew every savage that comes visiting, I'll stew every coyote that pokes his nose into camp, I'll stew the mosquitoes. By God, this American West is a bust, an absolute disaster. How am I to get a living?"

"Aiee!" howled Victoria. She was not opposed to this plan so long as she could be included.

It was a temptation. Skye didn't mind a good sousing. But there was something about all this that was menacing. Big drunks in wild lands were trouble.

"No," he said.

"What do you mean, no? This is my outfit and you're my employee."

"No."

"Are you defying me?"

"I always do what's necessary for the safety of people in my charge."

"Relax, Skye, and have a drink. Enjoy my hospitality. Where else can you get a good gin and bitters around a friendly campfire? The trip's a bust; let's celebrate the disaster."

In a way, Mercer's proposition was delightful. The man was making light of a bad trip and would head for other adventures in other corners of this great globe.

Skye had been there before. At the rendezvous of mountain men, when the fun sometimes turned deadly. At saturnalias where Indians, not used to spirits, came apart and went mad. He eyed Victoria, who would no doubt enjoy the rowdy times, and Mary, new to his life and white men, and vulnerable.

"No," he said. "If you and your party get stewed, I am resigning."

Mercer bared that row of pearly teeth once again. The man could melt the heart of a witch with a smile like that. "Not even one little toddy?"

"Not now. Not here. One would lead to another."

"Oh, come join us, just one, Skye."

"It's Mister Skye, sir. And in your present humor, it would

not be one. No, Mister Mercer. Pour and we'll pack up, my family and I."

That's when a voice rose out of the twilight. "Hello the camp," someone yelled.

# seventeen

*I*ntuitively, Skye and Victoria edged toward shadows even as Mercer welcomed whoever it was.

The approaching man towered taller than Skye thought a mortal could reach. Six and a half feet, perhaps. He had a gray slouch hat over jet hair. He was leading a black mule, laden with gear. If the man's height was striking, his face was even more so. He wore a jet beard as straight as spikes and sawed off horizontally at shoulder level, the shape of the beard as sharp and square as planed ebony. Above that was an aquiline nose and a pair of obsidian eyes. On first glance he seemed menacing, but Skye intuited that the man was not that way at all.

"Well, sirs, I see I am among my own. I'm Jacob Reese at your service," the man said in a voice that rattled out of his lungs. An odd voice it was, rising from the man's belly and reaching Skye's ears as something out of a cave.

Mercer took over. "Why, Mister Reese, I'm Graves Duplessis Mercer." Mercer was plainly waiting to be recognized, but the recognition didn't come, which just as plainly disappointed Mercer. "Ah, this is Mister Skye and his ladies, Missus and Missus Skye, and my assistants, Mister Corporal and Mister Winding. Won't you join us? We haven't started a meal, but soon we will."

"English are you. I saw it coming," Reese said, which puzzled Skye.

The man picketed his black mule and unloaded his gear, while Skye quietly observed. Reese seemed entirely competent in the wilds.

At last the man finished his chores and settled down beside the low flame. "I saw it coming," he said. "You would be here. I knew it this morning when I searched beyond the ready knowing and into the realm from which I draw gifts."

Mercer smiled, his teeth so achingly white in the firelight that they made almost a beacon of light in the darkness. "Well, sir, you can entertain us with visions. We're about to pour a libation. Would you care to imbibe?"

Reese paused, a certain cunning in his face, and nodded. "Yes, gin and bitters. That's what you're serving. I shall sample one, with gratitude."

"How did you know . . ."

"I don't know how I know. I just do. It comes to me. I have the inner eye. It's a gift and a curse. Did you know, sir, that silver has been discovered in Nevada? Yes, tons and mountains of it! But the word has not yet reached the States. I saw it spread upon the back of my mind. Don't ask me how. I saw it, and I shall be proven right!"

Mercer nodded to Floyd Corporal, the man who usually concocted the bitters and then added them to gin. The teamster set to work. Skye watched uneasily.

The stranger settled by the flickering flame in the twilight, and slapped away a mosquito. Skye didn't know what to make of him.

"What brings you here, Mister Reese?" he asked.

"Gold! Silver! Copper! Right in these northern mountains are giant bodies of ore, so rich it makes me dizzy. I saw it all; I know where to go. Gold, in filaments and flakes, in milky quartz, easy to pluck up if you wish. Fortunes to be made. Gold washing down creeks. Gold and silver buried in thick veins under the earth. Silver, crusted into strange shapes, ready to harvest."

"Where might that be?" Mercer asked.

"I will know it when the next vision is given to me."

"Then you don't know."

"Of course I know! I have come this far, first on a riverboat, and then overland, from Zebulon, North Carolina. I know exactly where I am going. Silver, gold, sir, draw me ever forward."

"But there's been very little silver found in North America," Mercer said. "Mexico, mainly."

"And that has changed! Even now, miners are hitting bonanzas."

"How do you know that?"

Reese sighed. "My inner vision, sir. I see I am not believed. And that's good. For it opens the field to me alone. Where I go, you will not follow."

Floyd Corporal began handing out the gin and bitters in sweating tin cups. Skye held his peace.

"Why do you tell us about the gold and silver? Why don't you keep it a secret?" Skye asked.

Reese fixed Skye with those obsidian eyes. "You do not believe."

Skye admitted to himself that he didn't. The man was half mad. In all the years Skye had roamed the northern lands, mountains and plains and deserts, no one had found gold or even a mineral seam. There was little gold here; little gold to the west where the Rockies climbed to the sky.

"Treasure stories. The world doesn't lack them," Mercer said. "On every continent, among every people. I don't put much stock in them. I couldn't even sell them to the *Times*. But I am looking for stories, Mister Reese. I write little things for British papers. Now, when you were coming upriver, did you see anything out of the ordinary?"

"It suits me that you don't believe," Reese said. "You see, I intend to claim it all and then put it to good use." He eyed each of the people sitting around that fire intently. "There's enough gold and silver and base metals within two hundred miles of here to transform the republic. We're a poor people, we Americans. We scratch livings out of the poor soil. We are roadless. We spin our cloth and hoe our gardens and barely get along. I'm going to change that. I will claim all these minerals before the greedy steal them and exploit them all for themselves. Yes, once I own these minerals, sirs, I will use every cent to bless the poor and the hungry. All a widow will need to do is apply. All an orphan needs to do is apply. The same for the sick and blind and wounded. I'll give a competence to those in need, and better than that, I'll set up people in business. A poor orphan might become a shopkeeper. A lame man an artist. You see? For once in human history, the wealth in the earth will be spent entirely on those in need."

Skye marveled. The man might be mad, but never had he heard such a visionary and noble design.

Reese stopped suddenly, waiting for a response, perhaps waiting for objections, but no one objected.

"I am being led by Divine Providence," Reese said. "Just as surely as I have seen the future, I will harvest the wealth and devote it to the needful."

Mercer seemed amused. The teamsters kept silent. Victoria accorded Reese all the respect that her people gave to madmen.

"This is a fine libation," Reese said. "You might suppose that I would not approve; that I teetotal. You would be wrong. I am not a puritan or a fanatic. Anglican, if you wish to know my background."

"Truly noble, Mister Reese," Mercer said. "But I do have a question. How will you claim these fields and mountains of minerals? Has your republic laws that permit it? This is public land, isn't it? Has it been surveyed? Can you file a claim somewhere?"

Reese sat up. Even sitting, he towered over them all. "What I find will be mine. What I claim will be mine. For I will know, while standing upon a bonanza, where it is and what is there. And once I know, that is all that is necessary. I will drive my corner stakes when I am called to drive them. Until then, the secret will reside in my soul."

"But, forgive me, how will you pass the secret on to others? Surely you don't expect to develop all these bodies of ore in one lifetime?"

"My nature is monkish," Reese said. "It is true that the secret abides only in my bosom. If I had heirs, they would fight over the spoils. So if I perish the vision will perish with me. This, too, I have seen, for it has been given to me to see things in the back of my mind."

"How far are we from gold? Right here, how far?" Mercer asked.

Reese closed his eyes, almost as if he were sliding into a

trance. "We are sixty-eight miles as the crow flies from gold. But that is not a large deposit," he said.

Skye had the uneasy feeling the man was exactly right.

"How far from this mountain of copper you mention?"

Again Reese seemed to draw into himself. He closed his eyes, and then opened them. "One hundred ninety-four miles to the mountain of copper, again as the crow flies. But the surface of that place has silver. The copper is lower."

"Where is the best gold?" Mercer asked.

"One hundred and seventy-eight miles southwest," Reese said.

"How do you know that?"

Reese looked affronted. "Have I not told you how I know? I could take you there. We could start this moment and I could take you to the exact place, a river so full of nuggets that it will yield millions and millions of dollars."

"Where is the nearest silver, Mister Reese?" Mercer was obviously enjoying this game.

"Not far. There's a rich carbonate ore of silver one hundred and eight miles distant."

"Very good, Mister Reese. I wish you luck," Mercer said.

"It is not luck, sir. If it were luck, I would spend my life meandering. No, I am being taken where I am being taken, and for the good of the Republic." He finished his cup, stood, and addressed them all.

"I thank you for the hospitality. I cherish a good gin and bitters. Now I'll be on my way."

"At night? You'll not stay for a supper? We've some buffalo tongue."

"Night and day make no difference to me, Mister Mercer. It is all one. Sleep and wakefulness make no difference. When I rest, it is for my mule's sake, not mine."

With that, Reese retrieved his black mule, loaded it, and vanished upriver. In utter silence they watched the man go, and then there was only the night.

"I come to North America looking for a good story, looking for something, anything, to promote science and entertain London, and what do I find? A madman," Mercer said. "There's not a good story anywhere. The trip's a bust."

## eighteen

T he night was black velvet but her flesh felt silky and the welcoming clasp of her arms was as tender as lamb's wool. They lay apart from the others. Victoria slept upriver. Mercer, as usual, slumbered in his stained wall tent. The teamsters were bedded under the wagon. This summer's night was serene but broken by the playful love songs of wolves on distant ridges.

He lay on the thick robe, she beside him, staring at the star-girt sky. So far, his new union had been joyous and yet he worried. He could not help it.

He asked her a white man's question. No Shoshone male would even think of asking such a thing.

"Are you happy?" he said.

"I do not know this. Why do you ask?"

"You are my woman. Is it good? Are you at peace?"

"I have all that I ever dreamed of, Mister Skye."

It was too much a white man's question, he thought, but then she slid her hand across his beard, toying with it.

"It is good. I am the woman of Mister Skye. How could it not be good?"

"I am glad. I am very happy too," he said.

"Maybe you will tell me what we will do next," she said.

"We'll take Mercer to the big bones. It makes my head ache to think of the creatures when they were alive. Lizards bigger than the tallest lodge."

"We must be very respectful. Their spirits will linger there. The spirit of an animal so big must be very strong."

"I think Mercer wants to measure them, sketch them, take a good look, and then guess what sort of beast they were."

"Why is this?"

"He likes to find things his people have never heard of, so he can write about them, tell stories about them."

"Our storytellers like to talk about the things we have always known."

Skye stared at the mysterious heavens. "Just now, bold men are looking everywhere for new things and new places, things unheard of, animals unknown, plants strange and exotic. They sail the seas. They go to the south and the north. They go to islands where no one has ever been. They go to a place called Africa and see strange people. And all this is being carefully recorded. Mercer is doing that, and has become a great storyteller there in England, and is making much money from it."

"He is strange himself," she said. "He says this trip is no good and yet his eyes don't see."

Skye liked that. He slid an arm around her and pulled her close until her head nestled in the hollow of his shoulder, her raven hair tumbling over his chest. "It's because he has an idea of what he wants and keeps looking for it. In other places he saw strange animals and strange people, and oddities of nature. In Africa there are horses with black and white stripes called zebras. But here, the animals are familiar, and the people, your people, have been known to English people for two centuries."

"He will be happy when he sees the bones."

"I think so. The geysers would have fascinated him too. Who in his land has ever seen hot water and steam explode from the ground?"

"He makes happy smiles but he is restless," she said. "Mister Skye, in my heart I fear that he will get us into trouble, and I am afraid of him."

Skye thought about that, seeing some realism in it. "We will need to be careful, then," he said. "It will only be for a while. And then he will buy a boat and go down the Big River."

A twig snapped near the stream and Skye instantly grew alert. Something was passing through. He sensed a large animal, and waited to hear more, but there was nothing to hear. He peered into the darkness and saw Jawbone looming over him.

"Go eat," he said.

The horse snorted softly, nudged Skye, and meandered away.

Mary relaxed too. On a summer's night the whole world moved from place to place. Over the years of living outside he had learned to sort out the shifting of animals, and could sometimes even tell which animal, but most often he knew only that some creature was making its way through the darkness. Somehow, human movement was different. Night sounds ceased, as if humans moving through the night were entombed in silence. He did not sense this silence now.

She was sitting up, the pale light reflecting off her bare

shoulders, so he pulled her close again, and she responded with delight.

The Musselshell turned north here, and they would follow it clear to the Missouri River, enjoying its flowing water and whatever game might be lurking in its bottoms. It would be a pleasant trip even if Mercer didn't much like the pace.

With the dawn, the explorer was up, shaved, and restless as his teamsters heated water for his tea and began some biscuits in a Dutch oven. Skye washed in the river, studied himself for a moment in the shimmering water, finding himself grayer than he had supposed, and then joined Victoria and Mary at the cook fire.

As Skye somehow expected, Mercer headed his way as soon as it was proper.

"I say, Skye, I'd like to hurry this along. Can we make better time? I'd like to get across this wasteland in a day or two and get on with it. If I have a peek at the bones, I can be in St. Louis in a few weeks and England before Christmas."

"With your wagon, sir, it's four days, maybe five to the Missouri, and a couple more to the bones."

"That long? Gad, Skye, I'm trapped."

"All right. We can go much faster if you abandon the wagon."

"No, unthinkable." He smiled. "It's got a hogshead of gin in it. And a cask of bitters decocted in a mountain stream. You wouldn't want to ditch that now, would you?"

Skye nodded. Mercer would have only himself to blame for the lumbering progress across the anonymous plain.

They toiled down the river and didn't seem to make progress. Ahead a vast land rose to meet the sky. To the east the land vanished in haze. Skye rode Jawbone to any prominence where he could get a good look at the surrounding country. It all seemed too quiet. The midday heat discouraged even the ravens, and drew sweat from dust-caked horses and humans alike.

Skye pulled up beside Mercer, who was stretching his legs and walking beside his horse.

"We might happen on some buffalo. Not just a cluster, but a herd that could run miles wide and more miles long. They drift south and north with the seasons right through here. If you saw a herd like that, Mister Mercer, you'd never forget it. I imagine there are hundreds of thousands in one herd. If they run, or stampede, you'd see something rarely seen by a European. You would have a fine story."

"I'm glad you think so," Mercer retorted.

But they spotted no giant herd. In fact, Skye saw no sign of buffalo, no broad pathway of torn-up short grass, dung, and dust. This day the August heat built up to unbearable force, and Skye called a halt at a copse of willows on the bank of the Musselshell. The teamsters unhooked the big draft horses and let them drink. Big black horseflies were tormenting man and beast, so Skye pushed on, hoping to find a windswept bench where the cloud of flies wouldn't drive them half mad.

The sun didn't relent and no cloud offered mercy. But just ahead, on a grassy flat beside the river, a dozen vultures lifted into the sun-bleached blue and flapped away. Skye halted at once and watched the vultures flap blackly into the heat of afternoon. Victoria halted too, studied the black birds, and slipped off her horse. She trotted swiftly toward a river bluff and scaled it to gain some perspective on what lay ahead.

Behind, the wagon drew to a halt, and Mercer sat his horse impatiently. "Well, what's the slowdown this time?" he asked.

"Vultures."

"Something is dead."

"It would seem that way."

At Victoria's signal, Skye proceeded the remaining half mile to the flat, his rifle at the ready. And there, close to the river, were bodies, four in all. Indians, young men, so newly killed that nothing had damaged their flesh except for the arrows protruding from each of them.

"Mister Mercer, look to your safety. Make sure your men are armed and keeping an eye on the bluffs."

"An attack?"

"The warriors who did this aren't likely to return. They dread the spirits of the dead. But never take anything for granted, especially in war."

Mercer reached for his rifle, a handsome Sharps model that evoked envy in Skye.

Victoria, ever bold, slipped into the carnage and studied the dead.

"Assiniboine," she said, poking a moccasin. Then she tugged gently until an arrow pulled loose from a man's thigh, and she squinted at it. "Atsina! Sneaky thieves!"

"What on earth are Atsina?" Mercer asked.

"Gros Ventres, Big Bellies," Skye said. "Allies of the Blackfeet, famous for begging and thievery."

"Never heard of them," Mercer said. "Not much of an item for my journal, I'm afraid."

"Not the same as a giraffe," said Skye, tartly.

Here was evidence of tragedy, of war and death, yet the explorer dismissed what he saw. Skye dismounted, studied this place for its story, and soon understood what had happened.

Mercer watched impatiently, eager to be on the road again.

## nineteen

great sadness tore through Skye. It was all easy to read. Three Assiniboine boys and an older war leader had camped for the night here. They were on a horse-stealing raid, the first test of a young warrior and the classic medallion of maturity among the plains tribes. And here their dreams came to a brutal end.

They had been jumped by Gros Ventres, perhaps also young men looking for war honors, and the Gros Ventres had killed every Assiniboine and made off with the Assiniboine ponies. And it had all happened only a few hours earlier. Rigor mortis had not yet stiffened the bodies. The Gros Ventres could be only a few miles distant. They could even be watching.

There were signs of struggle. The older one, whose gray hair was worn in coarse braids, had four arrows in him, two in the abdomen, one in the chest, and one through the neck. His bow was shattered. He had several ancient war wounds, puckered flesh that spoke of bloody fighting. The ground around him was disturbed. He had not surrendered easily. The neck wound, which must have pierced an artery, had bled and now bright blood, not yet browned by time, covered his flesh.

The others had come to swift ends. One youth's skull had been split by a war axe. Another had died of an arrow through his mouth. Another had a belly wound and had been mutilated in a way that suggested revenge or maybe triumph. Another had been cleaved at the back of the neck, and probably had been trying to run away from his pursuer.

Victoria knew better than he did what people these were and who the attackers had been. Each tribe made moccasins its own way, and signed their arrows their own way. Trying to memorize all that made Skye dizzy but she knew at a glance. The Gros Ventres had few arts; everything from arrows to clothing was coarse. The Assiniboine were gifted workers of leather and bead and all the bone and flesh and hair of the buffalo. These boys wore handsome moccasins.

Mercer stood at the edge of the bloody field, not wanting to get too close, his gaze on the hills, vigilant against attack. Maybe this was more story than he or his London readers wanted to read over their breakfast tea.

"Are you sure we're safe here?" he asked.

"I'm not sure of anything."

"They could be lurking over the hill."

"They could, but probably aren't."

"I'll keep watch," Mercer said, his gaze resolutely on the ridges.

Death draws the eye, even if one doesn't want to look. The four bodies seemed to blot out everything else; the bright hot day, the green of the river bottoms, the copses of willows and chokecherry, the flight of birds.

"Well, we'd better be going," Mercer said. "Losing time."

"No," said Skye. "I will bury them."

Victoria looked sharply at him. She didn't want to bury these enemies.

"But they mean nothing to us; I understand these tribes were enemies of your wives."

"The death of anyone is an occasion for grief," Skye said. "Their families would want us to care for these men."

"But shoveling four graves—"

"I will put them on scaffolds; that is how these people bury their own."

"Well, as long as you're in my employ, I'll ask you to push on. We can make another ten miles today."

Skye ignored the man. He probably would do this task all alone. Victoria would be wary of the lingering and angry spirits of the dead. Mary would watch quietly.

He fetched his axe and headed for a great cottonwood tree with overspreading limbs, some of which were horizontal. Nearby were green cottonwood saplings, still straight and true.

Victoria caught up with him, hatchet in hand. "Damn," was all she said.

They hacked and limbed the poles, working steadily while Mercer paced and glared. The adventurer would not discharge Skye; not here, Skye thought. Mary dug into the skimpy possessions of the Skye household and found a ball of thong. When twenty poles had been readied, Skye lifted each one onto the cottonwood limbs and the women anchored the poles to the limbs with thong. It was taking a long time, and Mercer was watching thunderously but saying nothing. He drifted closer now, studying the dead, putting them into his mental notebook if not his journal.

There were ancient blankets lying about; some half ruined by blood. Blankets not even the Atsinas wanted. They would do.

Skye spread one next to the older warrior, the war leader, and then cut away the arrows with his Green River knife. He nodded to Victoria. Together they lifted the warrior onto the center of the ancient red blanket, covered the man's empty face, and tied the bundle tight with thong.

Skye wished someone would help him lift this burden, but the two teamsters were on the nearby bluff, rifles ready, keeping an eye out, and maybe that was best.

It was hot and getting hotter. Hard to breathe. Flies swarmed around the bodies. Slowly, he and Victoria wrapped the Assiniboine boys in their tattered blankets. One had an ancient buffalo robe that would serve as a shroud.

"What is this turtle thing he's got around his neck?" Mercer asked, studying the youngest of the dead youths.

Skye saw that the boy was wearing a turtle totem, a small leather pouch that rested on his bronze chest.

"It's his natal totem," Skye said. "His umbilical cord's probably inside. It's who he is, all compressed into that totem."

"I want it," Mercer said.

"No! It belongs to this boy."

"Do not take it," Victoria added. "The boy's ghost will follow you the rest of your life, and bad things will happen."

Mercer smiled, even white teeth, his chiseled features lighting up.

"All the more reason for me to have it. I love to own the things that have stories in them."

With that, he knelt, slipped the leather turtle totem up and over the youth's head, and put it into his pocket.

Victoria muttered. Mary cast her gaze elsewhere, not wanting to see what she had seen.

Skye paused. "Mister Mercer, out of respect for the dead,

you'll wish to place the turtle totem inside the boy's funeral wrapping."

Mercer smiled. "I carry a good-luck coin, a shilling, actually. Here. Put that in. We'll trade luck." He withdrew the coin from his britches and dropped it on the blanket.

Skye stared at the coin. All right, he thought. A fair trade. Maybe.

Victoria stared, uncertain about the swap. Skye wrapped the youth in the old blue blanket and quietly tied the bundle shut.

And then they were ready: Skye slid his arms under the bundle containing the war leader, the enemy of his wife's people, who was far heavier than the boys. He staggered under the weight, and Victoria helped by lifting the warrior's feet. But finally Skye had the body in hand, and he struggled to the benevolent cottonwood, with its deep shade and noble height, and they hoisted the warrior to his grave, just above Skye's own height, and straightened him out. The other three would barely fit.

Mercer paced but did not assist. That was fine. Skye somehow didn't want him here under the funeral tree, thinking of journal entries instead of burying the dead and respecting the lives that were lost this hot and windless day.

One by one, Skye and his women lifted the youths, carried them to their aerial grave, lined them up side by side, until at last all four rested on the scaffold. Skye removed his old top hat.

"Rest in peace," he said.

Their bones wouldn't. The carrion birds would be at them soon, tearing through the tattered blankets.

"That was touching," Mercer said. "A wilderness massacre, a burial, the possibility of another raid always with us."

Skye thought that he was beginning to understand the soul of the man. He was hungry for a story and that hunger trumped everything else including ordinary compassion. Did Mercer have any feeling at all for these dead men? Did he see them as mortal? Did he see them as boys with mothers and fathers and brothers and sisters? Did he see them as youths hungry to be men, out on a raid for the first time, only to lose everything?

"Let's go," he said to Mercer, who smiled brightly with the three-hour delay ended.

Skye rode ahead. If there were hostile Indians about and they were in a fighting mood, he would need to be on guard. The teamsters got the wagon rolling. Mary and Victoria started their travois-laden horses.

Mercer spurred his sleek horse and pulled up beside Skye, who didn't want the company.

"Mister Skye, I've come to apologize."

That surprised Skye.

"You did the right thing, burying those chaps. That's the golden rule, isn't it? Treat 'em as we'd like to be treated."

"It is."

"I was going to discharge you. Disobeying and all that. I won't. You've taught me a thing or two."

"You've taught me a thing or two, Mister Mercer."

"Do you really think bad luck's going to follow me because I've got the chap's turtle in my pocket?"

"My women think so. They think you'll regret it."

"But I don't believe in that stuff. You could never get me to believe in a ghost even if half of England's got a dozen in every attic. The dead are dead. But that isn't it. I didn't just take the chap's turtle; I traded for it. I gave the chap a shining shilling, a good bit of cash to get him where he's going, wouldn't you say? He's not going to haunt me. The chap's going to be my guardian. If a man needs a friendly ghost, this chap will do just fine, eh? You just watch. From now on, everything that happens will be lucky. Hired me a genuine Indian chap to keep an eye on me."

Skye nodded. Then he smiled. What was it about Mercer? You couldn't dislike the fellow for more than two minutes even if there were a dozen bad patches in every day.

# *twenty*

The day turned hot. Not much air was moving. The sun pummeled them. Black horseflies circled like dreadnoughts waiting to bite. The blue was bleached out of the sky. The mountains to the west slid into white haze.

It was the time of year Skye liked least of all. The land was parched. The spring monsoons had ended in June, and now the grasses had been toasted to a tan color, and the stalks of dried-out weeds skipped over the ground with every gust of furnace air. The heat sapped the horses and slowed the caravan as it struggled north. The Musselshell River water wasn't cold enough to refresh man or beast, but it helped to pour it over one's head. Skye soaked his hair in it and clamped his black top hat over the soggy hair and got some relief out of it.

The teamsters took the wagon along the higher ground west of the river, where there were fewer impediments such as fallen logs to stay their progress. Away from the stream the way was easier. Skye roamed ahead, wary of trouble, while his women trailed their ponies along their own route, different from the wagon's. Mercer had fallen into deep silence, wearing his frustration like a hair shirt. This would not be a good trip, and his plain objective was to get it over with as soon as he could manage it.

Burying the bodies had turned the day sour, but the unbearable heat worsened the mood of them all. Skye yearned for some mountain valleys with icy creeks tumbling through them. But as far as he could see there was only haze and white skies and air so hot it sapped his will.

It also made him edgy. He couldn't say what it was, but the whole world seemed poised at the edge of disaster.

Mercer rode up to Skye.

"It's bloody awful. It drains me. How long do these hot spells last?"

Skye shrugged. "Long time, sometimes."

"You mean we're stuck with it."

"I don't know of any way to escape it unless you want to head due west into those mountains and find a cool valley. But that's fifty miles at the least."

Mercer shook his head. "Take me to the Missouri. At this point I don't care about seeing some bones. I don't care about anything except floating my way out of here."

"As you wish, Mister Mercer."

The adventurer turned his sweat-stained horse away and retreated to his wagon and the patient teamsters.

Skye spotted an antelope racing north, and then a pack of them, maybe a dozen. Something had stirred them up. Some crows flapped due north.

There was something on the breeze that troubled Skye, some portent of trouble he could not pin down. As always, when his instincts were jabbing him, he paused to consider what danger there might be. He sucked the hot air into his lungs and then got it: fire. Smoke. The first tendrils of smoke hastened along by a quickening south wind.

Now he saw mule deer racing north, and some coyotes loping steadily north, and a nervous bull elk on a crown of a hill. At a high point he turned in his saddle to take a sharp look at his back trail, and saw what he dreaded most. Maybe ten or fifteen miles to the south, a gray wall of billowing smoke crossed the whole horizon, and he could see no break or end to it east or west. It was a prairie fire, a grandfather of all prairie fires, loping along.

Just about then Victoria and Mary figured it out, and Victoria spurred her pony to reach Skye. She pointed. Skye nodded. He needed to find a safe harbor. He needed a wide river or a massive cliff. He needed some place to shelter the livestock and protect the wagon. And he saw none at all. Whatever decision he made now would determine their fate. If he chose wisely, they might have a chance. If not, they would die the most miserable of deaths, not necessarily of flame and furnace heat, but of asphyxiation. A prairie fire sucked oxygen out of the air; there would be nothing left to breathe.

Now Mercer spotted the ominous dark wall behind them and so did the teamsters. The sinister wall, sometimes yellow-gray, sometimes almost purple, was rolling along and would overtake them soon. Who could say when?

"Where, Skye?" Mercer yelled.

"I don't know."

"Tell me, man. Are we dead?"

Skye shook his head. His gaze raked the rolling plain, the river bottoms, the horizons. Jawbone shifted under him, his terror evident in his every twitch. It was all Skye could do to rein him tight.

"Head for the river. Don't head for an island. An island in

a narrow river's worthless. Head for a pool deep enough for your horses. Deep enough for your wagon. Make it a pool in a grassy area. Not a pool where the river runs through woods or brush. Then unhitch your draft horses. Go!"

Mercer didn't argue. The teamsters had already made their own decisions, and were veering downslope toward the river, toward a broad island in the braided stream.

Skye heard Mercer yelling at them.

Jawbone trembled.

"River's all we've got," he said to Victoria. She would do the best she could with whatever she had.

But the next mile of stream bottom was packed with dense cottonwoods and willows and chokecherry brush, all of which would turn into a furnace that would snuff life out of anyone or anything trying to shelter in the river itself. A ten-yard-wide shallow stream would hardly shelter a mouse. If they could get to the river downstream, where the bankside forest thinned and gave way to brush, that would help. If they managed another mile, where the river flowed through a grassy flat, that would be best, especially if they hit a hole where they could stay submerged.

He pointed, the best he could manage, and the whole caravan careened toward the north. Now small animals raced by them; frenzied hares, raccoons, otter, skunks, all of them oblivious of the men and livestock. Rattlesnakes coiled and slithered, thousands of them, racing north.

Victoria's ponies began running, their travois careening and bobbing and threatening to pitch out everything in Skye's household. Victoria and Mary fought the animals, barely keeping them from bolting. But one of the travois snapped loose, dumping parfleches of pemmican and kitchen supplies.

Behind, the gray smoke to the south had climbed the sky, rising into a giant wall that would soon obscure the sun. The teamsters had the worst of it, working their way down the bluffs to the floor of the valley, doing their utmost to keep Mercer's heavy wagon from toppling over. Behind them, the smoke advanced like the shadow of night, streamers of gray extending far in front, and reaching directly overhead.

Skye felt parched. Jawbone's sweated flanks had dried, leaving a white rime on them. The horse wanted to run. But prairie fires often moved so fast they overtook everything in their paths. And this one, riding the hot wind out of the southwest, was wasting no time. Gusts of hot smoky air coiled through the river bottoms. A breeze rattled the parched cottonwood leaves. Skye steered toward the teamsters, who had gotten the wagon down from the high plains and were heading toward water.

"Get beyond the woods," he yelled. "Look for a hole. Cut the horses free if you have to."

"Can't. Got to save the wagon at all costs. Orders. Mercer's journals," Winding yelled.

Mercer's journals. They could kill the teamsters, kill the horses, and perish anyway when the wagon burned. But there was no time to argue.

Still, these were savvy, trail-hardened men and Skye liked what he saw. They were keeping the draft horses at a steady trot, steering them away from boulders, fallen trees, ditches and ridges, somehow in control of twelve-hundred-pound draft horses.

Now live sparks began dropping, each an angry hornet capable of starting fires in advance of the main blaze. Skye watched Victoria and Mary race the ponies forward. Another travois had fallen apart, this one carrying the lodgepoles. And the lodge cover was working loose from the third travois.

A dry cottonwood tree to the right suddenly exploded into flame, as if lightning had struck it. Skye felt heat at his back, sucked smoky air, and heard for the first time a rolling thunder behind him, the roar of a conflagration that was rolling down on them, eating everything in its path. Above, blue sky had vanished and a gray smoke cast deep shadow over the land. The sun died suddenly, and a great darkness slid over them. Still, the fire was far enough back that Skye saw no flames.

A deer burst from a thicket startling Jawbone, who reared and danced and then bolted ahead, while Skye hung on. Ahead, the woods surrendered to brush, walls of chokecherry lining the stream, as dangerous as the wooded bottoms they were leaving.

Mercer's wagon fell behind. Skye feared the teamsters would stick with it, killing themselves and their horses. But they were far from succor, far from a hole in the river, far from meadows. He heard shouts, turned, and saw Winding and Mercer yelling at each other, while Floyd Corporal was unhitching the big draft horses. Mercer was screaming. Then the draft horses were loose, and they lumbered forward at speeds Skye had never dreamed possible in such beasts. They raced past, with the teamsters and Mercer just behind. The wagon stood forlorn, cocked to one side, its wagon sheet smoking on the bows, doomed.

Skye took one last glance, lamenting not the journals but the cask of gin, and then spurred Jawbone ahead. A half mile up was open land where the river narrowed and ran quiet, a sign of some depth. A place of salvation. A slim chance, but the only chance. Behind and gaining every second was a streak of orange flame higher than the tallest bankside trees, boiling into the heavens, ascending higher and higher until Skye thought the flame touched the sun.

## twenty-one

_F_light. Now it was a race to that pool. Heat behind them, heat beside them, a moving furnace gaining on them. Jawbone needed no encouragement, but plunged pell-mell toward the quiet waters ahead. Victoria rode a pony that trailed a broken travois behind it; Mary's pony bucked and leaped, but she held on.

Mercer, on a lean roman-nosed beast, sailed past, and amazingly the big Belgians thundered by, even as heat blistered hair. The teamsters were riding too, but one's hat was smoking and embers were driving their horses mad. A flash and boom behind them told Skye that the powder keg in Mercer's burning wagon had detonated. Some smaller booms from his own travois debris told him that fire had consumed his own powder, save for what was in the horn on his chest.

They reached the pool all at once. The draft horses plunged in, splashing deep into cool water. Jawbone hit the water with a giant splash, and Skye was shocked to discover him plunging straight toward a black bear sow, with two cubs, up to their noses. Two deer and an elk stood nervously at the far side of the pond, their heads barely visible. With a great roiling of water, the rest plunged in. Skye dismounted, filled his top hat with water and poured it over himself. Then he poured more water over the horses' backs. Victoria dropped straight underwater and emerged draining water from her braids. Mercer and the teamsters struggled to dismount in all that turmoil and dipped themselves in water. The horses splashed furiously as fiery missiles dropped from the black sky frying any flesh they touched.

Skye coughed. It was hard to breathe. The air was so bad one wanted not to suck it into lungs. He filled his top hat over and over, splashing water on Victoria, on Mary, on Jawbone. The heat was so brutal it evaporated water as fast as he threw it on the horses; it pushed itself straight through their hair, his clothing, his beard.

The bears slid lower and lower in the frothing water, until their snouts barely showed. The deer and elk writhed in pain as a storm of embers blistered their backs. He saw rattlers swimming in every direction.

Now they were surrounded by orange walls, no succor, no air, no relief. But here the river ran through meadow, not woods, and Skye had been counting on that. The grasses flared briefly and moments later there was only charred earth as the wall of flame rolled past them, driven by sharp dry wind out of the south. But heat and smoke followed, the streamside trees and brush still burnt furiously, casting blankets of choking smoke straight over Skye and his party.

It was each to his own safety. Skye dipped under the water, which was clogged now with black debris, burst upward, tried to breathe air that would not support life, felt his lungs ache, threw water over the suffering horses, and plunged under again.

Jawbone shrieked as a burning missile landed on his rump, and he bucked furiously in the water, which actually sprayed lifesaving water everywhere.

Skye felt himself weakening. No air. He was gasping and drawing only brutal, acrid smoke into his lungs. A quick glance told him that the others were done for too. They hung on to horses' manes, worn-out, not far from doom. Skye saw the future clearly. They had escaped the worse burning but were going to die of asphyxiation. And there wasn't anything anyone could do.

He slid backward into the roiling water, and discovered blue sky above him. The black wall of smoke had vanished. The hot south wind had driven most of the smoke to the north. But it didn't matter. He couldn't breathe. None of them could. He clung to Jawbone's mane. He saw Victoria faint, and somehow reached her before she slid into the water and drowned. He tugged her close and kept her head up and tried to keep her from sucking water into her lungs.

The river itself had turned hot, as if it would soon begin to boil, and there was no more coolness to comfort a body. So this was how it would end. Rattlers swam by. His mind was so fogged that he no longer cared. He could not think. Thinking required air and without air his mind simply drifted toward oblivion.

And so life was suspended. He didn't know how the others fared. Black river debris slid past him, bumped into his arms. He was holding Victoria above the surface with his last strength; that is all he knew.

Then oddly a tendril of clean air reached him. He knew it was good air. He sucked it into his chest, exhaled it, sucked again, exhaled again, and did not cough as much. The merciless south wind that had driven this galloping fire was also driving clean air past this place of death.

Yet no one moved. Not an animal stirred. The bears remained submerged, only their snouts showing. The horses, half out of water in that shallow pond, stood stock-still. They had terrible burns on their backs where the fire had scorched away their hair and fried their flesh.

"Help me," said Mercer. He could no longer keep his head out of water, and slid under the surface. Skye bestirred himself, as if coming from some distant shore, and waded toward the explorer, catching him as he drifted downstream. Skye yanked Mercer's head up, clapped him on the back until Mercer coughed and began to breathe again. Skye held him up. He counted heads. Mary, Victoria, Mercer, Whiting, Corporal. Alive. Draft horses alive and suffering cruel flesh wounds. The ponies all suffering.

There was little he could do. Little anyone could do. He hadn't the strength to help himself, much less help the others. In every direction there was nothing but char, blackness, black earth, black rock, black forest debris. A blackened earth cleaved by the shallow river, under a harsh sky.

Some unfathomed amount of time passed. The river water cooled and cleared somewhat, but it still carried a full charge of charred limbs, logs, and debris, along with dead animals, rabbits, a skunk, a porcupine, an antelope, belly-up snakes, slowly floating and whirling as the waters carried them toward their final destiny. An acrid smell hung over the whole area, the smell of charred wood and grass, smoke-saturated clothing, ash that clogged one's nostrils and ears and collected around the eyes.

The bears were the first to leave. The sow herded her cubs

147

out of the pool and lumbered downstream without a glance backward toward those who had shared the refuge with her. The deer stood frozen, not ready to move anywhere. There was no place to go. Not a blade of grass or a leaf to succor the creature. Skye felt the need to return to hard ground, and pulled his way out, feeling dirty water run off his soggy buckskins. He fell to the charred ground and lay there. The act of getting out of the water had exhausted him.

The women seemed more resilient, pulled themselves out, wrung their skirts, and began walking upstream to see what might be salvaged. But one of the teamsters, Floyd Corporal, was in a bad way. He pulled himself out of the water and fell down on the black ground and wept softly. Mercer and Winding were better off. But no one was ready to look after the animals, and they spent another hour beside the Musselshell just recovering what they could of their strength and wits.

At last Skye led Jawbone out of the pool. The horse had a blister on his rump that looked ugly. There was little Skye could do about it. The saddle was charred but intact. Skye's old Hawken still rested in its sheath. It was soaked and Skye would have to pull the wet charge. He hoped he still had dry powder in his horn. The others were now unarmed unless some of their weapons had survived the conflagration that consumed their wagon.

Skye discovered that most of the hair on his head had been singed, and now it fell off whenever he touched it. Still, the hair had protected his neck and head. He could grow more. Much of Victoria's jet hair was gone. Mary's hair had survived. Somehow, Mary had done best of all, and except for some ruined buckskins and moccasins, seemed much the same. Mercer and Winding began to look after their horses. The big Belgians had several blisters, and their other horses were little better off. No one would be riding them for a long time.

No one talked. Skye didn't want to. He nursed his thoughts deep down inside of himself, as if talking would shatter a healing process that had to occur in silence. He stood wearily, pulled the rifle from its sheath, and began to pull the wet charge. It involved a complex process in which a spiral worm on a hardwood stick was screwed into the lead ball until it could be pulled free.

He sat quietly, working the wet charge loose, and finally succeeded. Then he ran a patch down the barrel to wipe it clean, poured powder, which had stayed dry in the horn, patched a ball, and drove it home. The fulminate cap was still good, so he let it stay on the nipple. He was armed, but there were no animals to shoot and no defenses needed. Skye had no intention of shooting the deer that had shared the pool with them. The deer had survived; let it live.

Off to the north the wall of smoke continued to roll away, burning everything before it. They could no longer follow the river. There was not a blade of grass for the horses, not a deer or antelope or buffalo to eat. Nothing for man or beast. Blackness ahead, blackness behind. They would need to cut sideways, either east or west, and Skye already knew the answer. They would head west where the mountains still were dark green, unburnt. There, life could continue if they could find a way to start over.

Mercer broke the silence. "We don't have a thing. Everything in the wagon's gone. The blankets, stores, my journals, some tools. The rifles are twisted and worthless. We have only the clothing on our backs and some horses we can't use or ride. We're going to be hungry and haven't even a pound of flour. It seems to me we survived that fire, only to perish in a few days from every imaginable want."

Skye lifted his soggy top hat. "It's bad," he said.

"Worse than bad. We have nothing. How will we live? You don't have anything either."

"We might not live," Skye said. "Then again, we might."

Mercer stared, annoyed, at such enigmatic conversation, and wheeled away.

Skye didn't feel like talking. He studied the mountains lying to the west perhaps thirty miles, a hard day's walk in the best of conditions, but two or three days in the shape they were in. Two or three days without food or water or grass for the animals, under a brutal sun.

## twenty-two

sorrier collection of people and animals Skye had never seen. The backs of the horses were peppered with blisters. Both of the teamsters had lost most of the hair on their heads. Skye had lost much of his. Victoria had lost most of hers. Somehow most of Mary's hair had survived. Corporal had a blistered neck and hands. Mercer himself had blisters across his neck. Their lungs hurt. They wanted nothing more than to curl up in shade and rest.

Mercer, hollow-eyed, patrolled the banks, looking for anything that wasn't ruined. Victoria worked back along the bank to the place where the travois had fallen apart and discovered an axe head minus its burnt handle, and a hatchet with a half-burned handle. Actually, they were treasures. But the lodge was a smoking ruin, the lodgepoles gone, the parfleches of clothing and food lost.

She returned, showed the metal to Skye, who took note of it. Those two items could save their lives.

They were all caked with soot, their clothing a black ruin,

their moccasins soggy. The waters of the Musselshell were un-drinkable and filled with floating corpses.

Mercer, his face haggard, approached Skye. "We're dead men. That's plain. Dead men."

"How so?"

"Nothing but charred ground. Horses can't be ridden, blistered backs. No feed for them. Smoke's ruined our lungs. I can't walk a hundred yards. Same for my men. Not a thing left of our wagon. Even the iron wheels are twisted. No food. No drinkable water. Clothing falling off. The blisters will mortify. Nights are cold now. We've not a blanket among us. It's all plain enough."

It did look that way, and Skye knew that there was little he could say to hearten the explorer. "We'll try for grass. It's a hard day's walk. Day and a night, maybe."

Mercer stared at Skye as if Skye were daft.

"I'm taking my women and horses to grass. You want to come along?"

"I'd like to stay here. At least there's water."

"There'll be water where I'm going. Place I once trapped long ago, called Flatwillow Creek."

"It'll be burnt."

Skye pointed. "Those are the Little Snowies. Big Snowies beyond that. They didn't burn."

Mercer squinted. "How can you tell?"

"Are they smoking? Forest fires burn for hours, days, weeks."

Mercer whirled away and settled beside the river. "Go ahead," he said. "I'm staying."

"You're quitting."

Mercer turned his back on Skye.

Skye and his women collected what little they had, herded

the horses into a group, and started west, cutting across scorched earth that was sometimes hot under their moccasins. He didn't know whether they would make it. He knew it was the only choice. The brutal sun swiftly pummeled the wet out of their clothing, and then it really got hot.

He heard a shout and discovered Mercer and his teamsters a hundred yards back. He let them catch up. They had collected their few things and were pushing the horses ahead of them. The draft horses, in particular, were badly blistered; their backs were the highest out of the water. Not a horse in the whole party could be ridden.

Skye nodded. For some reason he liked Mercer though he often wondered why.

They hiked west through a dehydrating south wind, pausing every little while to breathe. Not a blade of grass nurtured the horses. Not a chokecherry bush, not a willow thicket. The fire had scraped the earth naked, and there was only yellow clay and ash and a brassy sky.

For a long while they struggled west, even as the sun marched west, as if to impede them. Skye rested frequently. His feet were bloody. Corporal had stepped into the remains of some prickly pear and was nursing a painful left foot. But no one complained, least of all Mercer, who had that British grit to him.

Then, as the sun began to slide, they struck a broad coulee issuing out of the mountains, and suddenly there was grass on its south slope, while the north slope was charred. The wind-driven flames had leaped over half the coulee.

They paused in grass. It seemed a miracle, tawny brown grass as high as their calves, something at last that wasn't ash. The horses spread out and devoured it. But soon it was time to push on. Skye led them straight up the coulee, which was going where he wanted to go more or less, and the horses nipped grass along the way. At one point they scattered a herd of antelope that had found refuge in the unburnt strip of land.

"I say, Mister Skye, it's a rule of exploring to find a trustworthy guide and follow his counsel," Mercer said.

Suddenly there was Mercer's mile-wide grin.

Skye nodded, smiled, and something was healed.

But now thirst loomed. He felt parched. He saw Victoria slip a pebble into her mouth and suck on it to activate the saliva. The murderous sun could kill them if nothing else did. And Corporal was slowing down, not able to keep up.

Skye found a shaded place and halted them. "We'll wait for twilight," he said. "Water ahead five miles; creek I know of."

Five miles seemed a continent away but that was the only choice they had. Corporal pulled off his boot, wrapped his injured foot in some shirttail, and tugged the boot on again.

"All right, we're going to cut northwest over burnt land again," Skye said. "I think we'll strike a creek in about two hours."

"Are you sure, are you absolutely sure?" Mercer asked.

"No, sir. I'm never sure. A man roams this land and makes a map in his head. In the beaver days we came through here a few times. But maps fade, and so does our memory. No, I am not at all sure."

Mercer's two teamsters stared, waiting for a decision from their boss. But then he nodded.

"We'll have a time of it pulling these horses off the grass," Skye said.

They did have a time of it. Two of Skye's ponies curled around to the grass; both of Mercer's draft horses refused to budge.

But then Jawbone set to work, snapping and snarling and

sinking teeth into blistered butts, while Skye marveled. There were times when he swore Jawbone knew his mind. They set off at a good clip, covering three miles in an hour, always over burnt land as desolate as the Sahara. But a half hour later Jawbone, and then the ponies, and lastly Mercer's horses, began trotting, and then loping, and finally the whole lot of them raced ahead, down a grade, into a burnt-out valley where leafless trees stood in wintry death, and poked their heads into a clean, swift creek.

Skye and his hobbling bunch found the horses sated and comfortable, standing beside the creek in the twilight. The men drank. Skye's women retreated around a bend and washed themselves. In purple twilight they all started up the creek, plodding toward the looming mountains, and then suddenly they hit grass. It was if a knife had severed the land; burnt black to east, placid golden grasslands with thickets of cottonwoods dotting the creek bottoms to the west.

Mercer stood at the knife edge of the fire and marveled. "Mister Skye," he said, "we're not out of it, but you brought us here."

Indeed, before them was succor and water, deadwood for a fire to drive the frost away at night and cook meat. The horses tore into the long grasses, eating as they all ambled westward into the twilight.

Skye was thinking about food. So were they all. He checked his Hawken. He had a fresh charge in the barrel and a patched ball pressed hard against the load.

"I'll go ahead, mates," he said. "Stay back."

They saw he was ready to hunt, and knew as well as Skye did that this grass-lined creek would be a haven and refuge for plenty of animals driven there by the fire.

But it was growing dark. Skye could only hope that if he

found game it would be at once, and not when he couldn't see to shoot. He walked only a few minutes when he made out great dark beasts ahead, so many that it startled him. His heart lifted. He was downwind and had a good chance. Up there were meat and robes, tools and clothing, moccasins and steaks.

He drifted close, knowing the shaggies did not have good hearing and only mediocre sight, but did have a keen sense of smell; that one whiff of him would send them running. But he had hunted them many times before, and slipped his way toward the shifting herd, maybe twenty or thirty; plenty of meat, plenty of everything they might need. He slipped toward the creek and settled behind a downed cottonwood, using the log for a bench rest. There were three cows he wanted, each grazing quietly. He set his horn beside him, uncapped it, readied some patches and balls, pulled out his ramrod, and then leveled his rifle, sighted on the heart-lung spot of one farther back.

The first shot dropped the cow in her tracks. She caved slowly while he dumped powder down the barrel, rammed a patched ball home, slid a cap over the nipple, and aimed at the next cow. The herd had shifted restlessly but had not run. The cow turned toward him, ruining his aim. He lined up a shot at a young bull, and squeezed. Again the boom shattered the peace. The bull trotted a few dozen steps and collapsed. Skye swiftly reloaded, and dropped a second cow, just as the herd decided, in some collective and mysterious judgment, it was time to run. The big animals raced upslope, out of the intimate Flatwillow Valley, and vanished into the night. One of the cows was thrashing on the ground, and then he saw Victoria cut its throat. That was a dangerous thing to do, but she did it.

By the time the others arrived, all three buffalo lay dead.

"Three, Mister Skye? Why so much waste?"

Skye reloaded, pondering an answer. "No waste at all, sir. There are six robes, two to a hide, to keep us warm. Meat for a few days. Tools to make from bone. Moccasins for your feet, a shirt or vest for your body, a hat to keep the summer sun from blistering your head, saddles and girth straps to replace the horse tack and harness you lost, and if you want to make a pillow out of the beard of the bull, it's there too."

"I'll settle for some hump meat," said Winding. "I'll eat one shaggy and you can share the rest."

# twenty-three

*P*eople seemed to know what to do without being asked. All set to work except Floyd Corporal, who was too sick to do anything at all. Winding looked to the horses. Mercer gathered deadwood from the patches of cottonwoods and pine near the creek. The women began sawing out the buffalo tongues, the easiest meat to get at fast, and one of the most delicious parts.

Skye studied this haven, bathed in lavender twilight, and decided to have one last look. Too many trappers he knew had come to a bad end by unwittingly camping close to trouble. He clasped his Hawken, slowly and painfully climbed the north slope of the Flatwillow Creek valley until he reached a ridge above it where he could see the bright blue sky in the west where the sun had vanished. To the east, the burnt-over land spread blackly to the horizon. A sharp line separated the burned from the lush valley grasses they had made their haven this night. He studied the lonesome land, so big and empty it sometimes made his heart ache. He saw no trouble. No smoke from other camps. No new flame on the horizon.

No burning mountain. No storm clouds. Just a vast, quiet, and achingly sweet land that flooded him with gratitude.

Below, a bright fire flared. The women had collected tinder from beneath rotted cottonwood bark and had ignited the wood that Mercer had collected. They were jabbing green willow wands through two buffalo tongues to suspend them at the fire, and in a while everyone in this ragged band would be fed.

Skye was reluctant to come down from the ridge. As cruel as this land could be, it was his own land, now bathed in soft and gentle light that made the whole world serene and quiet. But there was much to be done. He tore himself away from the views that entranced him, made his way down to the camp, and found the tongues sizzling beside a lively fire. The horses grazed peacefully on good grass. Their backs were a mass of suppurating blisters, and some might never be good saddlers again. But they could pull travois.

Even as the fire licked the tongues, the women had tackled the first cow with their skinning knives. Pulling a hide free was hard, messy labor. But ere long they had cut the belly, spilled entrails, set aside the intestines that would make a great feast, severed the head, cut the legs loose, and had started the tugging and cutting that would gradually pull the vermin-infested hide free of the great bulk of the cow. Three hides. Six robes, and plenty of hide left over for moccasins, which would be the most urgent of their needs. It would be a long time before anyone rode those horses.

The tongues sizzled; Mary occasionally rose to turn the meat, or see to it that the tongues didn't burn. Mercer and Winding stared hungrily. They all had food on their mind. Skye thought to go after a liver, always a choice piece eaten raw by Indians and mountain men. Indeed, Corporal had revived enough so that he began poking into the stomach cavity of the eviscerated cow, and did finally produce the purplish slab of meat. But instead of eating it raw, he skewered it and began to cook it alongside of the two tongues.

That suited Skye. Buffalo liver was legendary for its powers of rejuvenation. Let Floyd Corporal devour the whole of it. The man wheezed and coughed, and Skye wondered if the teamster would make it.

Oddly, no one spoke. And yet there was a silent language that flowed between them all. An occasional smile. A bright nod toward the cooking meat. A sigh as they glanced at this demi-paradise, the quiet groves of trees, jack pine, lodgepoles, willows, chokecherry, rushes, and a narrow creek of clean, cold water rippling boldly through the narrow valley. Only a mile or so away was a far grimmer world.

When the tongues were more or less cooked, Victoria pulled one from the fierce fire and carried it with her skinning knife to a slab of rock, and there she began sawing, one juicy slice after another, hot, steaming meat that fell to the rock.

Winding came first, but she shooed him away.

"Burn your fingers," she said.

He grinned, pulled out his Barlow knife, and stabbed a fat slice. He began whirling it around and around, letting the air cool the tongue, and finally sank his incisors into it, making obscene noises as he chewed.

That was the start. They all stabbed their pieces of meat, cooled them, and began gnawing. They ate both tongues, and Corporal ate the liver too, sharing small pieces with Winding, their fingers dripping.

"A respite, anyway," Mercer said, licking his fingers. "What's the old saying? Eat, drink, and be merry, for tomorrow we die."

Skye finished his tongue and wiped his hands on the tan grass. He felt so weary he could barely stay awake.

"Tomorrow the hard work starts," he said. "If we all work hard, we'll pull through."

Mercer smiled, but there was something fatalistic in the smile, as if he believed that Skye was simply trying to boost their spirits. Mercer was about to get a lesson in living Indian style.

"These downed buffalo will draw predators," Skye said. "I want each of you to collect a pile of rocks, something to throw at the varmints. Coyotes are no problem. Wolves could be. A catamount might be trouble. But I'm worried about bears. We haven't the means to hoist any of the meat into a tree; there's not a rope among us. The one other prospect is to bury each of the carcasses under pine limbs. Do you want to do it?"

"I don't have the strength left," Mercer said.

Skye didn't think he did, either. "All right, it's rocks, then." He turned to Floyd Corporal. "Tomorrow, I would like you to whittle a new haft for the axe head we salvaged. Not from pine. Try willow or aspen. That's mostly quiet work, something you can do while your lungs heal."

"It'll be done," Corporal said, and then coughed violently.

"Good. Tomorrow we'll pull hides, start fleshing them with the hatchet blade, braid some rawhide rope, try to raise some meat up high to keep it safe, start making some rawhide harness and packsaddles, and a few other things I have in mind."

Mercer laughed. "Factory workers."

Skye decided not to let it pass. "That's what tribes do, Mister Mercer. They are factory workers, turning what they hunt and gather into everything they need."

The flames dimmed to orange coals. There would be little

comfort this night with no robes or blankets to warm their bodies against a night breeze that would drop close to freezing. There would be no spare clothing, no sheeted wagon overhead to stop the wind.

"Let's keep this fire going," Mercer said.

"That's good. It'll throw heat and maybe keep animals at bay. Did you bring in enough wood?" Skye asked.

Mercer hadn't. "Maybe when the moon comes up I can find some."

"Maybe you can," Skye said. "You'll be in charge of keeping us warm."

Mercer laughed again. He was, it seemed, a pretty good sport.

The night passed quietly. Perhaps there was too much of the acrid odor of fire in the air. Perhaps predators were having a banquet upon all the fire-wounded creatures elsewhere. Mercer managed to keep a flame going all night, and asked no relief from anyone. Skye slept soundly; he was far too exhausted not to sleep, even if his backside was freezing while his front side roasted. He was awake at first light, as always. He studied the ridges for danger, as always. Around him lay the rest, each in a place hollowed in the turf. The great carcasses of the buffalo lay untouched, at least by large predators, thirty or forty yards distant. He arose stiffly, wishing he had some tea. But there wasn't even a kettle, much less a tin cup. He saw that Mercer had finally fallen into sleep, the explorer's face somehow soft and innocent.

Victoria was staring at Skye. She arose softly, padded to him, and he drew her tight. It was something they always did. They greeted each other with a fierce hug as each day began. She vanished into the bush while he washed his face in the flowing creek, which offered up the music of soft laughter. Then he washed his Green River knife and settled beside the buffalo cow. This fine morning they would all enjoy the most succulent and tender part of a buffalo, the hump meat. The women had pulled as much hide free as they could, but now the cow needed to be turned over so they could tear the rest of the hide free. It was a task beyond his strength, but when Mercer suddenly appeared, they tugged on the legs and finally flipped the cow over, so Victoria and Mary could continue.

Slowly and carefully, Skye sliced a rib roast out of the cow while Mercer gathered sticks and built up the fire from its coals. Skye hurt; yesterday's ordeal had left his body aching in every muscle. His lungs ached. The smoke had done something terrible to them. But he was used to it. No man lived close to the wilds without pain.

He cut two roasts out of the hump and set them to cooking while suspended on green willow sticks. As the meat sizzled, he continued butchering, gradually building a great heap of meat that would nourish them all this day. The women would find time to start jerking some of it for future emergencies. A lazy smoke lifted off the wavering fire while the meat sizzled. The scent woke up the teamsters, and then Mary. A feast at dawn. An odd breakfast, but just fine this big, hot day in paradise.

Skye watched them all. People were different at dawn, shaking sleep out of their bodies, and sometimes shaking the pain away too. But one by one they settled near the fire while the flame blackened the outside of the roasts and the fat dripped steadily from the meat.

They had a boss rib breakfast, and it was as fine a meal as

any Skye had ever enjoyed, though he might have savored a pinch of salt on the tender meat.

Mercer ate heartily and seemed as ready as the rest for a day of toil. And strangely, he no longer talked about the certitude of perishing in the wilds of North America.

# twenty-four

Factory indeed. The want of everything was so urgent that Skye scarcely knew what required the most attention. But these things sorted themselves out their own way. The women swiftly pulled hides off the remaining buffalo and staked them to the ground, hair-side down. Then, using the hatchet blade, Victoria began fleshing the hides while Mary brain-tanned them, using a rounded river cobble to grind the fatty brain into the hides.

Graves Mercer turned to joking, but at least he stayed busy butchering meat, which he did so poorly that Skye feared the man would sever a finger. Still, the amount of salvaged meat that could be turned into jerky or pemmican began to grow.

Silas Winding turned to what he knew best, and began slicing strips of rawhide from one of the hides and braiding it into rope. Some of this new rope would soon hang haunches above the reach of bears, while the rest of it would become lead lines, halters, bridles, reins, and other tack. Floyd Corporal, the weakest among them, was still able to whittle a new handle of willow and fit it to the axe head, gather firewood, tend camp, cook meat, and keep an eye out for danger. But he looked bad, haggard, and Skye wondered about him.

Skye patrolled the hillsides periodically, looking for trouble, but then he helped butcher for a while and found along the creek abundant chokecherries and sarvis berries to make pemmican. The horses grazed peacefully in the valley, content to stay near water. It would be many days before they might be healed enough to drag a travois.

After Corporal had fashioned a workable axe, with wedges pinning the head on the haft, Skye felled young lodgepole pines and turned them into usable travois and lodgepoles. It felt good to draw upon the world around them and make shelter and transportation from whatever nature provided.

When the women finished fleshing and brain-tanning one hide, they headed for a nearby tree and whipsawed the stiff hide back and forth around the trunk, softening the leather. There would not be time to turn it into velvety soft leather, but this hide, severed in two, would provide warm robes for two of the party.

Because one of the hides would be devoted to horse tack and parfleches and clothing, they were still short of leather. Skye hoped to remedy that the next evening, when he would slip out at twilight, heading up the creek in search of an elk or at least a mule deer. He wouldn't mind finding a moose or a black bear, either.

Floyd Corporal took over the cooking, and kept meat broiling all day. So hard was the labor, and so ravenous were the toiling people, that they simply stopped now and then for another slab of buffalo roast that rested on a flat rock, ready for all comers.

By the end of that first day there were crudely tanned

robes for two, plus the remaining hides to shelter the rest of them against the sharp cold of late-summer nights.

"Let's rest and have a bite, mates," Skye said.

They collected around a table rock where Corporal had piled the cooked meat, and helped themselves. It was a messy business, gnawing at large slabs of dripping hot meat held in bare hands. But a satisfying repast.

"Well, Mister Skye, we've survived another day," Mercer said. "I'll be the first to say you've opened my eyes."

"The Indians opened the eyes of many a trapper who came here," Skye said. "Here was everything they needed and they knew what to do with it."

"But the work! All I've done is slave all day," Winding said.

"And we'll slave for another week," Skye said. "Then maybe one or two of the horses can pull a travois."

"We'll head straight for Fort Benton," Mercer said.

"Why?" Skye asked.

"Because we lost everything. This is all make-do. We need to outfit."

Skye shrugged. "If that's what you want, I'll take you there. But there's no need. You came to see what you could see, and there's still two months of good weather."

"But, Skye. There's only one rifle among us. A few belt knives. Makeshift tools. No paper for a journal. I lack even a pencil."

"Then I guess we'll just have to live like Indians," Skye said.

"I shall want a dozen wives," said the explorer, and then laughed at his witticism. Skye did too. There was that quality about the man that made him good company.

"Ain't no damned Absaroka that would marry him," Victoria said.

"No Shoshone," Mary said.

"No Nez Perce. No Hidatsa. No Lakota," said Victoria.

"No Piegan. No Assiniboine. No Gros Ventre," said Mary.

"Maybe a damn ugly Arapaho with warts," Victoria said. "Someone with her nose cut off."

The women laughed merrily. A cut-off nose was the punishment some tribesmen imposed on adulterous wives.

"I don't know what's so funny," Mercer said.

"They're having a very good time with your ambitions," Skye replied. "In some tribes, a woman with a severed nose is a woman punished for unfaithfulness."

"Ah! Then I shall look for half a dozen of the bobbed nose beauties!"

Floyd Corporal thought that was capital, and wheezed cheerfully.

Skye found his ancient Hawken, checked the load, and slipped into the twilight. Behind him, the party sat around the fire, enjoying the evening even as chill air slid down from the mountains. He felt the soft rush of air as something silent flapped by and realized it was a large owl. He would not tell Victoria. An owl was an omen of big trouble.

He padded softly up the creek valley, looking for those shapes of large animals that would offer him more meat and hide. Elk hide made especially fine moccasins as well as good waistcoats or pantalones. A man could live just fine in a cotton shirt, elk-hide vest, elk leggins, and moccasins.

He was a fine hunter who glided softly through the cottony dark, pausing to listen, instinctively understanding where animals might water or graze or simply stand quietly. Jawbone had not followed, so Skye slipped along as silently as that owl.

Then he froze. Ahead was a cow elk and a late-born baby,

scarcely two months old. The little one butted her bag and suckled. He lowered his Hawken intuitively, but stopped. It was not in him to kill her and orphan that baby. He might if he were desperately hungry but that was not the case. He watched quietly as the calf suckled and then meandered away from his mother. She sensed his presence. Her head jerked upward, she stared at him, sniffed the air, and then hightailed away, dancing ahead like a proud trotter. The calf froze, ancient instinct telling it not to move. Then a soft whistle, or was it just an odd breath, and the calf tripped away into the gloom.

"Hope you grow into a big fellow," Skye muttered.

He worked his way into deep night, following the melodic creek, and then turned back toward camp, empty-handed. Jawbone whickered softly, trotted up and bumped his massive head into Skye's chest.

"Avast," he said softly. He scarcely dared touch the animal. The horse's mane had burnt away in places, and there were painful blisters on Jawbone's rump. Big black horseflies were tormenting all the horses now, crawling over the blisters, and Skye wondered what to do about it. Maybe river mud plastered over the blisters would help. He would try in the morning and hope he didn't get kicked to death.

He found the camp still busy. Mercer and Winding had hung two haunches of buffalo from a stout willow tree. The women toiled on the next hide, now staked down where the previous hide had been worked. Corporal, whose wheeze had worsened, was fitting together a little rack next to the fire where he intended to smoke-cure some buffalo meat. With indefatigable people like this, Skye thought, they would soon be outfitted and on their way.

That night Skye and Victoria shared one hide, spread out under them. The hair warmed them and offered protection from the hard earth. And they warmed each other. Floyd Corporal gladly took a robe. His wheeze had shifted to a rattling cough and Skye worried about the man. Too much searing hot air, too much smoke, too much chill and hard living and walking through corrosive ash, had taken their toll. Skye didn't like the black flesh around the man's eyes, the rasping of his breath, the desperate look in the man's face.

Mary gratefully took the other new robe, while Graves Mercer and Silas Winding settled on the remaining uncured hide, finding some comfort in it. This night was even colder than the previous one. It was that time of year when days remained hot but the nights turned icy. Several times, Skye awakened and added wood to the flickering fire, but its faint heat did little to drive away the chill, and Skye got more comfort out of stirring about than he got from the miserable flame.

He eyed the night heavens anxiously. The worst thing that could happen now, when they were so ill prepared, would be a cold rain or worse, an early winter storm. But for the moment, their luck held.

No predators showed up that night, either. The fire probably kept them at bay. But when Skye pried open his eyes at dawn, he swore he was staring at a wolf not far distant. Whatever the case, by the time he was fully awake, the wraith had vanished.

The camp was slow to awaken. A cold blue dawn slowly expanded into daylight. Victoria sat up suddenly, alarm in her features.

"He is dead," she said.

"He was all right a while ago. I checked."

"Dead."

She arose, padded softly across dewy ground, and knelt beside the still form of Floyd Corporal. Slowly she lowered her head to listen. Then she slipped the robe open and touched the man's face. Then she shook him.

There was no response.

Skye knew that they hadn't escaped the prairie fire after all.

*twenty-five*

eath in their midst. They gathered around Floyd Corporal, absorbing the great silence of him. It had happened suddenly and mysteriously. Yesterday, he had been well enough to whittle an axe handle and gather firewood. Late in the day he was wheezing. This morning he was gone. Of just what cause no one could say, but surely that fire and its lethal smoke had much to do with it.

He looked smaller in death than in life. Alive, he had been a quiet, able teamster who was well versed in wilderness ways, kept his livestock in good shape, knew what could be gotten from a horse or mule or ox, and said very little. There he was now, dark-haired, hollow-faced. His eyes were closed.

"This is bloody awful," Mercer said.

"Floyd Corporal was a good man," Skye responded. "He got you here."

"What'll we do? We haven't a shovel."

"We're living by Indian ways," Skye said. "We will give him to the sun rather than the earth."

"A tree burial! But that's for Indians, not white men. I wish I had a journal to record it."

Skye was put off by the remark. "We will bury him with respect," he said.

Corporal was some mother's son, perhaps someone's brother, maybe someone's father. He would be missed by someone, somewhere.

"Do you know his family?" Skye asked Winding.

"I can't say as I do. Missouri folks."

"I would like you to make it your mission to get word to them, whoever they may be."

Winding nodded. "I have that in my mind."

"Let's be about it," Skye said. He took the axe and headed for a grove of saplings, where he began to harvest poles. Mary slashed branches from the poles with the hatchet. Victoria cut rawhide strips. Mercer and Winding, not knowing what else to do, watched.

When Skye had cut eight poles, he and his women built a scaffold in a willow tree whose limbs overarched the meadow. The rawhide strips anchored the scaffold to two horizontal limbs, and in a while a bed of poles rested aboveground, under a leafy canopy. It would be a good place for a mortal to meet eternity.

Without hesitation, Mary and Victoria wrapped Corporal in the brand-new buffalo robe, the very robe that had cost them a day of hard labor, and tied the robe tight with the thong, making a snug leather coffin for Corporal.

Mercer looked like he was about to protest; to say that the robe was needed and valuable. Skye could almost read the man's mind. But Mercer held his peace. The dead deserved whatever honor could be accorded them, including the precious robe.

Skye nodded, and he and Winding and Mercer lifted the body and carried it slowly to the willow tree, and then hoisted it as high as they could reach, until they settled it evenly on the poles.

Skye pulled his battered top hat from his graying locks and addressed Mercer. "Do you wish to say anything?"

Mercer looked about, at Victoria and Mary and Winding and Skye, all of them suffering from fire blisters, scorched-away hair, soot-blackened clothing.

"Floyd Corporal was a fine man. May he rest in peace," Mercer said. "I know little enough of the man. He kept to himself. But a man reveals himself in his work and his conduct. He left no task undone, angered no man, wounded no man, and gave his best at all times. I should be proud to call him a noble Yankee."

Skye liked that. He found himself gazing into the eyes of that other teamster, Winding, and found tears there in that sun-blasted chestnut flesh under his eyes.

"The Lord is my shepherd, I shall not want," Mercer said, and recited the psalm.

Then it was finished. And still a mystery. Corporal's life had played out almost before anyone grasped how close he was to death.

The sun had not yet transcended the surrounding ridges.

"We have a few more days of work here," Skye said.

The next days were devoted to hard toil. The women fleshed the remaining hides, brain-tanned them, softened them, and sliced them into robes. Mercer gathered buffalo berries and sarvis berries, shredded the cooked meat, collected bone marrow grease, pounded the berries with river cobbles, and made pemmican. Winding looked after the horses and made horse tack from the remaining rawhide. Skye hunted, at last bagging a mighty elk. It took a combined effort to drag it into camp, with Jawbone providing most of the motive power.

"Moccasins!" Victoria exclaimed.

And more. Before the women were done, there were moccasins for two men, a parfleche to store the pemmican, and enough left over to make a vest.

Mercer was growing restless, but Skye and the women were far from done. Mary harvested pieces of buffalo small intestine, washed it, turned it inside out, and stuffed it with shredded meat, which she then roasted. Victoria sliced the lean meat into strips and set them to drying in the hot sun on racks of her devising.

Bits of rawhide became belts or hobbles. A piece of green rawhide wrapped over the head and haft of the axe, soaked and left to dry, anchored the axe head to Corporal's improvised haft.

Skye cut the buffalo horns free, hollowed them out for ladles and spoons, while Winding swiftly learned to weave the shaggy hair of the bull into braids that would end up as halters for his horses. The women carefully freed the sinew from the backbones of the great beasts. The sinew would have various uses as a form of thread, and could be turned into bowstrings.

But at last the day came to move along. The carcasses were reeking. The surrounding meadows had been grazed down to bare earth, and the horses were wandering farther afield to feed themselves. One of the draft horses seemed well healed, and the simple belly-band harness for a travois would do the beast no harm. Skye and the women had fashioned a long travois, poles and crossbars, and now hooked it to the draft horse. They piled the new robes and the parfleche and tools onto the crossbars, and carefully anchored everything down. During the fire everything had been lost; now the robes and tools and emergency foods needed to survive rested on those poles.

Mercer had slipped into a respectful silence. From the aftermath of the fire unto this day, his perception of events had changed. He thought himself doomed after the fire, when every one of his European tools, save for a belt knife, had been consumed. But now much had been restored. To be sure, an axe head and hatchet had contributed. And Skye's salvaged rifle and powder had helped. Robes and clothing and tools and food had been extracted from nature. The lesson of living Indian style had sunk deep into Mercer's mind.

They looked at one another, and at the brook and meadow that had nurtured them.

"Fort Benton?" Mercer asked.

"Why there? I thought you came here for stories."

"My notes are ash. I haven't a scrap of paper."

"Then record your stories Indian style. On the back of your robe."

Mercer thought about it. "I've seen these," he said. "Pictographs, each evoking an episode. Each triggering a communal memory." He walked to the creek and stared into the babbling water. And then returned. "Would your ladies teach me?"

Mary nodded shyly. She was a good artist.

Mercer brightened. "Then we're off to see the big bones."

Silas Winding spent one last moment, head bowed, his slouch hat in hand, at the scaffold and then began driving the horses before him. The blisters had scabbed over, but the horses were far from being useful.

Skye took the caravan straight north, out of the intimate

valley, over ridges dotted with pines and into brush-choked coulees. There were unnamed mountains to the west, clad darkly in pine, but he steered through open country as much as he could. They were on the move but defenseless against a host of troubles, most notably a cold downpour, and unless they could make peace with passing bands of Indians, they could find themselves in big trouble.

Skye rode Jawbone, who seemed none the worse for wear, and stayed well ahead of the rest, scouting for trouble and hunting game. He shot an antelope and left it on the trail for the rest. The meat would be fine; the hide would make a new parfleche or a vest for someone else. The summer was waning, and leather clothing would be welcome.

For days they toiled north through open country. Graves Mercer was growing restless again. He was an adventurer, and when no great adventure greeted him, he fell into distemper. This took the form of small complaints about food, or lack of shelter, or the slow progress.

"Find me a tribe, Mister Skye. I wish to meet them."

"You won't wish it if we run into Piegans, Mister Mercer."

"Piegans?"

"The southernmost of the Blackfeet. And deadly enemies of Yanks in particular. But they buy their weapons from Hudson's Bay, and suffer the British."

"What would make a good story about them? You know, for London readers? Do the chiefs have a dozen wives? Are they lecherous?"

"I think, Mister Mercer, that no tribe has social arrangements that Europeans think are proper."

"That's what I'm after! Find me some."

Skye laughed.

The next day, while riding up a ridge well ahead of his party, he stopped suddenly. On the ridge were two mounted warriors, waiting for him to reach them.

He did what he usually did in those circumstances, spurred his horse straight toward them, his hand high, palm forward, the peace and friendship posture of the plains.

When he reached the ridge he found two young men, both with bows and nocked arrows, but these were pointed away from Skye.

Gros Ventres, Big Bellies, or Atsina, allies of the Blackfeet, famous moochers, famous thieves, famous tricksters, famous for their endless visits. And maybe the killers of those Assiniboine youths back on the trail.

# twenty-six

The young warriors were wreathed in smiles. They eyed Skye, studied Jawbone, who stood with his ears laid back, and then examined Skye's party, visible a mile back from that ridge.

"Come. Visit. Smoke. People that way," one of the warriors signed. He pointed northwest.

Skye would rather not, but saw little choice in it. All he could do was warn his people to keep an eye on their horses. There wasn't much else that they could call property or that the Gros Ventres would prize.

Skye nodded. His hands worked swiftly. He would return to his people and guide them to the village.

The sign-talker's hands responded. "We go with you."

Skye acknowledged it and turned Jawbone back to his party, trailing along behind.

When he rode in, flanked by the Gros Ventres, his women watched warily, ready for trouble. But Skye possessed the only weapon among them, something the Gros Ventres swiftly realized.

"Mister Mercer, these gents are Gros Ventres, a tribe allied with the Blackfeet. They want us to visit them," Skye said.

"Well, we'll do it."

Skye studied the two warriors, who sat impassively on good ponies. They didn't grasp English.

"We'll go. Not much choice. These people can be very friendly or not, as the mood strikes them. Watch your possessions. Especially the horses."

"Thieves are they?"

Skye shrugged. He wouldn't single out the Gros Ventres as being any more light-fingered than many others.

But Winding knew these people. "They've a reputation as moochers."

"That's a Yank word I'm not familiar with."

"They are known to overstay their welcome," Skye said.

Mercer chuckled. "Very like us all. Let's go."

Escorted by the young Gros Ventres, the party topped the ridge, descended into a grassy bowl, and discovered the village camped along Box Elder Creek. They had obviously had a successful hunt. Buffalo hides were staked to the grass, jerky was drying on racks, and the women were busy fleshing hides, making pemmican, and cooking.

The party was soon being scrutinized by the whole band, who crowded around, examining the blistered horses, the sole travois, the lack of weapons, and Mister Skye, the one person they knew.

"Sonofabitch!" said Victoria, walking beside Skye. She didn't like any people allied with the Blackfeet, and Skye guessed she despised these most of all for their sticky-fingered ways.

"I feel like a rabbit in an eagle's talons," Winding said.

Nonetheless, the throng seemed perfectly cheerful, and

Skye spotted plenty of smiles along with rank curiosity as they all studied Skye's harmless and near-desperate group.

There would be the ritual visit to the chief or headman. He hardly needed to explain what had happened. The singed hair on horse and man, the soot-smeared clothing, the blistered backs of the horses, the makeshift tack, all told a story to anyone with eyes to see.

"Is there anything I should know about these people?" Mercer asked. "Do they worship a dragon goddess? Eat sheep's eyes? Sacrifice virgins to the sun god?"

"They're cannibals, mate. You'll end up in their stewpot."

"Ho, ho. You make dangerous jokes, Mister Skye."

"Anything for a good story, Mister Mercer."

This was an ill-kempt camp. The lodges were scattered in random clumps. Latrine odors sifted through it. Middens of offal and bones lay everywhere. Mangy mutts circled the newcomers, some of them yapping or howling. The lodges sagged in the sun, many of them fashioned of ancient buffalo skins that had seen their day. This was a place of castaways. Still, this was not a permanent camp; it was a hunting camp, intended to serve its purpose for a few days. But Skye found himself aware of poverty here. These people had no wealth, unlike the proud Blackfeet to whom they were allied. He wondered if they were simply shiftless, or whether misfortune had afflicted them.

But they seemed cheerful enough. The crowd throbbed along beside them, scampering children, the boys naked; bronze women in summer calico. Chestnut-tinted old men wrapped in grimy white and red and black trade blankets. Toothless grandmothers, built like barrels, smiling through wrinkles in their corduroy faces, their faded dresses hanging loose.

The chief's lodge proved to be no larger than the rest. The headman waited, dressed only in a loincloth and moccasins, some scars of battle puckering across his ribs and arms.

Several elders flanked him. Clearly, they had received word and had arrayed themselves for guests.

The chief held up a hand in welcome, his face crinkled in pleasure. These people plainly were enjoying the prospect of guests. Then he signaled a word, bear, and pointed at himself.

There was no one who could translate, so Skye found himself using the time-honored sign language of the plains. Swiftly, he introduced his party. The Englishman, the Missouri man, the Snake woman and Absaroka woman who were his wives. He recounted the fire that had destroyed nearly everything. And told the chief he was glad to be welcomed among the Atsina. He used the name they gave themselves, not the French name trappers had bestowed on them.

The chief rambled, barely accompanying his long talk with signs, so that Skye caught little of what was being said. Still, there were scraps of information. The great prairie fires had pushed the buffalo this way, and hunting was good here. The People had no enemies, only friends. The visitors would be welcome to share the meat. Everything the village possessed now belonged to the visitors for their use, and everything the visitors possessed now belonged to the Atsina for the People's use.

That gave Skye pause. Was it rhetoric? Was it something larger, a justification for copping some horses? Uneasily Skye worked his way through the welcoming ritual, and then the chief summoned a pipe-bearer to bring him the peace pipe. There would be a smoke, a sacred affirmation that no harm would be received or given, and then his party would be free to make camp.

"And what have our visitors brought us?" the chief asked, his fingers filling in for words.

Skye knew at once that a gift was required. A gift he and Mercer didn't have.

"Nothing. We are poor. The great fire took everything."

"That is a good horse." The chief waved at Jawbone.

"You would find him dangerous, Chief Bear."

"Then he would make good meat."

Victoria watched, horror in her face.

"What's he saying, Mister Skye?" Mercer asked.

"He is expecting a gift and has his eye on Jawbone."

"Tell him I will give him the giant horse. Not the one bearing our travois, but the other."

Skye felt a flood of gratitude toward the explorer. "Chief Bear, grandfather," he signaled. "It is our wish to give you the largest horse of all, that giant standing there. You will have the biggest horse you have ever seen. He is recovering from some wounds caused by fire, but in a short while, you will have a giant. He can pull twice as much as other horses."

"Ah! So it will be! Welcome. The Atsina welcome our friend Skye. Welcome. Be our guests!"

"What's he saying?"

"He's welcoming us. He accepts the draft horse. He wants us to be at home among the Atsina."

Skye felt momentary relief, but worries crowded his mind and he wanted nothing more than to escape gracefully, without arousing trouble that seemed to lurk in every corner. He wondered how many more horses this visit would cost.

Mercer led the great animal to the chief, who waved a hand and one of the younger of his family took the line. They peered at it, stood beside it, marveled at its height, carefully scrutinized the crusted-over wounds, talked much among themselves, and seemed pleased. Now everything was smiles again.

Some tension dissolved and Skye's party was led to a place just outside the village where there was some grass remaining for their stock. Mercer and Winding picketed their remaining draft horse and saddle horses while Skye turned Jawbone loose. If an Atsina tried to catch him, he'd have his hands full. And they had all been warned. Jawbone was no horse to trifle with.

Mercer seemed content to wander the village, study men, women, and children, his sharp eye missing nothing. Skye was plenty hungry, and so were they all, but so far they had not been invited to any feast.

But at twilight all that changed. Chief Bear summoned them all to a feast of buffalo hump, the finest meat available on the plains, and soon Skye and his wives were gorging on well-done, succulent meat that was roasted in such plenitude that they all ate more than their fill.

"Skye, this is the best boss rib I've ever sampled," Mercer said.

And so it was. It came without adornment, no prairie turnips, no greens, no berries, but it sufficed this pleasant evening, as the sun swept toward its bed behind the western hills, and a lavender darkness crept over the cheerful camp.

He began to relax. Tomorrow, early, they would slip away, probably before any of these people stirred. They were not known for industry, or getting up at dawn to spend daylight at toil.

"I say, Mister Skye, this is capital. But I haven't a story. Can you think of something worth writing about?" Mercer asked, gnawing on a stem of grass.

"You could write about the white men wandering these plains. You've met two unusual sorts," Skye said.

But Mercer dismissed the thought with a grunt.

Then an emissary arrived from Chief Bear, summoning Skye once again to the headman's lodge, where he sat upon a reed backrest, enjoying the company of half a dozen comely women.

"Mister Skye," the chief signaled. "Night comes, the owl flies. And at night we think of other things. I will give you a gift. Take one of my wives this night. Send your men here and take them all. Enjoy them. They are very beautiful."

Skye was afraid of that.

"And, Mister Skye, send your wives to me. The younger one catches my eye."

# twenty-seven

Over many years, Skye had learned to cope with practices and beliefs of the native people of North America. Often they didn't accord with his own. And now he was caught in a dilemma that instantly tortured him. Chief Bear was being hospitable. Lending an honored guest a wife or two was a mark of esteem. Offering the chief a wife or two was a mark of the visitor's respect. All this was simply the commerce of the plains, ordinary except to a European like Skye whose instincts were utterly different.

"Sonofabitch," said Victoria.

"What did he say, man?" Graves Mercer asked.

Skye could hardly bring the words to his lips. "He's offered us the pleasure of his wives and wants me to reciprocate."

"No! Really?"

"Hell yes," said Victoria.

"Ah! At last! Something to write about! I've wandered over half of North America looking for a sensation, and finally I've found one!"

"Mister Skye," said Mary, "I am honored. I will be the one-night wife of this fine Atsina chief. I will bring smiles to him, and feel rewarded by his happiness."

"Dammit, Skye, tell him I am old and full of bad diseases," Victoria said.

Skye lifted his top hat and settled it on graying locks, for once not only wordless but with no plan rising to mind. Beside Chief Bear, a dozen women smiled broadly. They could read the chief's sign language as well as Victoria and Mary could. Skye spotted the sits-beside-him wife, older, stern, gray, with great authority in her demeanor. She showed no pleasure in the honor of sleeping with guests but the younger ladies trilled and cooed and smiled broadly.

Skye surveyed them all and admitted to himself that Chief Bear had an eye for comely young women. In fact, most of these Atsina ladies were gorgeous, with flashing brown eyes, glossy jet hair in braids or hanging loose, golden flesh, and trim ankles. One in particular stared at him quietly, her young, golden face warm with anticipation, even as she stood higher and prouder that he might notice her. One glance at her, slim and sweet and eager, stirred him.

Skye puckered his lips. He wished to speak, but all he could manage was some fierce puckering of lip.

"By the Lord Harry, I hope you'll spare me a pair of them," Mercer said. "What a dainty dish to set before the king."

"Serially or at the same time?" Skye asked.

"Ho, ho, ho," Mercer retorted.

Matters were getting out of hand.

"You must realize, Mister Mercer, that some of these lovelies might be infected. The venereal is common among them, and white men are more vulnerable to it than they are."

"Trying to scare me off, are you, Skye?"

"What you do is up to you, Mister Mercer."

"Will they expect anything from me, Mister Skye?"

"A baby."

"Baby? Surely you don't mean it."

"The Atsina would be enchanted if you were, ah, to father a child among them."

Mercer began to shuffle, one foot and another, contemplating that. "Do I have my choice of lovelies?"

"You might offer another horse, seeing as how you don't have a wife to bargain away."

"And Winding?"

"I imagine a horse would do it."

"Absolutely delightful. How do I proceed? I can't even signal them, unless I just point at the lady . . . maybe that one there, standing behind the rest. A slim beauty, solemn, not a bit of eagerness in her face."

"I'm afraid, Mister Mercer, that the object of your desire is the chief's daughter. If you ask for her, you might get her for life."

"Oh. Blast. Bad luck." But then he brightened. "But good story. Shock London, you know. Old boys'll turn beet-red over their tea. Oh, what it'll do the prime minister. Ah, what it'll do in every rectory! Oh, what a stir at the Royal Society! Half the old dogs will run snuff up their nostrils, the other half will be envious of me."

"Confession is good for the soul," said Skye.

"How'm I going to write all this down? Have they paper and pencil?"

"Not likely. You can record it on your robe, using the greasepaint Victoria gave you, and a reed."

"I'd have to smuggle the bloody robe into England."

"Mister Skye, just choose a few," Victoria said.

He knew she wouldn't mind it a bit if he wandered into the night with three ladies on his arm, even if she herself didn't want to become Chief Bear's paramour. But the Crow were like that.

"Please, Mister Skye, give me the honor," said Mary, aglow.

Around them eager Atsina had collected. This was a good show, and word had spread through the whole camp. They would enjoy seeing who Skye selected, and would enjoy Skye's presentation of his ladies to Chief Bear, and maybe Bear's sons and sons-in-law.

All in all, it seemed a cheerful prospect.

But something was raking Skye's soul.

He stepped forward, and immediately the merriment and gossip stopped. What he would say with his fingers would be there for all to see, all to interpret. It would not be easy. The finger-talk lacked nuance and was unclear, sometimes dangerously unclear.

"My medicine," he signaled, "is to live only with my wives. It is not in me to share them with you. It is not in me to take any of yours. It is the way I am. It is in me to believe this comes from the Great Spirit. You are good to offer these things to me. This is good according to your medicine. I wish you happiness and peace."

"What's all that about?" Mercer asked.

"I was turning down Chief Bear. I said it isn't my medicine."

"But, Skye, what about my story?"

"I impose my own rules of life on no man but myself," Skye said.

"But you're employed by me. You didn't ask me."

"Yes, sir, I am. No, I did not ask you. My domestic arrangements are my own."

189

The chief thought about Skye's response for a while, frowned, and nodded. But there was grudge in his nod. Plainly he had been affronted. And plainly Skye's party was on perilous ground. But it was an ironclad rule of the plains tribes that hosts treated their guests with respect. Nothing would happen within this village. Probably nothing would happen at all. And yet Skye found himself ill at ease.

Mercer seethed all the way back to their campsite. As soon as he was out of earshot of the Atsina, he lashed out.

"I've walked across this continent looking for a sensation. I've suffered indignities, lost my outfit, lost a man, and lost my journals. Nothing happens over here. It's not like Africa or the Near East. All I've found is a big blank. What will I send to the seven newspapers that employ me? What sort of papers will I present to the Royal Society? Answer me that, eh?"

Skye stood stock-still.

"Now at last something happens. A chief with the morals of a rutting dog wants to trade women. A sensation. I can sell the story ten times over. At long last, after squandering months and a small fortune, we have something worth writing about. And what happens? You scotch the whole thing. I never thought I'd be hiring some missionary. I never imagined you'd wreck this entire trip. What's left, eh? Bones. I don't want fossil bones. I want sensation. You've taken a year out of my life. That's what this is about. A year out of my life. Lost. Gone. Dead."

Skye had hoped for good pay, but now he knew he would get nothing at all.

"If you're discharging me I think we will head for Victoria's people, Mister Mercer."

"What? And leave me here? Without a guide? Without a translator? Without anyone who knows the hand-talk? Without a weapon? You signed on for the whole trip. You'll take me through."

"Very well. My advice is that we pack up and leave immediately. There's trouble here."

"Don't be absurd, Skye. They're fixing to do some drumming, have a party, throw a fandango in our honor, and you want to sneak out."

"Do you reckon one of those blistered saddlers which ain't ever gonna be good for much would fetch me a lady?" Winding asked. "I'm plumb lonesome."

Winding's yearnings seemed to settle it for Mercer. "Are those nags good for anything?" he asked.

"Not for saddling, anyway," Winding said. "Maybe you and me, we'd be getting the real bargain, eh?"

Victoria laughed; it was her rowdy, raucous laugh, the sort of laugh that evoked midsummer saturnalias among the Absaroka people.

"I don't know as how I'd want the chief's sits-beside-him woman anyhow," Winding said.

Skye nodded. His women were already drifting into the village, full of merriment, full of devil-may-care, ready for a howl. And Mercer and Winding were headed for the horses, which were picketed on grass alongside some trees two or three hundred yards away.

Skye found himself alone. The whole world, in all its diverse tribes, enjoyed a happy time. Fiestas, potlatches, parties, balls, dances. He wondered why he felt so ill at ease about all that. Maybe it was because he had ended up a man without a country. His only land was not a place, but lay in the heart.

# twenty-eight

Skye wasn't going to have a night by himself after all. Victoria came for him and told him he was needed.

Reluctantly, for he was not comfortable with these people, he followed her into the village, where a great congregation had collected before the lodge of Chief Bear. The wrath of the earlier hour had melted away and he eyed Skye affably.

"Ah, Mister Skye. Help me, please," Mercer said. "They've inquired what I do, who I am, and I thought to tell them I am a storyteller. That's as close as I can come to a journalist. Victoria did the sign-talk. And now, nothing will do but stories. They're gathered here, whole bloody village, to hear me tell stories!"

"We will have stories!" Victoria said. "They have a young man who knows English."

"Then why me?"

"Just a little English. He worked at Fort Benton a few moons."

"Two sign-talkers and a translator?"

Victoria grinned.

Spread on robes in every direction was a great crowd, some wrapped in blankets against the chill, most of them eager for this delightful event to begin. A small fire cast up gray smoke and shot wavering light into the multitude.

"What'll you talk about, Mister Mercer?"

"I don't know a thing about stories but I can tell them where I've been, what I've seen. Monkeys. Zebras. Giraffes. Lions. Crocodiles. Anteaters."

Chief Bear, seeing Skye at hand, rose and lifted an arm, gaining attention swiftly. He was going to orate first, and Skye hoped the young translator could convey the gist of it.

Bear began in a monotone that somehow projected outward to the farthest reaches of the crowd.

"He says, storytellers are the greatest of all people. He says storytellers bring us the rest of the world. They give us mighty lessons, and show us good and bad. They fill our minds with wonders. And here is a man who is said to be the greatest storyteller on earth, this man Mercer. So listen well my children, for there is no one else like him."

The young man was converting the Gros Ventre tongue into English well enough, which relieved Skye. He had no idea how he would convey the idea of a giraffe or a hippopotamus to these Atsina people.

"Ready, Mister Skye?"

"No, but go ahead."

Graves Duplessis Mercer stood gracefully among the Indians that cool night, lit only by the flames of a fire before him. He spoke in a loud sonorous voice, thanking them for inviting him, and expressing his wish that they would all profit from his talk.

Skye knew at once that Mercer possessed some sort of

magic. It would not matter what he said, but that he was there among the Gros Ventres, making a memorable night out of a fall evening.

"I have sailed across the great waters. I have been to lands we call Asia and Africa and South America. I have been to a vast land called Australia where there are strange animals. I have been far north to an island covered with ice called Greenland. I have been to small islands in the south seas, where the waves crash on white beaches, and everyone is beautiful."

Skye intuitively followed the dialogue with his hands, even as the youth who knew a little English intoned his translation. No one consulted Mercer about the accuracy of any of it; it didn't matter. A good story did not need to be true.

"I have seen snakes called anacondas and boa constrictors so big that they are as thick as a tree trunk and five or seven paces long. I have seen animals called anteaters that have a long snout and dig up ants."

"Ah!" said someone. People laughed politely. This man's stories were becoming more and more strange, and that made them all the better.

"There is a tribe in Africa that pierces the flesh below the lower lip of young women and puts a wooden plug in the hole. And then every little while they put a larger plug in, until the lower lip protrudes outward like a small platter. They think this is beautiful."

Women clacked and giggled at that.

"I have been among people who tattoo their whole bodies. Do you know what a tattoo is? It is body art, pricked under the skin, and some people have covered all of themselves with body art. It cannot be washed off. It is their medicine forever," Mercer said. Clearly, he was reaching for anything exotic, and was getting exactly the result he hoped for.

"Zebras! Horses with black and white stripes! Can you imagine it?"

No one could.

"And pygmies! Little people, only this high." He gestured in the direction of his waist. "Little people, great warriors."

"Some people in Africa have blowguns. I suppose I'll have to tell you what a blowgun is. It's a big reed. The little people put a poison dart into it and blow it toward their enemies and kill them with poison."

Ah! That evoked a stir. Skye's fingers were incapable of telling these stories but he kept up manfully. The Gros Ventres were getting most of it from their translator. Whenever the fire flickered low, a young woman fed its flames, so all could see Skye's sign language and watch Mercer talk.

The man had a genius for it. He paused dramatically to let his interpreters translate. He gestured. He didn't try to tell stories, the kind with beginnings and endings, but simply described the wonders he had seen, and that was more than enough.

People edged closer, so they could study the sign language and hear the translator, who stumbled along, as taxed as Skye was. But somehow they got it, or something close to what Mercer was saying.

The explorer catalogued all the wonders of the world. Giant lizards, parrots as bright as sunsets, scorpions, camels with great humps on them that could walk across deserts and go for a while without water. He talked of fierce tribes of marauders in North Africa, blond people in Scandinavia, striped tigers that prowled the jungles. He talked of naval battles between big wooden ships with cannon on them. His talk roamed everywhere, the seas, the deserts, the woods, the mountaintops, the jungles, the rivers a mile wide.

Then, finally, as the chill turned to sharp cold, he stopped. By now, the whole village had edged close, jammed together for warmth.

The hour was late but one could not know that from watching Mercer, who had an odd glow about him. He was a storyteller, and he had recounted many of the wonders of the world.

Chief Bear stood. He seemed oddly animated, as if Mercer's great catalogue of wonders had triggered some excitement in the seamed old man. He spoke quietly in the Gros Ventre tongue to some youths who slipped away, and there was an air of expectation.

After a while, the boys returned leading two horses. These were handsome ponies, each equipped with a saddle and hackamore.

Chief Bear made the sign for a gift.

"These are gifts to you," Skye said.

"A gift? I thought they were moochers. Isn't that what you told me?"

"A gift," Skye said. "Accept them."

Mercer stepped forward, accepted the reins, and nodded to the chief.

But more followed. Now others in the village brought three horses to Mercer and Skye and his women, two of them saddled. Others brought lodgepoles. Then a group of Gros Ventre women dragged a whole smoke-darkened lodge into the circle of light, and presented it to Skye's party. Others brought parfleches filled with pemmican or jerky. Young men brought bows and quivers and left them at Mercer's feet.

Mercer accepted them all gratefully, making his delight known to these people. Skye signaled his own great pleasure and offered the friendship sign to them all.

"What's the protocol, Mister Skye? How do I thank them? My Lord, what have I done?"

"All the world loves a storyteller, mate. They're honoring you. This night they heard of wonders they'd never imagined. Creatures beyond anything they'd heard of. People different from any they'd seen. Customs they never knew. Foods they never tasted. Weapons they sent shivers through them. But yes, you can return a gift or two. Good idea. It's called a potlatch, and it's very big among some of the tribes. Maybe the nags blistered by the fire. These people could use them after they're healed."

"Done!" Mercer said.

Winding needed no instruction, but plunged off toward Skye's camp to collect the animals. They now had six new ones, all sound and saddled, and could surrender the blistered ones. And now they had a lodge and lodgepoles. They had gone in one evening from fire-chastened poor to rich.

Soon Winding returned with the nags, and Mercer gave them to Chief Bear, who was pleased to have them.

The evening was over. Skye's party lugged all their newfound wealth toward their own camp. Mary and Victoria swiftly spread the lodgepole pyramid, and laid lodgepoles into it, and then raised the soft, worn buffalo-hide cover. They would have shelter that chill night. It wasn't large, but it would house the five of them.

"What have I done? I still don't quite grasp all this," Mercer said.

"You gave them wonders. You do just the same in England. Why do all those papers and journals pay you well? You give them, in your words, sensations. You even hunt for sensations to write about. This is no different. The person who can tell stories is the most valued of all among many peoples."

"Well, that's a bit of a twist, eh? I thought I was a talebearer to the English, but now I'm a tale-teller to the Indians. The only trouble is, there's hardly a blessed thing to write about in North America."

Skye kept his thoughts about that to himself.

"I say, Skye, will we be intruding? There in the lodge with two women?" Mercer asked. "A little bit too close for comfort, eh?"

"You are gentlemen," Skye responded.

"Not exactly, Mister Skye. When I'm pressed, or desperate, I can be a gentleman. But don't push your luck."

# twenty-nine

Suddenly they were affluent. Each had a saddle horse. The remaining draft horse pulled one travois bearing the buffalo-hide lodge; another horse pulled the lodgepoles. Spare horses carted the rest of the gear, the robes, the parfleches, on packsaddles.

They pulled out at dawn while the Gros Ventre camp slept. Those people were late risers and their village would not come to life until nearly noon. A few horse herders silently watched them leave. In the quiet chill, Skye led his party north through broken country, largely open range land, a paradise of deer, antelope, and elk.

"How far is it to Fort Benton, Mister Skye?" asked Mercer.

"I thought we were heading for the bones," Skye said.

"But I am unequipped to write about them. I lack even a blank page and a pencil for my journal. Those pictographs won't do, you know."

"The bones are not far now."

"Oh, well, I'll have a glance."

"I've seen them only once but I won't ever forget them.

You can't imagine how big. Victoria tells me they're the bones of giant birds, three times taller than a man."

Mercer laughed. "Never let the truth get in the way of a good story. I believe that's your motto?"

"We'll see," said Skye. He didn't blame Mercer for doubting.

They were crossing an empty land where a man could watch cloud shadows scrape across the breeze-bent grasses, cured tan now by a hot summer's heat. The clouds sometimes took the form of animals, bizarre heads, horned creatures floating through the blue. There were shapes to heat the imagination, clouds to trigger campfire stories.

Victoria's people swore that some clouds reflected the world they were passing over, and one could see buffalo or a migration of some other tribe mirrored in the bottoms of the clouds. But Skye had never seen any such thing.

They nooned at a willow grove beside a slow spring that fed water into an algae-topped pool. The horses nuzzled the water but drank little.

Victoria approached Mercer with a request: "You let me shoot that bow a little?"

"You know how to shoot it?"

"Hell yes."

"You're a warrior woman?"

"You want to bet? Make a match?"

"I should warn you. I'm very good with a bow and arrow," Mercer said.

"Whoever wins gets the bow and quiver, eh?"

Skye watched all this with joy. Victoria coveted that bow and quiver that the Gros Ventres had given Mercer. It was a handsome reflex bow of yew wood, strung with buffalo sinew. The quilled quiver contained a dozen arrows wrought from reed and tipped with Hudson's Bay sheet-iron points. That bow and its arrows could down an elk or deer; maybe a buffalo if the shooter was close enough to the heart-lung spot.

"And what'll you give me if you lose?"

"My robe."

"Oh ho, this will be a contest."

Victoria smiled. "You pick a target."

Mercer studied her, noting the thin arms, the wiry frame, the feminine hand. "I think I will go for some distance," he said. He selected a willow tree perhaps thirty yards distant and gashed an X in its bark. Ninety or a hundred feet, Skye judged. For a plains Indian bow, an ample distance.

"Three arrows apiece? Closest one wins?" Victoria asked.

"Do we practice first?"

She smiled. "Practice one arrow if you want."

Winding finished watering and picketing the horses and watched quietly. Mary was digging into parfleches, extracting some jerky for their meal.

Mercer easily flexed the bow with his knee and slid the bowstring into its slot. He pulled back the string, getting some sense of the bow's power.

"It pulls easily, but I'll wager it'll put an arrow some distance," he said. "Mister Skye, will you join the competition?"

"I couldn't hit an elephant," Skye said. He hoped Victoria would win. She was a fine hunter and many a time made meat, especially when rain had ruined his powder.

Mercer slid an arrow from the quiver, eyed it, and frowned. "This shaft isn't exactly true," he said.

Victoria smiled.

"I suppose you mastered a bow and arrow as a young woman," Mercer said. "I shall have to redouble my effort. I learned, actually, in the Near East. No one thinks of that as a place of bowmen, but it is."

He nocked his arrow, took a long time aiming, and let it fly. It buried itself in the old willow trunk only a foot above the center of the cross scraped in the bark. He smiled and handed her the bow.

"I will shoot four," she said. "The first for practice. The rest will count."

She took no time at all. Some ingrained instinct made her draw the string and loose the arrow all in one swift movement. The practice arrow was about as far from center as his; the next three grouped closer, within seven or eight inches. She had hardly squandered thirty seconds at it.

"Oh, my," said Graves Mercer. "The lady can aim."

"Let's mark her arrows," Skye said. "Pull the practice arrow and tie a bit of something to these."

They did that. Victoria tied a little doeskin thong cut from her skirt to each of her arrows.

"Ah, here goes your robe, madam," Mercer said. "It'll keep me warm."

He drew and aimed slowly, taking his time, settling his body into steadiness. He loosed the first arrow, and Skye saw at once that it was true. It plunked home only an inch farther out than the best of Victoria's.

"Two more," he said. There he was, those even white teeth bared in a cheerful smile.

He aimed the next one carefully, taking all the time in the world, only to see it miss the target willow altogether.

"That means it all rides on this one," he said. "I'll keep that in mind."

He nocked that arrow after studying it, and took his time once again, lifting and lowering the bow, flexing it, studying that distant crude X clawed out of the gray bark of the tree.

Then, when the wind had died and the sun was burning down on them all, he loosed the arrow. It slapped squarely into the center of the X, easily the best shot.

"Oh, ho! You owe me a robe!" he said, unstringing the bow. They all walked to the willow tree where his final arrow had sunk true into the very place where the bars of the X joined. They patiently retrieved the valuable arrows, working the metal points loose, and restored them to the quilled quiver. Then Victoria headed for the packhorses, found her robe, folded it, and carried it to Mercer, who accepted it.

"Time for a little potlatch of my own," he said. "These both belong to you." He handed her robe back, and then added the quiver and the yew-wood bow.

"Sonofabitch!" she said, accepting the gifts.

"Well put, madam. You get right to the heart of it with your pithy remarks. The truth of it is that I'm no hunter. By the time I line up a shot the deer would be over the hill."

That was true, Skye thought. It felt just fine to have Victoria armed and able to help defend them if need be.

They rested through some midday heat and then headed north once again, toiling through an empty, lonely land that seemed never to change. Some landscapes were boring. But Skye knew that the best hunting was often in the dullest country. The coulees ran north now, the dry washes steering their occasional charge of water toward the mighty river that had cut its way deep below the level of the tumbling plains to either side of it.

They camped that night at a seep that supported a few cottonwoods. Winding cleared out some debris from a hollow and let the water form a tiny pool scarcely two feet in diameter. It would do. With a little patience, they could water all the stock and themselves. The savvy teamster set to work, deepening the pool even as he brought the horses one by one to the cool water.

Skye could have used some real meat that night, but they made do with pemmican and some prairie turnips they roasted beside a fire. Not much of a meal, but a thousand times over the years Skye had fared worse. And it only made the promise of some buffalo boss rib all the more delicious.

Jawbone drank heartily in the twilight and began gnawing the short grass, making a meal of almost anything that grew. Then suddenly his head bobbed upward and he snorted softly. That was all Skye needed to grab his rifle and begin a slow, steady search of distant hills, soft in the twilight. He saw nothing. Victoria and Mary saw nothing either. Winding noticed that all the horses were pointed in one direction, their ears forward, and finally it was he who spotted whatever there was to see.

It was a mustang, plainly a wild stallion, standing erect, silhouetted by the fading blue of the day far to the northwest. And flowing below him as grazing dictated was a band of mares and foals and yearlings. The stallion lifted his head and sniffed the wind, a noble animal with an arched neck, a long broom tail, a proud demeanor. Now the mustang mares were alerted. The old lead mare stared squarely at the camp, her ears pricked forward, ready to run. That was how the mustangs lived. The king stallion would fight; the mares, under the old boss lady, would retreat.

Nothing happened for what seemed an eternity. No animal moved. The stallion stood there, the setting sun dropping below the horizon behind him. The mares and young stuff stood stock-still, assessing trouble.

Then everything happened at once. Jawbone squealed and broke straight toward the mustang stallion. The mares saw him coming, and bolted to the south, driving their young with them. But the stallion didn't move.

"No!" yelled Skye, but it was like bawling at the wind.

Jawbone loped straight at the old mustang, and Skye knew that blood would flow.

# thirty

Winding raced for the horses, which were tugging on the picket pins. Skye followed the teamster, grabbing a lead line just as a young stallion yanked free. Victoria and Mary each caught a mare before it bolted, and Mercer, last to act because he scarcely grasped what was happening, caught two yearlings. All the horses tugged and fought their lines in wild-eyed excitement.

"Hang on," Winding yelled. The livestock man had taken charge. That mighty mustang stallion out there was fixing to pirate the whole herd and had sent shocks of terror through the horses in camp. There was something eerie about it; his screech on that distant ridge had galvanized the horses, as if lightning had struck nearby.

The mustang stallion danced on the ridge, its neck arched, its nostrils flared, looking to make all the trouble it could. With each of its bellows, the domestic horses reared and danced and snorted. It was all Victoria and Mary could do to hold on, and Skye feared that those braided lead lines would snap.

The world of wild horses was a cruel one. Stallions fought for mares; a powerful stallion acquired a harem. He killed rivals, kicking and biting them to death. He drove away yearlings and old horses. The lead mare, and every such mustang band had one, was his partner, leading the mares and younger animals to safety, disciplining the other horses with kicks and bites. But it was also nature's way of preserving the bands. Horses relied on flight, and everything in the behavior of the band was geared to flight.

Now Jawbone danced outward, his very soul reverted to the primitive instincts of a young stallion about to square off with an older one. This was not the Jawbone Skye knew, but some brute of a horse, murder in his eye, ready for deadly combat with the intruder. Skye could no more stop him than he could stop the sun in its tracks.

Skye's and Mercer's horses quieted suddenly. The boss mare of the wild band stopped, and nipped the rumps of the mares that didn't stop. They knew somehow to await the outcome. This was going to be war, horse against horse, to the death. The stallion, lit red by the setting sun, stood stock-still, a statue on a ridge, while Jawbone slowed to a mincing walk like a boxer circling around his opponent. The old stallion bore the scars of battle. Half an ear was missing. Its flesh was puckered. Its broom tail reached the grass. Its burr-choked mane rested in lumps on its neck. There was nothing beautiful about this wild animal, but rather something sinister and proud. Its tail switched back and forth as it waited patiently to slaughter yet another rival.

Jawbone slowed, and then walked up the ridge until the setting sun limned his gray body. The wild stallion watched almost quietly, except for the arch of its neck and an occasional shuffle of its feet. He was magnificent, far more handsome in his raw fashion than Jawbone. The low sun glinted off the dun coat of the wild one, setting it afire or so it seemed to Skye's eye.

The two horses stood a few feet apart on the ridge, just out of kicking range, studying each other. Time stopped. Jawbone lifted his neck, bared his teeth, and sawed the air, his head bobbing up and down in some act of challenge known only to horses. The wild stallion did much the same, its lips forming a rictus, its head sawing the air, issuing his own challenge. And then things quieted. The two stallions stared at each other. Skye wondered if there would be a fight at all; whether Jawbone might turn tail and walk back to camp.

The wild mares and young ones stood two hundred yards distant, ready to bolt. High in the evening sky a large hawk of some sort rode the breeze. Skye found it easy now to hold on to the lead lines of the three horses under his control. They stood as quietly as the two rivals on the ridge.

Then the wild stallion slowly turned around until its rump was to Jawbone, and seemed to gaze into the deepening twilight, ignoring his rival. But Skye knew better.

Jawbone sawed the air again and stepped closer. The wild dun whirled, squealed, and planted rear hooves squarely into Jawbone's chest, with such shock that Jawbone staggered, seemed paralyzed a moment, and then righted himself just as the wild one's lethal teeth bit into Jawbone's neck. Now the mares stirred.

But Jawbone did not flee. That was the thing about Jawbone. He ran straight toward trouble. Instead of stumbling away, chastened and defeated, he sprang straight for the wild one, slamming the wild one with his chest, staggering the wild one. Now it was Jawbone's turn, in close, too tight to receive a lethal kick, slowly crowding the stallion off the ridge, pushing forward steadily, impervious to the wild one's bites. Once the wild one reared upward, intending to crush Jawbone under falling forehooves, but instead, Jawbone plowed into the belly of the rearing wild horse and unbalanced him so he tumbled to earth, rolled, sprang to his feet even as Jawbone's own hooves crashed down on the wild one's rump.

The wild stallion staggered up and retreated. Jawbone followed relentlessly, crowding inside those brutal hooves, always chest to rump, chest to belly, chest to neck. And then the stallion fled. Jawbone followed, crowding the wild one with every bound, not letting him escape. The wild one would not walk away from this fight. Jawbone ran him hard, over the ridge and out of sight, and suddenly Skye and his party hadn't the faintest idea what was occurring out there in the twilight.

They stared at each other, still mesmerized by the drama they had witnessed. The sun vanished, leaving rosy light in its wake, and a cloud the color of blood. Silence crept over the land. Jawbone had disappeared. Minutes passed and they seemed longer to Skye; as if each were an hour. The mystery deepened. Wherever the stallions were, far to the south, their combat was veiled to Skye's party.

Then, as the day turned dusky, Jawbone reappeared alone, nipping at the wild mares, disciplining the boss mare with teeth planted in her neck, driving the wild one's entire harem straight toward Skye's party. They clearly didn't want to approach the human beings there but Jawbone was making them, doing it brutally, knowing he was king of the herd and intending to let every animal know it. The lead mare veered away from Skye's party, but Jawbone cut her off, his teeth snapping, until her fear of him was larger than her fear of the people watching this amazing spectacle.

Then, as swiftly as it had started, the run ceased. The wild

ones milled before the group, terrified of both the human beings and of Jawbone. The domesticated horses jerked on their
tethers, excited by all of this.

Jawbone quietly circled them, a living corral that prevented
escape. Proudly, calmly, he proclaimed his lordship over them,
even while his sides still heaved from a long run.

"Mister Skye, I do believe that you are suddenly a rich
man, if wealth is measured in horses," Mercer said.

"It appears that way, if Mister Winding can gentle them."

"I think I can," said Winding. "Most, anyway."

"You will be rewarded for it," Skye said.

"Wasn't that something! Damn, Mister Skye, you should
have ten wives, like Jawbone," Victoria said.

"It appears that Jawbone is going to leave his progeny all
over the northern plains, Mister Skye," said Mercer.

Jawbone knew they were talking about him. He aban-
doned his guardianship of the harem for a moment, walked
straight toward Skye, and gently butted Skye in the chest. It
was his way of giving Skye the gift of mares and foals and
yearlings.

"Avast!"

"Ah, Mister Skye, he has more ladies than you do," Mary
said.

Mary was teasing him! He was used to it from Victoria,
but now Mary was doing it too.

"I prefer quality to quantity," he retorted.

"What do them damn words mean?" Victoria asked.

"They were compliments." Skye was feeling testy.

All that evening the mares looked ready to bolt but Jawbone disciplined them. The slightest infraction won a nip or a
kick. By deep dark, the wild bunch was grazing quietly. Everything depended on Jawbone. It would be a long time before

any human could touch that bunch or turn them into saddle horses. Skye's and Mercer's own horses were allowed to drift among the wild ones. The sooner they became acquainted, the better. As long as Jawbone remained the king of this herd, there would be little trouble.

They built an evening fire and roasted some antelope. The meat tasted just fine.

Every now and then the wild horses stirred in the darkness, and sometimes Jawbone's policing squeal drifted through the darkness.

"Jawbone has his work cut out for him," Mercer said. "But I think he's equal to it."

"He's a lucky stallion," Winding said.

"Luckier than you, Mister Skye." That was Mary, of all people, but Skye ignored the insult. The women were giggling. He lifted his top hat and settled it, contemplating whether to rebuke them. But their laughter dissolved his displeasure.

They put up the lodge by firelight and moved the robes and parfleches inside.

"I say, old boy, it's a fine night for sleeping out. I think Winding and I'll just catch our robes and hightail away for the evening," Mercer said.

There it was, right out in public, but Skye didn't mind. "Get yourselves a good rest, mates," he said.

The Briton and his teamster drifted into the night, laden with warm robes.

From out of the darkness, Jawbone squealed. Skye knew that squeal. So did his women.

Mary and Victoria were grinning at him and he thought that was just fine.

# *thirty-one*

No one slept well that night, least of all Skye. The quiet was punctuated with squeals, the clatter of hooves, snorts, nickering, and the sounds of passage.

Jawbone spent the whole night patrolling his new harem, disciplining rebel mares, sinking teeth into rumps and necks, kicking the unruly, and above all circling the whole herd to keep it from bolting. The wild mares and yearlings and foals weren't used to the presence of human beings. Neither were they used to the domestic horses in their midst and spent the night taxing Jawbone's energies.

Skye and his two wives spent the night side by side in their buffalo robes, Victoria on his left, Mary on his right, his own arms catching them both. But the night did not turn out in the way of Mercer's imaginings. Skye and his women rested peacefully, protected from weather and cold by the Gros Ventre lodge, happy to share a quiet moment. It was, in that respect, a sweet night, except for the hubbub outside of the lodge as Jawbone established his command over his new family.

As always, Skye awakened at dawn when the first light shone in the smoke vent at the top of the lodge, silhouetting the poles where they collected together. His women breathed quietly. Skye slipped out of his robe and into the chill predawn, sucked cold air into his lungs, and studied the country. Off a few dozen yards, Mercer and Winding lay in their robes beside the ashes of a small fire they had built. Dew lay on the grass. Patches of fog blanketed the hollows. The air was cold indeed to have condensed moisture out of the air.

Jawbone stood guard over his herd but he was plainly exhausted. His head hung low. His alert and fierce gaze had vanished under the obligations he now faced. The wild mares shifted nervously as Skye drifted toward them, and Jawbone's head popped up. The mares didn't run but edged away from this alien thing in their lives, and Jawbone minced along beside them, each step taken as if on springs, his way of telling the mares that he would catch and punish any runaways.

All but one. A yearling stood awkwardly, and staggered when it tried to follow the drifting mares. Even in that soft gray light, Skye knew at once that its foreleg was broken. As he edged closer he could see that the shinbone had splintered and pierced flesh.

Skye knew what he had to do. It was never easy, but he never asked anyone else to do these things for him. It was a part of being a citizen of the wilds. He feared the day might come when he would have to do this very thing to Jawbone. It was why he tried not to love an animal, but he did anyway. He remembered horses he treasured, a dog he once owned, and his deep respect for Jawbone, whose mysterious medicine made him an animal he would honor all of his days.

The yearling tried to limp away as Skye approached, but finally stopped, quivering and in obvious pain. The night's uproars had destroyed him. A night spent racing around on treacherous ground, a night bumping into fleeing mares, tumbling under Jawbone's onslaught, had finally snapped this fellow's leg. And there was nothing anyone could do except end its suffering.

Skye slipped his Green River knife from its sheath at his waist.

"Whoa, boy," he said.

The yearling was too far gone to resist, but it trembled as Skye approached.

The wounded leg was terrible to look at. Splintered bone stabbed through flesh. Black blood soaked the pastern and hoof.

That didn't make it any easier.

Skye lifted a hand to the colt's mane. It trembled. Then swiftly, hoping to give swift peace and not lingering agony, he jammed his knife under the ear, sliced downward under the cheek and across the throat, feeling his keen blade sever life from death. The horse shook a moment, and then tumbled down.

"Well done, Mister Skye," said Winding, who was standing ten yards away.

Death is never well done, Skye thought. But he nodded, acknowledging the teamster's expert opinion. The swift sharp knife had lessened the torment of the wounded animal, offering a merciful death, and that was what the teamster meant.

Skye wiped his blade on grass and restored it to its sheath. It was a rotten way to start a new day.

He would not ride Jawbone. The young stallion would be busy this day and many more herding his harem, and the task would draw on the horse's last reserves of strength. It would be good to put one of those fine Gros Ventre ponies under saddle and see what sort of gift those people had given Mercer for the magical night he gave them.

Jawbone was young. He had whipped a proud old mustang and driven him away. Skye wondered how that old horse must feel this dawn. Yesterday, he was king of his little herd. Yesterday he was a lord of all horses, breeding mares, stamping foals with his own nature, disdainfully chasing away all the young stallions who meant to steal his band from him. Today he was a broken old stallion, an outcast who had surrendered to the law of life: the young replace the old; the young conquer from the old.

Was he quietly grazing somewhere, nursing the wounds Jawbone had inflicted on him? Did horses have feelings? Was he bereft? Or was he merely a bundle of instincts, without understanding of his new and humbler condition? Skye didn't know, but he wished he might find the old stallion and wish peace and comfortable old age upon him. Maybe now, free of responsibility, the old fellow would graze peacefully, enjoy the warm sun, look upon his world as a good place, and think upon his own glory. It was a fanciful thought, so Skye set it aside. There was much to do this morning.

The light was quickening now. Mercer swung out of his robe and stretched. Skye's women emerged from the lodge and headed toward the seep. Skye remembered there was little water here; not enough for a herd of horses. They would need to move on.

"Didn't sleep. Not a bloody wink all night," Mercer said. "Jawbone was breeding, I take it."

"No, it was more than that," Skye said. "He was making himself king."

"A monarch! Well, whatever. It spoiled my night," Mercer said. "The horse world is no democracy. God save the king."

With that, he smiled, those even white teeth flashing again.

He caught up his robe and brought it to Skye, turning it over so the hair side was down. "Now, what'll I record for yesterday, eh? The day Jawbone captured a harem? And how do I paint that, eh?"

Mercer had indeed kept a pictograph journal of sorts on the fleshed side of his buffalo robe, very like the winter count of many a tribal elder. Mary had shown him how to make paints of grease and colored clay, usually ochre, and how to turn various fibrous reeds or twigs into brushes. She had even sewn a tiny bag for Mercer, so tightly done that he could store his greasepaint within it and tie it shut.

"Not much to record, Mister Skye. Nothing that would cause a sensation in London. Just horse doings. Anyone in England is entirely familiar with horses."

"Wild horses, sir? You could make something of it. I'd be interested in reading it."

"Well, it's not the stuff of a good story. I should have headed for Salt Lake. A piece or two on the Saints would've rocked London on its heels. This North America, sir, it's a bust. There's not a story in the whole continent."

Skye had heard it all too many times.

Nonetheless, Mercer opened his little paint bag, softened the fibers of his stick brush, and began to draw some stick-figure mares and foals, and two stick-figure stallions rearing. It was not bad art. Mercer could be expressive with a few strokes of brown paint. There was, actually, an impressive collection of symbols and figures known only to the adventurer himself. But the saw-toothed fire symbols were plain enough.

"There now. I'll take this moth-eaten thing to London. But I'll write most of the stories on board ship across the Atlantic and pop them onto desks when I get back. Not that my scribbling will ever pay for this trip."

Mercer rolled up his robe and put away his little paint bag.

"I say, Mister Skye, what do the bones look like?"

"They're poking out of rock. There's a skull several feet long, teeth six or eight inches high."

"What do the Indians think of them?"

"Hard to say, sir. Each tribe has its own stories. But Victoria's people think they are the bones of a huge bird, maybe the big black bird of their people, their namesake."

"How big did you say?"

"Bigger than any animal known to modern man, sir. Maybe three times the height of a tall man."

"These birds, did they fly?"

"I can't say. Ask her."

"Well, bones are bones. I hardly think there's a sensation in them."

"The tribes all have legends about them, Mister Mercer. The Crows do. I'll wager you'd get a different story from the Sioux or Blackfeet or Assiniboine. It's also a sacred place, sir. We won't touch those bones. The spirits of those animals are there, ready to destroy anyone who tampers with them. That's the story one gets from the people who live here. It's taboo. It's forbidden."

"Forbidden! I have been to a hundred forbidden places in Asia and Africa. At last I might have a story, Mister Skye."

# thirty-two

Skye's party continued to cross broken prairie in autumnal weather, as if it were all a picnic. Maybe Graves Mercer was simply a lucky man, Skye thought. Everything seemed to go right, just because he wanted it to go right.

The man lost an outfit in the fire and won another one. The gods were smiling. It was as if Mercer, the great explorer, could conjure up whatever he needed. And now he needed a sensation. A bigger sensation than anything that other explorers might uncover. The man had rivals. Who could find the most exotic thing lurking in the unexplored world?

Skye thought about that as they pushed northward toward the great ditch of the Missouri River. What the man really meant by a sensation was something that would shock his English countrymen. Shock was in the air. In modern times the queen's men had radiated outward to the farthest reaches of the unknown world, penetrating into the Amazon jungles, pausing at South Sea islands, probing toward the poles, trekking up the Nile, climbing higher and higher toward the peaks of the Himalayas. But it was the customs of foreign peoples that shocked the English. Wicked things. Erotic things. Cruel things. Sacrifice a virgin to the morning star and the civilized world would be duly horrified.

Mercer was really engaged in shock. Whatever he could unearth that would rattle his countrymen, that's what would ensure his own fame. How different this was from other times, when people sought the comforts of orthodoxy, or the healing of faith, or the blessings of a strong crown.

Even as Skye mused, a good buffalo runner gotten from the Atsina chief was carrying him northward ahead of the rest of the party, the horse lithe and young under him. Skye never stopped scanning the open country, for it was his duty to keep his people safe, to spot trouble, to give those behind him time to regroup or defend. His women were riding now, thanks to the plenitude of horses. They kept the travois ponies and packhorses moving steadily along. Winding and Jawbone brought up the rear, keeping an eye on the wild bunch.

Mercer, also riding now, never seemed content and was forever spurring forward, or pulling off to one side or the other, or dashing somewhere to examine something. But now he urged his pony forward and joined Skye as they crossed an empty land.

"When you say forbidden, Mister Skye, what do you mean?"

"I meant that the Indians revere these bones, respect them, and would not want anything to damage them. In the case of the Absarokas, these are the bones of creation, the bones from which they derive their visions of where they came from, and who they are."

"Ah, mythology! I suppose most people have some of that to explain themselves. The Greeks and Romans did. All those stories were displaced by Christian religion but they linger on, half submerged, and one still sees villagers at the old pagan shrines. I've seen them myself. I suppose when Europeans settle this country, these old stories will linger in the hollows and hills."

"They are more than stories, Mister Mercer. The tribes feel a kinship to these bones. The bones are their ancestors. And I should tell you, there's never been warfare at the place of the bones. Blackfeet, Crows, Sioux, other tribes that fight each other, they gather here, enemies at all other times, but quiet and respectful and at peace. Parties come and go, camp there, sit for hours before these giants, and are perfectly safe. The next day, a mile away, they might kill each other but not there where the bones poke up from rock. That's how powerful this place is."

"Well, I'm ready for it. There's nothing else around here. Of course I discount all the stories about the size of the bones. Those things get exaggerated, you know. The more sacred they are, the bigger they get. It'll be a guffaw or two when I start some measuring and find they're maybe as big as an ostrich. Now that's a big bird, an ostrich. And I'll probably end up writing about this very thing: the natives worship at a pile of fossilized ostrich bones and have turned them into the bones of giants."

The man was saying he didn't believe Victoria or Skye, but there was no point in protesting it. He would see for himself. But Skye supposed that was all part of being a sensationalist writer. If you debunk a local legend that's quite as good as confirming it.

"I say, Skye, these bones. They're caught in sandstone?"

"Fossils, yes."

"How do you suppose that happened?"

"They are very old, Mister Mercer."

"How old?"

Skye had no answer. "Older than anyone imagines; what else can one say?"

"Maybe a trick of God to fool the unfaithful? Wasn't the world created in six days, about six thousand years ago?"

There were things Skye did not feel he could respond to, and that was one. He scarcely grasped theology. But he had a few notions.

"Some things are written as poetry, Mister Mercer, because they were too much for the prophets to explain. Genesis is poetry, I imagine. I read Genesis once, and saw that it was fanciful."

"Ah, you're a heretic, like me!"

"No, sir, not that. I am a faithful man in my own way. Let me put it this way. Most of the natural world has yet to be revealed to us. Someday maybe God will open our eyes."

"That's a gracious response, Mister Skye. How did you get here, in this corner of the unknown world?"

"I was a pressed seaman, ended up in the Royal Navy, snatched as a boy right off the streets of London. I made my escape when I could."

"Ah, a deserter."

"Think what you will. I consider myself a freedman. My liberty was taken away; I took it back."

"But you cannot return to England."

"Never."

"I've met wanderers like you from one end of the world to the other, Mister Skye. England has its exiles. Convicts sent to Van Diemen's Land, the refuse of the Napoleonic wars, criminals who fled the island, and republicans at war with monarchy, or Irish opposed to English rule. But mostly, Mister Skye,

221

outcasts. Social transgressors. Women who became enamored of another man and paid for it by fleeing from disgrace. Men who professed atheism and found themselves ostracized. Bigamous men. Banished men. Odd quacks who declare themselves nobility. I met a chap in Spain who said he was pretender to the throne and he was collecting a fleet to topple the queen. Of course most Englishmen flee to France, but there are exiled Englishmen in every corner of the world. And you're one."

"By accident, sir. I would probably be an import-export merchant like my father if a press gang of laughing sailors had not pinned my arms behind my back and dragged me over the cobbles to the wharf. I have no very great quarrel with England. It's still my land, my people. In fact, after meeting a few Yanks, I prefer Englishmen. I won't make myself a Yank. I'm a man without a country."

"That answers my next question, Mister Skye. What a good day this is. We've been weeks on the trail, and only now do I sense that I know you."

"I guard my privacy, Mister Mercer."

"Out here, beyond society, beyond law? But why?"

"I'll respond with a question: Are you planning to write about your guide Skye in the North American wilds, the one with two Indian wives, one young and very beautiful?"

Mercer grinned. "You have me, Mister Skye."

"And shock London with it?"

"Yes, but what difference does it make?"

"I have not seen my family for decades. I don't know whether my parents or my sister live. I don't know whether she married or has children. I haven't heard about my cousins, either. Would you make sport of me?"

"Probably. If it's true, and if it catches the eye, I would publish it."

"Then say that I love my wives. Both of them. Say that it is the Indian custom. Say that when native women's burden is shared they are happier. Tell them that I was and am an Anglican. And tell them that a man yanked off the streets and stuffed into a royal sloop deserves his liberty."

"As you wish, Mister Skye." Mercer's tone was earnest. Somehow, he always managed to redeem himself.

They rode on in silence, though no antagonism remained between them. The land forms changed. Now great grassy gulches tumbled northward. Skye consulted with Victoria, who pointed westerly. Skye turned their caravan down a long trough where the grass was thicker in the bottom than on its sides.

The horses seemed eager, and pushed ahead almost without urging, so that sometimes the travois bounced. The walls of the great trench of the Missouri River rose higher and higher as they plunged into a giant ditch that seemed devoid of all life.

They came at last to narrow bottoms and beyond a slender flat the great cold river purled its way to its union with the Mississippi. Skye dismounted and let the buffalo runner poke his ugly nose in the icy, clear water. Skye studied the bluffs, looking for trouble, and found none.

The women dismounted and let their horses drink. And then, one by one, watered the packhorses and the draft horse and the spare mounts, while Winding ran a well-versed teamster's hand over pasterns and fetlocks and shins.

A narrow trail ran west here.

Victoria spotted the broken arrow and summoned Skye.

Directly ahead, on the trail they soon would take, was an arrow plunged point-down in the ground, with its back broken and the feathered part lying beside it.

Mercer hastened to the spot.

"What's that about, Mister Skye?"

"It's a warning. It says, do not go farther."

"For us?"

"Yes."

"But we will, of course. I haven't come across an ocean and a continent just to be put off by this."

"You would be risking your life, Mister Mercer," Victoria said.

"Well, I'll just risk it. Missus Skye," he said. "What tribe's arrow is this?"

She picked up the feathered end, and pulled the shaft out of the moist earth.

"I don't know," she said. "I have never seen an arrow marked like this."

# thirty-three

The arrow was unlike any Skye had ever seen. The entire shaft was enameled bloodred. Large feathers, maybe hawk or falcon, adorned it. It lacked an arrowhead or iron point. A ceremonial arrow, then, and all the more ominous for it.

"This is big medicine, Mister Mercer," he said. "See how it's made. No point. All red. This is a medicine arrow, a message arrow."

"Who made it?"

"Damned if I know," said Victoria. "Makes me unhappy, I don't know. Maybe the spirits made it."

"Spirits?"

"Stuff you and me don't know about."

"Surely you don't . . ." Mercer stopped himself.

Skye smiled. Mercer was dismissing Indian legend but was being polite about it.

Victoria studied the arrow, cussing softly. "Owl feathers. Owl feathers! That's what these are. This is very bad, owl feathers."

"And what does it tell you, eh?"

Victoria squinted at him. "We better damn well stay away. That's what."

Mercer studied the red arrow, turned it over and over. "A taboo. A message. Oh, this is delightful. I love a taboo! I shall record it on the backside of my robe tonight. This makes the whole trip over here much more promising. Something to scribble about. There's nothing like a good taboo to titillate a Londoner over his morning tea."

Skye was growing restless. "I think maybe we should consider it a threat, Mister Mercer. Someone might have some rather lethal plans for you."

"Oh, pshaw! This is legend, and legend is my meat! We shall carry on."

"I think not. You should not take this lightly, sir."

"Don't be a tiddlywink, Mister Skye. This is grand. I haven't seen the like since a human head the size of my fist was set in my path in the Mato Grosso of Brazil." He turned to Winding. "Have you an opinion on it?"

"It would be more comfortable if we were armed, sir."

"But I am armed in ways unknown to you. I know how to deal with all of this. Why, I've dealt with bushmen, cannibals, Zulus, and Lord Admirals of the Fleet. And never had to draw so much as a pocketknife. Here's the secret. We're big medicine ourselves. I make magic. My magic is bigger than their magic, eh?"

He thumped his head and then his skull as a sort of exclamation point or two. "I am the great Wazoo, Moomumba, Atlatl, Kitchikitchi Bugaboo, Lord of the Universe."

"Wazoo, I ain't going," said Victoria.

Mercer's smile was all teeth again. "Very well, then. The men will carry on."

She glared at Mercer.

The explorer mounted his nag, nodded to Winding, and the pair of them proceeded upriver, past the threshold of warning. Skye knew he could either try to protect his client or turn back. There was no stopping Mercer. Uneasily, he climbed aboard the buffalo runner and followed. The women resolutely started their pack animals upriver too.

The going was peaceful enough. Here there was enough bottomland for a river road. Here and there the Missouri was hemmed by great cliffs, often weathered to odd formations, and at these points the trail climbed to the high plain and then down again to the bottoms.

Skye kept a sharp look for ambush, for a glint of metal along the bluffs, or movement around the crenellated rock, or the startled flight of a bird, or a sudden shadow. But he saw naught but silent bluffs and he was tempted to think the warning wasn't for his party. He knew better. He kept his old Hawken across his lap ready for use. But whatever befell them would be larger than a lone man with a lone rifle could cope with.

The river flowed quietly here, the icy water hurrying on its way to the Gulf of Mexico an impossible distance away. He saw an eagle floating above, an osprey, an otter, and something he couldn't identify. The canyon narrowed but a trail carried them to the plains above. The day was utterly peaceful. Mercer was enjoying himself; the thought of doing something forbidden had transformed the man into a daredevil, but also into a sort of invincible, invulnerable purveyor of magic.

They paused at a place where the trail dived downward into the gloomy valley, where the rock changed from chalky to tan, and then oddly blue. The bones were not far ahead. Victoria squinted at Skye.

"Maybe we will walk the star-path together," she said.

She was saying she loved him and also saying good-bye. This plunge into the forbidden was tormenting her far more than she let on to Mercer or anyone else. Skye saw Mary sitting resolutely on her pony. She had kept her feelings to herself and would go wherever he went, be with him wherever and whenever she could be with him. Hers was utter faith.

He turned to Mercer. "The bones are close now. Maybe a mile ahead."

"Good. And no lightning bolts have struck us yet, Mister Skye."

But square on the trail before them was a blue arrow, this one unbroken, erect in the ground, made by the same arrow-maker as the red one. Skye dismounted and pulled it up. Its shaft was a deep blue, a dye not easily found in nature; maybe trading-post dye. It, too, had been fletched with owl feathers.

Victoria studied the arrow and sagged. "I don't know what the hell it means. It means something bad, but I don't know it."

"Ah! More taboos! More mystery! Skye, old boy, this is getting better and better," Mercer said.

"It's *Mister* Skye."

Mary studied the arrow. "This is an arrow of respect," she said. "We must honor what we see and maybe the spirits will not torment us."

"How do you know that?" Mercer asked.

Mary shrugged and turned silent.

Skye didn't know. He thought he would need to know what blue meant to whoever fashioned the arrow. He liked the color. The Blackfeet used it a great deal on their lodges, in their clothing, beadwork, and quilling. For him, blue was the color of liberty. When he thought of himself as a freeman, it was always somehow associated with blue.

"There you have it," Mercer said. "What does blue mean? Anything. We will be respectful." He nudged his horse forward, and suddenly they were all descending a rough path down into the shadowed bottoms of the Missouri past layers of blue-tinted sandstone, dropping precipitously, so much so that Skye worried that the travois might topple or twist the ponies off the trail. But soon they were at the river and entering a broad flat south of the water, a delta that had been carved from a tributary canyon and deposited there.

This was the place. Skye recollected it now from his sole trip there years earlier. And he had the same eerie feeling now that he had then, a sense that indeed he was trespassing. It was quiet here, perhaps because no wind found its way into this sunken vault far below the high plains. There was blue sandstone layered up the south slopes, topped with tan sandstone streaked with red. He had the sense that this was an ancient place, one where the river itself was a newcomer, slowly sawing its way downward.

They paused. Victoria pulled up her pony, and Mary did too. They were alert for trouble even without having any real reason to be alert. A great and old serenity lay upon the land. Skye felt a sort of sadness in him, and couldn't say why. Maybe it was because he was about to experience the world's darkness, something in these primeval bones that spoke of blood and ferocity and struggle.

Mercer pulled up too, and Winding.

"This is it?" the explorer asked.

Skye nodded. He pointed toward a far blue escarpment.

They rode quietly across the flat, which was sparsely vegetated with a coarse grass, and came at last to the blue sandstone wall.

"I don't see a thing," Mercer said.

"You will."

Skye noted evidence of other visitors. There was a medicine bundle hanging from a stunted cottonwood. On closer examination he found several amulets and totems, each suspended from a limb.

He pointed these out to Mercer. "This is a holy place. This is a place the Indians come to when they are looking for guidance or needing the story of their people."

"Medicine bundles. Why are they here?"

"They are put there in reverence," Skye said. "They are offerings to the spirits that live here."

They dismounted. The horses stood quietly, content to be in this sheltered flat. Skye led them slowly across the flat to the tumble of detritus that had fallen from the blue stone above. The strata were actually layered in stair steps, with the higher strata farther back from the river, and the lower strata closer.

Victoria knew the way better than Skye, and veered left toward a sector where the ancient tributary had cut its own passage through the sandstone.

She began climbing slowly, working past talus that erosion had tumbled from above. She reached a bench that lay at the foot of an overhang that sheltered everything that lay below it, paused, and decided to head right. The rest followed, somehow silent as they approached what amounted to a shrine carved out of a cliff.

Then she stopped, and stretched to the balls of her feet, proudly. The rest caught up and stared at what lay before them. Protruding from the rock was a long skull of unimaginable size, the head of a monster.

# thirty-four

It was oddly quiet. No breeze penetrated here. There was nothing to say. They stood side by side, studying an elongated skull that rose only a little out of the sandstone in which it was embedded, revealing perhaps ten percent of its mass. But it was enough. The ancient jaws held monstrous teeth, each larger than a man's hand, and shaped to pierce. The powerful jaw could catch large prey if indeed the beast was a meat-eater.

A huge eye socket, the hole larger than a human head, peered up at them. Slabs of humped skull bone formed a lengthy nose. The back of the skull stopped abruptly, almost as if broken off. Behind the skull, the spinal bones lay disordered, half buried in the stone. From the vertebrae rose flat-topped dorsal ribs, with smaller curved ribs below. From there, the fossil vanished into the stone, only to reemerge ten feet farther along. There were more vertebrae all in disarray, beyond the imaginings of the most learned doctors of nature. But here were giant ribs, familiar bones now that spoke of the chest cavity. And an array of tiny bones that formed forepaws.

These were so small that Skye could not believe they belonged to the same animal. Maybe this was all an ancient boneyard, the grave of all sorts of strange beasts.

There was a pathway that took them farther along, a path worn by countless visitors. A pathway recently used, with faint imprints in the dust. Next was a few square yards of disorder, a great jumble of ribs and vertebrae, and then odd-shaped pelvic bones, broken into several pieces, mostly buried in rock. And then the shocking thing: monstrous leg bones, each taller than a tall man, mostly buried in rock, but the outlines visible. These were impossible bones, larger than wild imagination could fathom. Bones of an animal as tall as a house. And a few yards away, a well-preserved three-toed foot, a bird's foot, delicately formed but still a pedestal that could support this monster. Beyond was a scatter of other bones, smaller and smaller, yard after yard, as if this strange beast had a twenty- or thirty-foot tail.

Skye had been here before, and now had the same response as before. Did this come from God?

Now he watched Mercer; watched the man visibly abandon the notion that this was a carved shrine, some religious artistry worked by an ancient sculptor. This beast had perished beside a river or on a beach and had been gradually covered with sand, and over aeons had become a fossil caught in sandstone until some giant upthrust had pushed this rock high, and erosion had worn through the sandstone and bared these unimaginable things.

Mercer took off his hat. He was not smiling this time.

"How old, do you think?" he asked.

Skye shook his head.

"There's more," Victoria said. She led them silently along

the worn path that skirted the sandstone outcrop, until they came to another ledge jammed with bones, these disordered so much a mortal could hardly put them together to mean anything. But there they were, a carpet of bones, mostly broken into small pieces, and yet parts of a beast as formidable as the more complete skeleton they had just visited. But no, this was not the same beast, for when they came to the skull, or the fragment left of it, they found a peculiar horn rising from its snout, a blade where no blade should be, an illogical blade that would serve no fathomable purpose. So here was another monster of the deep, another nightmare to float through a man's soul when sleep beckoned.

"How would you like to run into one of these on your path?" Winding asked.

"Why are they here?" Mercer asked.

Who could say? The sandstone overhang protected them; that was all Skye could make of it.

Mary was careful to touch every bone she could reach. She ran her small brown hand over the rock, her fingers into creases and over bulges, as if the bones were there to give her strength, and the more she touched them the stronger and wiser she would be. Victoria frowned. For her, the bones were sacred relics of her own origins, for she was one of the people of this bird. But Mary saw these bones her own way. Skye smiled at her and she smiled back. Touching the bones was giving medicine to her and she was harvesting the strange powers that lay within them.

"Many more," Victoria said, pointing. Indeed, the trail ran another fifty yards through the mortuary of giants somehow trapped here and hidden from air and sun and wind until recent times.

Slowly Mercer hiked to the end of the bone yard and retraced his steps back to the monster that lay almost intact, the very first they had seen.

"So you suppose the earth, the whole universe, is very old?" he asked. "I mean, hundreds of thousand of years. Maybe a million years. Do you imagine that God is recent; the universe is older than God?"

Skye smiled. "That sort of thing is beyond me." He would not speculate on things that seemed forever beyond understanding.

"Well, I've seen the bones," Mercer said. "Now let's measure them. As it happens, the length of my belt is exactly a yard, and I've marked off feet on the belt. It's my wilderness measure."

He pulled the belt from its loops. There indeed, on its interior side, were foot markers, and half-foot markers, and a set of six inches marked in some sort of ink or dye.

"How am I going to record all this when I lack so much as paper and pencil?" he asked.

It was a good question.

"I will bring your robe. We will put the marks on the robe," Mary said. The Shoshone was dealing with the bones a lot more easily than Victoria, who turned tight and silent and maybe angry.

Skye watched Mary head back to the travois. But Mercer was already heading for that giant skull.

"I say, Skye, I owe you an apology. I didn't imagine these bones could be real. Just a mystery or some madman's art. Not something that taxes my limited grasp of geology. Not something that turns my world, my theology, my universe, inside out. I'm glad you brought me here."

That was the thing about Mercer. He was always redeeming himself. Skye nodded and smiled.

Mercer crawled up on the shelf and began measuring. Victoria looked ready to explode. He ran his belt over the skull and finally pronounced his verdict: "Six feet four inches from the extremities." Then he measured the eye socket. "Over a foot. No make that fifteen inches." And then he measured the largest of the exposed teeth. "Can you imagine it? Eleven inches or so!"

Mary returned with the robe, some reed paintbrushes, and the small sack of ochre greasepaint. These she handed to Victoria. "I do not know how to make the marks," she said.

"Don't give it to me," Victoria snarled. The explosion was so dark and pained that Skye and the men paused.

"We'll be leaving directly, Victoria," Skye said. "We will be very respectful and do no harm."

Victoria sullenly turned her back on him. Skye had never seen her in such a state, and it worried him.

"Oh, not quite that fast, Mister Skye," Mercer said. "I'll want some sketches. Blast it for not having paper. But I'll do what I can on the back of the robe. What else can a man do?"

Mercer laid the robe, hairy side down, directly on the bones and began the slow process of painting line drawings of what he saw. There was little room left on the robe, which now was filled with stick figures and pictographs. Mary cheerfully helped him but Victoria stormed away.

Skye saw the depth of her anguish and headed her direction, catching her at last well out of earshot of the others.

"He will doom us," she said. "He has no respect."

Skye didn't argue.

"That is the Mother of my people. That is the great bird that came out of the heavens and gave birth to my people. That is the bird the ancient ones, the storytellers, speak of. We are the people of the great black bird. And whoever touches those bones will perish."

Skye didn't believe the legend. It was ingrained deeply in her very soul but he could not share it with her.

"You and I have not touched the bones or shown them disrespect," he said.

"But Mary has! And so have the white men."

"What will happen, Victoria? What does the legend of the Absaroka say?"

"We should not even be here. We should not even approach these bones without a purifying. A sweat and the smoke of sweetgrass and gifts to the spirits. You saw the gifts as we came here, bundles given to this spirit. The spirits of these birds are here. They are offended. Now we will perish, all of us, and I am at fault. I brought you here. I am a daughter of the People, a daughter of these ancient ones. They are my fathers and my grandfathers."

Tears filled her eyes.

"I'll fetch Mercer and the rest. We'll leave the grandfathers alone, Victoria."

"It is too late."

Skye left her and went back to the bones, now resting in deep and cool shade under the sandstone ledge. Mercer was busy painting ribs and vertebrae.

"I don't know what half these bones are," he said. "How am I going to persuade anyone I ever saw them? London is a city of skeptics. The Royal Society is a body of squinting old men."

"Time for us to leave, Mister Mercer. This is a holy place."

"Leave! I just got here. I don't have much to dig with, but I'm going to take a tooth. That'll shake a few timbers."

# thirty-five

Mercer began hunting for a tooth he could pry out with his belt knife but Skye tried to stay him.

"Mister Mercer, don't. This is sacred to Victoria's people. And other people who live here."

"Skye, it's nothing but a boneyard. Bones scattered everywhere. I plan to take a few with me. It'll be my contribution to science."

"Mister Mercer, let's think about this. If you took a tooth back to London they'd say exactly what you said before you got here. It's a fraud. Someone carved it. A few fossil bones won't make believers of them."

Mercer grinned. "Have to try, Skye. This is the biggest find of my life. My Lord, this'll make me a Knight of the Garter. Sir Graves Duplessis Mercer, K.G." He laughed. The idea tickled his fancy. The ancient order was the highest civil honor the crown could bestow and entitled the recipient to be called "Sir," and to add the K.G. after his name.

So Mercer was hell-bent to make himself a knight. Skye

chose another tack. "Mister Mercer, this is a holy place. If you pry up bones it would be no different from someone sacking Westminster Cathedral for relics."

"Oh, pshaw, old boy. The cathedral's a work of man. This is just an old boneyard that got covered with sand, and eventually the bones fossilized. Now, that's not a bit like someone walking into a cathedral and digging up a dead king or duke or two to steal a molar."

"I'm afraid it's just like that. For people who find their religion in nature, this is their cathedral. Those prayer bundles hanging from the limbs over there are oblations, sacrifices, gifts to the spirits here."

Mercer listened impatiently. "Well, I'll carve a few bones anyway and no one will know the difference. Why aren't you curious? Why aren't you excited? The biggest bloody bones in the universe. We've found a monster! Why aren't you dancing? Itching to share this treasure with the whole world? I am all of those things. What do you think these bones are? What sort of beast? I'm absolutely at a loss. A bird? Three-toed feet, eh? A lizard? How do you make out the little front paws and giant rear limbs? Is this some sort of giant kangaroo? By gad, Skye, these beasts are something unknown. Unimagined. Maybe the bones of a dragon? Who would have thought that Mercer would find a prehistoric dragon, eh? But the reality is, sir, that this monster from the deeps is nothing known to mortals. Not a bird nor a lizard, not a mammal nor a fish. This monster will shock the world, shock every single member of the Royal Society. What shall I do? Pretend that these are nothing, not worth the attention of science, not worth bringing to the attention of civilized people?"

Skye tried again, quietly: "As a favor to me and a favor to Victoria—"

Mercer shook his head. "We'll not impede science. Nothing will come of it. I've seen superstition on every continent I've visited. I've seen strange rituals, sacrifices that civilized people abominate. I've seen strange peoples worship a stone or a toad or cut open a carp to examine its entrails. I've seen a thousand religions and superstitions and this is just one more in the long parade."

"Then do this: Be an observer. Leave them alone. Don't dig them up. Measure them. Record them. Sketch them. Gather witnesses. I'll verify what you record. I'm sure Mister Winding will. But leave the bones alone. If you leave the bones unharmed, I believe you will leave here unharmed. If you harm these, I cannot say what will happen or which of us might get hurt. Maybe all of us."

But it was over. Mercer was shaking his head all the while that Skye pleaded with him. The adventurer had already made up his mind and no argument could stop him.

"Lend me your hatchet and your axe, Mister Skye."

"No, you're on your own."

"I'll use our knives if that's all that's available to us. It'll take longer, that's all. Some good hot fires over these bones will crack rock and loosen the bones. That and some careful digging. I'll get some bones, whether or not you're here to help."

Mercer smiled, that bright, relentless smile that announced he was going to have his way no matter what. "I refuse to argue. If you feel so strongly about it, we can part company here, Skye. I can make Fort Benton on my own. It's simply upriver. Winding and I'll go there after we're done. I'll send you a letter of credit for services rendered, care of the factor at Fort Laramie, or whatever you choose. What was it? A hundred pounds? Yes, and well spent. I'll thank you for services rendered. You and your lovely wives. Excellent service, Mister

Skye. You've been a fine guide and companion, and here we are. This is the finest of all my discoveries on four continents and nothing will put me off."

Skye saw that this was how it would end. He eyed Mercer and Winding, thinking of all they had been through, the fire, the loss of all equipment, the odd quest for sensation, and now the sacrilege. Of course Mercer didn't see it as sacrilege, and for that matter Skye didn't either, but over his long years in the wilds he had come to understand how his wife's beliefs governed her life, her choices, her tastes and feelings and very character, just as his own faith, however residual it might be, governed his own.

"Very well. I'm sorry to part company with the mission incomplete. I had hoped to deliver you safely to Fort Benton and with ample material for you to write about. There's one thing more, sir. I should like a receipt or financial instrument."

"But there's not a sheet of paper here, Mister Skye."

"You may write it on my robe, sir. And sign it."

"Well, that's fine, I'll do it. I'm a man of my word and you'll have your receipt for services performed, even if we're parting a few dozen miles shy of our destination."

Skye nodded. There was always that redeeming quality about Mercer. Mary, who had followed the conversation, was already heading back to the packs to fetch Skye's robe, and now she returned with it and spread it on the sandy pathway before the terrible bones.

Mercer knelt, and with his stick brush and little sack of greasy paint, dated and began his instrument. For services rendered, Mister Barnaby Skye shall be entitled to one hundred pounds, to be collected at an exchange of his choice. Signed this day, Graves Duplessis Mercer.

It took a while. Scratching text with a fibrous end of a stick required time. A midday brightness began to flood the canyon and its flat, even throwing light upon the great field of bones under the sandstone overhang.

"There you are. Present this at a post and they'll aim it toward Barclay's Bank in London via Hudson's Bay or Chouteau and Company."

Mercer lifted the heavy robe and handed it to Skye.

"I will do that." Skye lifted and settled his old top hat, as he always did when at a loss for words. "We've been through a lot together, sir. I wish you a safe passage home."

"Wish me a boatload of bones, Mister Skye!"

Victoria sprang at him, bristling, saying not a word, her glare so fierce that Skye wondered whether she would strike the Briton.

"We will never see you again. No one will ever see you again," she said.

Mercer, used to more politic language, was plainly at a loss for words but he nodded and bowed slightly.

But there were tears in Victoria's eyes. It was not just anger, but some anguish, some deep sadness that was moving her now.

Skye slipped over to her, wrapped an arm over her shoulder, but she violently shook herself free. Just then, white men were her enemies.

He hoped this great sadness would repair swiftly. There was little to do but collect Jawbone and lead his family and horses away from this quiet canyon off the Missouri River, and hope the high plains and wind in the waving grasses would brighten her heart.

An odd cloud drifted overhead, a momentary gray on a dry, brittle autumnal sky. An equally odd roll of distant thunder slipped into the canyon, muffled and low, as if it had come from a great distance, maybe aeons away through time and space. Victoria stood rigidly, hearing things that Skye could not hear, and then she stared long and sorrowfully at Mercer. For her, the gods had spoken.

Skye thought maybe the gods had spoken to himself as well, for the odd cloud was vanishing before his eyes and there was naught but hard blue heaven at last from one rim of the canyon to the other. Maybe, when they reached the high plains, they would discover the odd cloud drifting away.

Things did not feel right. He furtively eyed Mercer, wondering if he would be the last person ever to see the explorer alive. And Winding. He collected Jawbone, whose flesh shivered when Skye touched it. What was the matter with the horse?

He mounted, and felt the horse turn leaden under him, devoid of all energy. Mary seemed cheerful enough, but Victoria looked small and shriveled, temporarily an ancient woman as she collected her horse and made sure the travois were readied.

Then, softly, from some other passage into the river canyon mounted Indians came in a long file, all of them painted in ghastly fashion. There was no escaping them. The newcomers took in Mercer and Winding as well as Skye's party, and continued toward them, never pausing. Some wore black on one side of their head, red on the other. All were hideously painted. And for the life of him, Skye could not make out the tribe.

# thirty-six

Skye glanced at Victoria. She shook her head. She didn't know either. Mary studied the Indians and shook her head also. None of them could identify this band of painted men walking their ponies toward them.

Mercer saw them too, and hastily moved his robe so it did not cover any of the bones he was rendering to pictographs.

"Who?" he asked Skye.

"Don't know."

Mercer began his own preening, straightening hat, adjusting his shirt. Winding stood, watching the painted Indians, a certain resignation in him.

Now the warriors, walking their ponies single file, were close enough so Skye could make out details. The ponies were painted too. The lead horse had a set of pointed teeth across his chest, like an alligator jaw. The hideously painted warrior held a staff burdened with feathers. Not a weapon was visible among any of them. They were all splashed with umber and red, black and tan, with circles and giant eyes painted on their chests, and chevrons on their arms.

"Mercer. Stay quiet. They're not painted for war."

"Got it, old boy."

But Skye wondered whether the explorer did get it. The band now rode toward Mercer and Winding, parading their ponies along the path that bordered the bones, studying Mercer's pictographs painted on his robe.

Skye held up his hand, palm out, the peace sign, and then did the friend sign. The chief of this band did likewise. For the moment, anyway, trouble receded. Skye beheld about fifteen young men of unknown tribe, all silent, all dressed in outlandish ways, but plainly exhibiting the most powerful medicine they could manage from their paint pots.

They reined their ponies to a halt and stared at the white men.

"Who are they, Mister Skye?" Mercer whispered.

"No idea," Skye replied.

"Well find out, blast it."

The explorer who had just discharged his guide suddenly had need of him. Skye allowed himself a moment of amusement.

"I am Skye," he signaled, pointing to the sky and his chest. "Who you?"

"No Name here," the leader signaled back. A man who concealed his name.

"What people?"

The leader gave the sign for Sarsi but Skye didn't recognize it.

"Sarsi!" whispered Victoria.

"Sarsi? They're Sarsi," Skye said to Mercer.

"Never heard of 'em."

"Canadian."

"Ah, the queen's very own!"

"I doubt it," Skye retorted laconically.

He knew little about them. The band had lived on the Saskatchewan plains, been driven west by Cree about the turn of the century, and had found protection and support from their friends the Blackfeet.

"Sonofabitch," muttered Victoria, who was no friend of anyone associated with her mortal enemies.

"Who him?" signaled the one who owned no name, pointing to Mercer.

"He storyteller, makes pictures, from the land of the Great Mother."

Skye's hands flew, his fingers formed and re-formed image after image. Sign language was never easy.

"Why here?" No Name pointed at Mercer.

Skye paused. He had to be very careful.

"To tell story of bones."

No Name dismounted and stooped over the robe to study the pictographs.

"What's he doing, Mister Skye?" Mercer asked.

"He is reading your signs as best he can."

Others dismounted and crowded around the robe, pointing at this or that image. Mercer was plenty nervous and kept smiling, flashing a row of white teeth at one and another of the Sarsi. Then they began arguing in a tongue Skye could not grasp.

"What are they saying?" Mercer asked.

"Who knows?"

"I have to know!"

Skye smiled. "Mister Mercer, at this moment your life depends on the way you behave. Give no offense."

All of our lives, Skye added silently.

"What do you make of it, Victoria?"

"Secret society. Sarsi come here to get big medicine from bones. Maybe bone society. All young sonsofbitches, eh?"

"What are our chances?"

"No one ever got killed here. What you call it, a truce here. Big truce."

"But if they decide Mercer has done evil?"

She shrugged, not wanting to answer that one.

The dispute among the Sarsi seemed to escalate. And it involved the robe. That was plain from the gesticulating and pointing.

Skye signaled Mercer to be cautious but Mercer mixed right in with the young men, smiling, making friends or so he thought.

Finally, the Sarsi headman approached Skye, hands and fingers moving swiftly once again. "The storyteller. Does he know the story of the big bones?"

"No."

"But he has told the story on his robe."

Skye nodded.

"He will tell the story to us."

"He does not know the story."

"But he has painted it on his robe."

Skye sensed he was trapped. "Mister Mercer, they believe you know the story of the bones because of what you've put on the robe, and now they want to hear it. I'll have to use sign language."

"But, Skye, I'm really not a storyteller."

"I told them you are one."

"What'll I say?"

"Tell them what Victoria's people believe the bones to be."

Victoria glared at Skye and retreated into herself. But Skye sensed she was secretly pleased.

No Name signaled Skye. "We will learn the story of the sacred bones. The Storyteller will tell us. We will dance and pray. We have begged the four winds for the Storyteller and now he is here. This is a great omen. The Mystery of the Bones will be opened to my people. This day will be remembered for all times."

"What's he saying, Mister Skye?" Mercer asked.

Skye pondered how to put it. "Mister Mercer, they have waited a long time to learn the mysteries of the big bones. This is a pilgrimage. They come from the north. They have come here to pay their respects to the bones and learn about them. And now they will find out from you. For a long time they have pleaded for you to come here and now you are here. You are the high priest of the big bones. Perhaps one of their shamans prophesied that you would be here. I don't know. This evening they will listen to you, and dance and pray to the big bones."

"High priest?"

"You, yes. Behave accordingly. Consider yourself the archbishop of bones."

"Gad, Skye, I am not a high priest of anything except women." He was grinning again, even white teeth on display.

"Sir, take this seriously. I repeat, your life depends on it. False priests are the first to feel the battle-axe."

"But I am to make up a story? How can I take that seriously?"

"A myth is not made-up. The story of Victoria's people, the people of the great bird, is not simply manufactured. It's an ancient tradition to explain their origins."

Victoria absorbed that solemnly.

Mercer sighed. "Storytelling is my calling, it seems."

It was eerie. The Sarsi clearly believed this encounter was preordained, fated by the gods, and clearly had foreknowledge of Mercer's visit. There were powers of the universe that Skye didn't grasp, this understanding of the hours and days and months ahead.

The secret bones society of the Sarsi made camp on the flat close to the river. They had brought no tents, only a sleeping robe each, and necessaries. Some of the young men had drums; each had his own paints. They carried only a little jerky, just enough to stave off starvation.

That afternoon, they lionized Mercer, bringing gifts to lay at his feet. The high priest of the bones received two robes, a Hudson's Bay axe, a battle hatchet, an awl, a knife, a King James Bible from who knew where, a small medicine bundle carefully strung over his neck, a fringed elk-skin jacket, and a sacred pipe with a red pipestone bowl.

"Gad, Skye, I'm rich! Now I can dig bones!" Mercer said.

A cold fear coursed through Skye. "Leave them alone if you wish to live."

The great ceremony began at sundown, when chill suddenly pervaded the gloomy canyon of the Missouri and a soft lavender light replaced the bold blue of day.

Skye grasped that there would be no food; these Sarsi were fasting, and expected their guests to fast. This was the moment of the big bones and it would be remembered in their tribal history for all time.

At last No Name summoned his men to sit close to a fire, where they could see Skye's gestures and learn the story of the bones. One by one, these young men settled, mostly cross-legged, some of them with their robes cast over their shoulders.

"The floor is yours, Mister Mercer," Skye said.

"Blast it, Skye, I have no story to tell. So I'll tell them some science, at least as far as my addled mind can come up with some science. They want truth. From me, they'll get science, and not wild stories."

Skye waited with dread for the explorer to begin.

# thirty-seven

There was this quality about Mercer: he stood there like a Greek god, gathering the light about him, so confident and whole and magical that the expectant gaze of every Sarsi was upon him. What was it that Mercer radiated? Skye could not say. This man was Hermes, god of travelers, luck, roads, music, eloquence, commerce, young men, cheats, and thieves.

Mercer smiled at Skye and his women and then turned calmly toward his hosts, but now his gaze was different, mysterious, as if he were tapping some powers of heaven that eluded lesser men.

"The world is very old. Older than any person can imagine," he began, and Skye had no trouble translating that into hand-signs. The Sarsi followed easily enough.

"The world changes. Long ago there were oceans here. Mountains rise and fall. Rivers cut through rock and carry land into the sea. Ice carves valleys and cuts down mountains. All this happens so slowly that no one can imagine it. But there are fossils of seashells high in mountains. Nothing stays the same."

Skye marveled at this strange tale of a world so plastic that mountains rose out of seas and ice and rain wore them down again. The Sarsi were marveling too.

"The world is so old that people are newcomers. We have been here only a little while," Mercer continued, while Skye turned that into the universal language of the plains. Good. If Mercer stuck with simple words and ideas, Skye knew he would have no trouble conveying them.

Mercer spoke quietly, yet his voice carried easily to the farthest Sarsi, a boy sitting well behind the others.

"Long before there were people, there were creatures, large and small, creatures of the skies, the oceans, the land. They are all unknown to us. Many disappeared. Some became other things."

Skye suddenly realized that Mercer was flying a long way from the biblical beliefs of the English, the creation story found in Genesis.

"There were giants among them such as the giants whose bones you see here. They are gone forever. They lived before our type came. We do not know what they were or why they went away."

This was certainly not Genesis. This world was not made in six days. Skye meant to inquire about it, when he could catch Mercer afterward.

"These bones we have here, the bones you have come to honor, are the bones of that which has no name. But maybe these bones are the grandfather bones of creatures we know. Maybe these bones are the first bird or the first lizard."

How could that be? How could any species change? What God wrought was what God wrought. Was Mercer some sort of heretic?

Mercer talked of these things another little while, of

creatures forming and dying and changing into other creatures, of land rising and falling, of ice and rivers changing everything, of those bones and shells found in rock all over the world, the bones of creatures unknown to anyone.

The Sarsi were rapt. Mercer, whatever his other gifts, had the magic of the storyteller in him, and the stranger the story, the more attention he won from his auditors.

If the Sarsi were rapt, Skye was even more so. For this man was not talking about eternities, a world forever the same from beginning to end, but a world in endless flux, as if God could not make up his mind, and was forever erasing continents and species, and creating new ones. Was the world made of India rubber? Were creatures, including mankind, here today and gone tomorrow? Skye had never heard of such a thing, though his own observations had hinted at them sometimes. Who was Mercer? How could he know these things? Or even theorize about them?

By full dark, Mercer was done.

The Sarsi expressed their thanksgiving at this great revelation, and made camp down beside the river.

Skye was done with the sign language and it had become too dark for the Indians to follow his fingers and gestures anyway. He glanced at his bemused women, who were absorbing Mercer's strange talk of a world in flux, where nothing was permanent, and monsters of old became something else.

"I say, Skye, thank you. I was in a bit of a bind, you know, not being able to talk with those chaps."

"Yes, Mister Mercer, you were in a bind, all right. You are still alive."

"Right you are, old boy. You saved my bacon. That's an expression I got from the Yanks. What do you suppose it means, saved my bacon, eh? The thing I want to talk to you about, sir, is my mistake. I shouldn't have let you go. I need you. That was a scrape, all right. I simply must have someone with me who'll translate."

"I will take you to Fort Benton and you can hire a translator there, sir."

"Ah, you still object to my taking a few specimens."

"Exactly."

"Then we can't resolve it. I am going to take some specimens and thanks to these Sarsi chaps I have some tools to do it."

"Then I cannot be associated with you, Mister Mercer."

The explorer smiled. "I'll go it alone, eh?"

"This place is still a church to these people and I will not desecrate a church. But speaking of that, sir, would you tell me where all this came from? I've heard things this night that I never thought I'd hear from an Englishman or a Christian."

Mercer nodded and settled on the ground near the dying fire. "There's a ferment in England, sir. Seems most everyone looking at the natural world is objecting to the Genesis account of how it came to be. Blasphemy, my friend, and subject to action by the crown, you know, but that has hardly slowed anyone down."

"Tell me of it."

"You've been out here, far away from England, so I don't suppose you've heard of it. There's a fellow named Charles Lyell who's done a bang-up book about geology. I pretty closely followed his ideas when I talked to these Sarsi chaps tonight. He thinks the world is truly ancient, and there have been enormous changes wrought in it by natural forces. Land masses rising and falling, oceans now where they weren't before, and land now where it wasn't before. Mountains coming up out of the bed of the sea and that's why you find fossil seashells on mountaintops. A world of constant geological change, Mister Skye, but over aeons of time."

"How much time?"

Mercer shook his head. "No one can even fathom the time. But there's more. Chap named Darwin, Charles Darwin, one of that bright Wedgwood tribe, been on a long sea journey to South America. He's a keen observer and he's shared a few of his ideas with me, but cautiously. He doesn't want the crown on his neck. He's admitted to the Royal Society, 1839 that was, and also the Athenaeum, 1838 that was. That's a little club for the leading minds in the arts and sciences. And of course the Royal Geological Society. He's a man of parts, sir, and he's working on something that'll rock the world. It was 1842 that he did a little sketch about what he's up to, and he tells me he's about ready to publish his outline of a whole new hypothesis, drawn from observation of all forms of life, about species and where they came from. He thinks that they evolved from other forms of life. Too long to go into here but let me put it the other way. He doesn't think God thought up a bug or an elephant and plopped the creature down on earth full-made and ready for life."

"Heresy, then?"

"Oh, I wouldn't say that. But you might find most of the men in the natural sciences thinking that Genesis is a poetical account of creation, and not a literal one."

"This is what you call science, Mister Mercer?"

"Yes, exactly. Observation, analysis, deduction. Rational examination of a phenomenon."

"And that's what you brought to the Sarsi?"

"You have it just right, Mister Skye. You've called me a storyteller, and that's a good way to letting those fellows know what I do. So what does a storyteller do? In London, I'll tell them about the creation story of your wife's people and their belief that these are the ancestral bones, and let them marvel at the banquet table when I'm done. But here, among the Sarsi chaps, I'll tell them about Lyell and Darwin, and let them marvel. That's what a storyteller does, you know. I bring them new things, meat they never tasted before."

That was an insight into Mercer. Skye, who knew he had no storytelling gifts at all, felt a faint surprise at Mercer's ways of dealing with radically distinct audiences. Tell the creation legends of the plains tribes to Londoners; tell the latest ideas raking scientists to the tribes. Skye laughed. It took all types to make a world.

"Who's this Darwin, sir?"

"He's got a fine brain, if you ask me. He found the fossils of seashells at twelve thousand feet in the Andes and began asking the right questions. He found species on the islands off South America unlike others, and well adapted to their environment, and began asking questions. I tell you, sir, I can barely wait for his outline to come out. Last I know, and I talked to him just before coming to North America, he was ready for the printer. I hope it's out when I return. I tell you, Mister Skye, this man Darwin's going to rattle every cage."

"Rattle the idea of God?"

Mercer smiled. "It might. Some will argue that it might even overthrow God."

"That is not something I want to hear."

"Of course not, Mister Skye. I don't want to hear it. I'm a good Church of England man myself. Everything we are in England, it all flows from our beliefs and our faith. That's why I dread this a little, even while applauding it. There's Darwin and another chap named Wallace who thinks the same way, and many others asking questions. We're on the brink of an earthquake, I'd say."

It was odd, sitting there beside the embers of a campfire in one of the most remote corners on earth, listening to all the latest ferment in London. For a moment or two Skye wished he could be there, in his old home, following all of it. But he saw Victoria and Mary, sitting pensively, blotting all this up, and knew his home was here and always would be here.

"Well, Skye, are you going to help me pry up some bones tomorrow?" Mercer asked.

"No, sir, I won't," Skye said. "And we'll be far away."

## thirty-eight

Skye awoke to a sharp pain in his chest. He stared upward, found a Sarsi warrior over him, the man's lance stabbing into Skye's breast. He was one quick thrust from eternity.

He lay very quiet but stared up at the warrior. He could see that the women were similarly impaled. It was light; well past dawn. They had not erected the lodge but had made their beds in a private corner of the flat, well away from Mercer and Winding.

Now he stared in terror at the young man whose lance pinioned him to the earth. The Sarsi was not painted this morning. He and the others had scrubbed away the hideous designs and colors that had marked yesterday's ceremonial visit to the bones. He was simply an alert young man, dressed only in a breechclout, his hair loose around his head and neck, a red headband holding it in place. Suspended about his neck was a small medicine bundle shaped of leather.

All Skye could do was wait and pray. Even to open his mouth, to yell, to explode in anger, could be fatal. The warrior seemed to be waiting for something, and as the seconds ticked by, and Skye wondered whether this was his last day, he began to fathom what this was about.

He was not wrong. In a while more armed Sarsi warriors appeared, pushing Mercer and Winding before them with their lances. Other Sarsi men had arrows nocked into their strung bows, ready for anything.

Mercer was putting a brave face on it, smiling, standing erect, ignoring the half-dozen lance points that were hovering inches from his body; points that could turn him into a pincushion in no time at all. He carried a piece of rock in his hands.

"They don't take kindly to my digging, do they?" he asked.

Skye did not respond but his stare caught Mercer and somehow subdued the explorer.

"I went for a tooth, just one old tooth," Mercer said. "I tried the war hatchet and the axe, but all I did was shatter the blasted tooth. A man needs stone mason's chisels to cut out a bone or two."

"Westminster Abbey," Skye said.

Mercer managed a smile. An acknowledgment.

Skye felt the iron point dig into his chest and swiftly returned to silence. He waited, his pulse climbing, waited for death.

The older Sarsi, the only one with graying hair, appeared before Skye, and nodded to his young warriors. They withdrew the lances. Skye didn't dare sit up but a nod from the warrior told him he should. Slowly, he sat up. Slowly, the women were sitting up. Mary was very still. Victoria glared at Mercer with such heat in her face that Mercer could not escape the scathing rake of her gaze.

The chief began to say something in sign language, and

Skye followed carefully. The two men had taken the tooth of the ancient one. They had desecrated a holy place. They had offended the spirits. They had offended the Ancestors. They were worse than an enemy of the Sarsi; they were worse than a witch. They were the Evil Ones. The Sarsi would put them to death. Then they would decide what to do about Skye.

Skye turned to Mercer and Winding. "You've desecrated the ancient one, the holy place. You are more evil than enemies. You are more evil than a witch. You will die. They will decide what to do about the rest of us."

Mercer absorbed that bleakly.

No one spoke. The Sarsi were all watching Mercer, watching to see whether he was a god-man, a prophet of the bones. Mercer wilted as the reality gradually pervaded him.

"Tell them I'll give back the tooth! I don't want it!"

He thrust the tooth fragment toward the headman, No Name, only to see it fall to the clay. The broken fossil lay there, an accusation, the proof of evil. No one picked it up. Skye wondered whether these people were even allowed to touch the sacred bones.

He surveyed the scene. The light was quickening though this deep canyon of the Missouri still lay under shadow. Several lancers guarded the prisoners. Several more bowmen backed them. Two of the Sarsi had caught up the lines of Skye's horses and the one holding Jawbone was likely to get his head kicked in. But Jawbone, whose ears lay flat back, was behaving for the moment.

There was no escape.

Mercer must have been working from the earliest gray light, maybe hoping to chip out a tooth of the monster before anyone noticed. And now he was standing before the Sarsi, a condemned man.

259

"Tell them I will make it up. Tell them I am a priest of the bones."

Skye shook his head slowly, but the headman caught the gesture and wanted a translation.

"He says he is a priest of the bones and will make everything right," Skye translated, employing gestures.

The one with no name stared bleakly at Mercer.

He barked some sort of command to his group and they withdrew except for half a dozen who were guarding the prisoners. Skye watched them retreat out of earshot, toward the place of the bones, where they all paused to examine the ruptured rock, the damaged skull where the giant tooth had been torn out, taking some of the lower jaw with it judging from the rock still clinging to the tooth.

"What are they going to do, Mister Skye?" Mercer asked. He was now truly alarmed. It had taken him this while to grasp the trouble he was in; to understand that his luck, which had been with him across several continents and in all sorts of strange circumstances, had suddenly run out.

"They are going to decide our fate."

"But I've offered to make it up." It was a plaintive whisper from a man who had never grasped how different peoples are and how sharply they vary, and how goodness to one people is evil to another.

"Sonofabitch," grumbled Victoria. This time the expression was directed toward Mercer.

Skye didn't know what to do or whether he could do anything. Powerful warriors stood ready to slaughter them if they showed any signs of trouble.

Over at the bones below the sandstone overhang the Sarsi sat in a circle and began a discussion, sometimes animated, sometimes so quiet it was hard to know whether anyone was saying anything. But Skye gathered that an intense debate was in progress there, and he guessed the debate had much to do with Mercer's fate. The Sarsi did not want to anger the spirit whose bones lay just a few feet from them.

The sun rose, bathing the tops of the bluffs north of the river with gold. Mercer, weary of standing, slowly sat down. Winding joined him. Skye thought that Mercer's fate would probably be Winding's fate if both of them had been caught ripping the fossil tooth out of the sacred site.

The guards watched warily. Their lances had flat iron points made by Hudson's Bay Company, points that could pierce flesh as well as slice sideways. One point was caked in black dried blood. The guards were veterans, not a youth among them. They eyed Victoria and Mary, identifying the tribes by what the women wore.

The women would live. Skye was sure of it. He also suspected that they would become prisoners, maybe virtual slaves of the wives of these warriors. They might never see their own people again and might die far north in British possessions.

Skye drove such thoughts from his mind. If he focused on a way out of this, perhaps he could do something. But he didn't have the slightest idea of an escape.

As was often the case among plains Indians, the Sarsi took their time. But eventually the headman, who declined to reveal his name, rose, walked to the prisoners, and addressed Skye, his hands and arms forming quick, sure gestures.

"Not long ago a blackrobe came to us and told us about the religion of the white men," he said.

Skye nodded. That probably was Father De Smet, or one of his assistant priests, who had done so much missionary work among the Blackfeet and other tribes.

"He told us about the god-man, the high priest of the peo-ple. Is this man here, who destroyed the bones, the god-man of your people?"

The question startled Skye. Where was this chief's thought running?

"No," Skye signaled. "This man is a storyteller. He goes into strange lands and learns about them and goes back to his people across the big water and he tells his people what he has seen."

"But he called himself a priest of the ancient bones. He is a grandfather, is it not so?"

A grandfather could be a revered elder. Reluctantly, Skye acknowledged that it was so.

"The white men hung their god-man from a cross, is it not so?" the headman asked.

"It is so."

"Then we will do this. He must die. He angered the spirit whose bones these are."

"But it is not the same."

The headman stopped Skye's protest with a savage wave of the hand. "We will put him on a tree like the god-man of the whites."

Skye stared at the headman.

"What's he saying? Tell me!" Mercer said.

"I don't think you want to know," Skye said.

# thirty-nine

Mercer whitened. "Am I to die?"

Skye nodded.

"But why?"

"You already know."

"You must stop this! I didn't offend anything."

"I will try." Skye caught the eye of the headman and began the language of the signs. Let this man go. Do not hurt him. The spirit of the bones does not want him.

The headman, the one with the secret name, growled and abruptly slapped Skye's hands and arms with an arrow. The blow stung. It was a command: no protests, no resistance, no signs, no words. Skye felt rage boil through him, found himself staring into three lance points and a nocked arrow, and he subsided.

The morning sun caught the cliffs high above the river bottoms and painted them gold.

"What are they going to do to me, Skye?" Mercer asked.

But Skye simply shook his head.

Several of the Sarsi headed for a willow grove with axes and cut two stout poles, each about six feet long. These they laid on the ground and forced Mercer and Winding to lie across them, so the poles were under their shoulders. Then the Sarsi bound the arms of each man to his pole with sopping wet rawhide. Their arms were anchored at elbow and wrist. Skye knew that the rawhide would dry into a steely binding, and shrink in the process, gradually cutting off circulation at wrist and elbow.

Victoria muttered softly. Mary was horrified.

The Sarsi lifted each man to his feet. Now their arms were outstretched to either side and firmly anchored to the pole across their back. They could not eat or drink or perform any function with their hands. And in time the pain in their shoulders and arms would become excruciating.

Sharp commands from the headman made it clear that the Sarsi were leaving and taking their prisoners with them. A Sarsi youth collected the Skye horses. Jawbone had sense enough not to fight the cord that drew him. With a word, the headman started them all up a winding trail that climbed steeply through juniper to the rimrock high above.

"Where are they taking us, Skye?" Mercer asked.

Skye quickly shook his head. Silence was best just now.

It was hard for Mercer and Winding to climb that trail with their arms outstretched and tied to the pole. They were utterly helpless to balance themselves. Skye and Mary and Victoria followed, watched carefully. All of Skye's possessions followed, on the packhorses.

The Sarsi traveled quietly, padding up the steep grade, sometimes over rock ledges, sometimes up cliffs that were hard for the horses to negotiate.

"My arms are killing me, Skye. Make them cut me loose. Beg them. I'll do anything they ask. I'll be their slave if they want a slave. Just cut my arms loose."

The headman listened, no doubt surmising what Mercer was saying without requiring Skye's translation. But he said nothing. The trail was steep and just staying upright occupied all of them. Then suddenly it topped the bluff and they stepped into harsh sunlight blazing out of the east. It was already heating the sandstone. In a few minutes the whole party collected on the flats at the top of the bluff. Below, the Missouri River ran its silvery way toward the east, still caught in deep shadow. The river flat and the sandstone ledge that protected the bones lay directly below, perhaps three hundred feet. Skye could see the high plains stretching toward the heavens at some hazy horizon an infinity away. Every rise in the land cast its long shadow as the sun struggled upward from its night-bed.

The headman studied the cliff below him. About twenty feet below was a narrow sandstone ledge that capped a stratum of rock. A game trail led down to that ledge. He motioned Mercer and Winding to follow him down there, and motioned Skye and his women to stay put.

Mercer warily slid down the game trail, obviously knowing he was helpless to stop the descent if he should lose his balance. Winding followed. Several Sarsi followed them, carrying more of the well-soaked rawhide thong. On the ledge they bound Mercer's ankles and knees with the rawhide and tied the sopping leather tight. And then they did the same to Winding. Then they swung Mercer's legs around until they dangled over the ledge. And Winding's. Now both of them were poised on the lip of the ledge, their arms tied to the poles across their backs. They could not walk or stand. They could not untie themselves and escape. They could only sit on the brink of eternity.

Skye suddenly knew how this would end. When the

deepening pain in their shoulders, or the tightening rawhide cut the circulation in their hands or forearms, or their thirst, or the heat of the midday sun, became more then they could endure, they would do the one thing they could manage: kick themselves over the ledge and fall a hundred feet free and clear and then bounce another hundred or more over scree and talus. They would end up on the sandstone overhang protecting the bones, and add their bones to the boneyard. The Sarsi had arranged it so that Mercer and Winding would, of their own volition, give themselves to the spirit of the bones.

Mercer saw it all now, and craned his head upward to Skye.

"Good-bye, then," he said.

"I will do what I can, any way I can."

"You were right, Skye."

"We can go fast or slow," Winding said. "Our choice. They ain't killing us. We'll be doing the job ourselves."

"Tell the Royal Society. Write them. Don't leave out anything."

"How much time have we got?" Winding said.

Skye shook his head. How thirsty would they get? How hot? How long could they endure the pain in their shoulders and arms?

"Do not give up hope. I will return if I can, as soon as I can."

A sharp rap from the headman's arrow, which he employed as a nasty little club or crop, lashed Skye's face.

Then several of the Sarsi brought twists of sweetgrass, coarse and dry, and laid them between Mercer and Winding.

"What are they doing, Skye?"

"Sweetgrass smoke purifies you, cleans your bodies for the sacrifice to the spirits."

The headman glared at Skye but did not lash him.

The Sarsi struck flint to steel, showering the dry sweetgrass until it began to smolder. A pungent and pleasant smoke began to rise from the small pile, curling outward, drifting over Mercer and Winding. Skye had sometimes burned sweetgrass himself and bathed in its smoke. It was a tribal custom that he found comforting and cleansing, though he could not say why.

The sun rose higher, blinding the two on the ledge, who could not protect their eyes or turn away from its glare. Skye pitied them and felt sheer helpless anger roll through him. He searched wildly for a way, for a club. He would find a stick and wade in, crack heads, push Sarsi over the cliff, until the lances found him. But what good would that do?

It was all about religion again. Offend another man's religion and hell would break loose. Challenge belief, question faith, desecrate an altar, violate a taboo, laugh at rituals, and you would stir the most volcanic emotions residing in the soul. Mercer had violated a religion. Skye doubted he would ever see the man again, and hoped he would push himself over the edge sooner rather than later; avoid suffering rather than torment himself to the last. By afternoon, at most, if the day was hot, both men would be out of their heads.

The Sarsi sat quietly, watching the sweetgrass smoke wash the sacrificial victims, knowing the smoke would prepare the two men for their rendezvous with the spirit of the big bones. The Sarsi were in no hurry. It was well to sit and watch, and know how perfectly the two suffered from heat and pain and thirst and hopelessness.

The sun climbed until the sandstone around them radiated its heat. And then the headman, he of the secret name, rose, gestured, and the Sarsi bone worshipers collected their own possessions as well as Skye's laden horses, and prodded their other prisoners away from the fatal ledge. That country was impassable, and it was necessary to retreat from the headlands back to the high plains and pick up a trail there. Skye had no idea where he and Victoria and Mary were being taken. They were on the south side of the Missouri; the Sarsi lived far to the north. Fords of the Missouri were few and often dangerous.

He had been so absorbed with the explorer's fatal circumstances that he hadn't given much thought to his own or those of his wives. Now, back from the ledge, the prisoners were given their horses and Skye found himself astride Jawbone, who itched and twitched under him. He had all his possessions except his Hawken and axe, which the Sarsi wisely kept.

Victoria rode silently, her face stony, and Skye knew she thought the punishment was just and proper. Mary was far more anguished, fighting back her grief.

They rode west for miles, and then the headman of the unspoken name halted them at a high plains seep to water their horses and rest in the shade of two or three willows there. This was coulee country, a land of giant gullies each leading down miles of prairie to the Missouri River.

The women retreated to find some privacy down one of those giant grassy gulches, leading their horses with them. The Sarsi didn't much care. Eventually Victoria returned with her horse, but not Mary, and in the milling of packhorses and Jawbone's wild bunch no one noticed as they started west again, except Skye.

# forty

**M**ary's absence was soon discovered. The man whose name was secret approached Skye.

"Where wife?" he signaled.

"Don't know."

"Gone to bones?"

Skye shrugged.

The headman issued a sharp command. Several Sarsi trotted their ponies back toward the coulee where Mary was last seen. Skye waited quietly. Victoria looked grim. She probably didn't approve of Mary's rescue attempt but it was her code to let anyone do what he or she would, and bear the consequences.

In a few minutes the Sarsi returned and consulted with the headman. They plainly had lost Mary and the rock-hard clay of the area wasn't providing a track. Skye figured that Mary might even have a mile head start by then if she had urged her pony into a lope.

Still, she was four or more hours from the bones. And the sun this late summer day had been relentless. If she did escape, she probably would find Mercer and Winding dead at the foot of the bluff. But she would try, and he marveled at that quality in her. His Mary, so newly his wife, had the same courage and spirit as Victoria.

The Sarsi were engaged in debate, probably whether or not to return to the bones, catch Mary, prevent her from saving those who had been sacrificed. Skye eyed them, eyed his pack animals, eyed his rifle snugged on one of them, wondered how to make use of this, wondered how to escape the four bowmen and lancers who were steadfastly guarding him and Victoria.

He edged Jawbone toward the impromptu conference and signaled: "Permission to speak."

The headman stared, then nodded.

"Let us go. We have done you no harm. We did the bones no harm. Why do you keep us?"

The assembled Sarsi watched his hands work. Fingers were poor substitutes for talk, and he doubted he could do or say much that would persuade them. There were only a few hundred words in the sign language, and they had to do, and often didn't do.

The headman stared at the sun, which was heading west now, well after noon. It was very quiet. Skye could pretty well read his mind. If he released the white man now, could they return to the sacrificed ones in time? Why keep them longer? Keep them? Kill Skye and his wife? Chase Skye's younger woman who had escaped them?

The flinty headman stared proudly at Skye, and Skye wished he could befriend this one. He liked the man who had led a small group of young Sarsi to pay homage to the big bones. Maybe the headman liked Skye. He and his family had been treated with care and respect.

A bee hummed by, surprising them.

The headman with no name spoke abruptly to two of the boys. They trotted their ponies to the herd, cut out Skye's horses but not Mercer's, and brought them to Skye.

Skye lifted his hat. There was no good sign for thank you, so Skye signaled blessings.

The headman nodded. Skye took the reins, gave Victoria the lines of the pack animals, and turned away. For the briefest moment his back itched as if it would receive arrows, but nothing happened. Skye and Victoria walked their horses slowly back along the path they had taken, and in a while the Sarsi turned the opposite way, and receded from view.

"Oh, Skye," whispered Victoria.

He saw the tears.

With the pack animals they could not hurry, but Skye thought they did not need to: Mary was hurrying. She had her moccasin knife. She would do what she could do if she was in time.

They rode steadily through the heat and the waning day. The sun was plunging below the horizon earlier now but Skye thought they would reach the bluff by daylight.

They paused briefly at a seep in a coulee, and Victoria dismounted, stretched, and smiled.

"I am going to put the tooth back in the jaw of the grandfather," she said.

"Where is it?"

"Where it was dropped by the one whose name I will not say."

That would be Mercer, whom she believed was dead now. Once the spirit had fled no plains Indian would name the departed.

"I will help you if you want me to."

"It is for me alone. The bones are my grandmother."

"We will watch for it, Victoria."

Something in her face touched him just then. She loved him as much as he loved her. She loved him through best and worst, through times that challenged everything she clung to, believed in.

They mounted and rode steadily east, along the trail south of the Missouri River basin. The closer they came to the place of the bones, the more they rode deep inside of themselves. Familiar bluffs hove into view and finally the one that overlooked the flat, far below, where the monster lay in layers of sandstone, its bones a shrine to many peoples of the plains.

It was not easy to find the exact cliff; so many places like it crowded the river canyon, but slowly Skye and Victoria examined the likely places, one by one, until they did find the spot, and found fresh hoofprints in the dust. They dismounted. No one was sitting on that ledge below. Heat from the ledge still radiated fiercely, though the sun was now well to the northwest, and adding nothing to the temperature.

Skye walked down to the ledge itself, treading carefully because a misstep could send him sailing to his doom. He saw nothing there. He peered over the lip, and far below detected something crumpled, something he was sure was a body. He studied it, not knowing who, or whether the cloth heap down there was two bodies or one.

"Someone died," Victoria said when he returned to the top.

"Maybe both."

He stood a moment, feeling grief.

They mounted, followed the perilous trail down the cliff, and eventually reached the shadowed flat that lay very still, very lonely, in the late light of the day.

Skye was puzzled. Surely Mary would be here.

Then Victoria pointed. Mary was not near the big bones

but some distance away, at the bank of the river, doing something. Her horse stood quietly near her.

Jawbone whinnied and Mary's horse responded. Mary looked up, and then stood gently.

Skye and Victoria rode slowly there, through gloomy shadow.

At Mary's feet was the body of a man, legs dangling in the river. Skye and Victoria hurried close. It was Mercer, and he was alive, his body writhing now and then. They gazed down from their horses at a man whose limbs were monstrously swollen, whose shoulders had puffed up, whose hands were purple, whose face was sun-blistered, whose whole body was sun-poisoned, and whose blue eyes were filled with madness.

Mercer stared up at them from eyes sunk in puffed flesh.

"Ahhhh," he said.

"This man, I find him up there and cut him free. Somehow we get down to the river," Mary said.

She had been cooling him, pouring water over his shirt and trousers, finding a way for him to drink. But he plainly could barely move his tormented arms and hands, which projected out like bloated sausages to either side, in much the way they had been tied all day.

"Ahhhh," Mercer said.

Skye knelt, felt the man's forehead, and found it feverish, as he had expected.

Victoria headed for her packs. She kept herbs in them for many an illness, including some that broke fevers.

"Winding is gone?" Skye asked.

"Ahhh."

"You will survive this. You will be all right."

Mercer groaned.

273

Skye and Mary pulled Mercer's feet out of the water and laid him flat beside the river. The explorer stared.

Great shadows filled the canyon of the bones. Victoria returned with some bark in hand and began steeping it in a buffalo-horn cup.

Skye stood slowly, his gaze on that brooding cliff. Winding was somewhere partway up it. He felt saddened. He liked the teamster, a man excellent with horses and filled with the sage wisdom of the wild trail.

"I find him there, and he is still talking a little. I cut him free and help him down. Very hard, he cannot walk, so we drag down together. He falls into river, and I pull him out and get water into him. At first he talks a little, enough so I can get his words. The man who died, this man lasted until around the middle of the day. But the rawhide it tightens, making him crazy, and then bees come and sting, and he screams and pushes himself, and he goes down the cliff and his spirit leaves him," she said.

"Bees?"

"Bees sent by the spirit of the bones."

"Is Mercer bitten?"

"No, just the other." She, too, would no longer name Winding out of respect for his spirit.

Mercer gazed wildly upward at them, struggling for air and life, and sanity.

"How long has he been like this?" Skye asked.

"He is mad, his spirit gone to be with the owls," she said.

"The bones did it," Victoria added. "That was what happened."

# forty-one

Mercer was out of his head. Sometimes he wailed. Sometimes he glared at one or another of them. "You have no right!" he said once. "No story," he muttered. "Knight of the Garter."

Skye wondered if the man even knew where he was or who he was with. Victoria tried to draw Mercer's swollen arms to his sides but he howled with every gentle tug. He simply would not fold his arms to his sides; something about it was too painful.

The women began to make camp. Mary was propping up the lodgepole pyramid and laying the rest poles into it. They were going to get Mercer out of the night air if they could.

Skye saw he was not needed and decided to tend to the next business. He hiked slowly past the bones and then climbed the steep slope laden with scree at the foot of the cliff where Winding had jumped. Enough light remained to hunt for the teamster. Skye hoped to offer the man a respectful burial. He had no spade; it would have to be another scaffold burial but at least it would be that much.

He did not see Winding in the talus, and stumbled about the base of the cliff hunting for the body. But it was not there, nor visible in either direction. He was mystified. Then, looking up, he saw Winding dangling seventy or eighty feet up the cliff, caught by the pole across his arms that had wedged into stone there. He saw only sheer rock, gouged by cracks, and no foothold or handhold.

He could not bury the teamster. The birds would soon reduce that hanging flesh to bones and then indeed the last of him would tumble.

He pulled off his old top hat and stared upward. "Mister Winding, I'll send a letter to your folks in Missouri. I hope they'll get it. I'd do more if I could," he said.

A breeze turned the dangling feet.

A black bird, raven maybe, settled on Winding's arm. Skye found a rock and threw it upward. The bird flapped away.

It didn't seem right, didn't seem finished, but he didn't know what else to do so he retreated carefully down the talus, taking great care not to stumble and twist an ankle. Winding gone. Mercer out of his head. Corporal gone. What was left?

Slowly, in fading light, Skye descended the slope to the place of the monster bones and paused there. He felt the sacredness of the place. Generations of Indians had come to this place of mystery, taking away some intuition of the origins of life, giving something, reverencing the great bones projecting out of rock. Someone had restored the broken tooth. The piece, including the chunk of jaw, had been carefully restored to the monster's skull. Odd. He didn't remember Victoria or Mary coming to the bones to do that since they returned. They had been busy setting up the lodge and caring for Mercer.

Skye stood in the quiet, feeling the sour song of the bones churn in him. How old they were. It occurred to him that this monster might be one of God's mistakes. Maybe God didn't fashion creatures he was satisfied with and kept throwing them out. Maybe this one was evil, cruel and wicked, and God cast it into hell, or into oblivion, which might be the same thing. Maybe heaven was merely the place for what was selected to survive, a place for what proved to be good. These seemed older than a hundred thousand lifetimes. God's early mistake, not a recent one.

His mind drifted back to the idea that these were sinister monsters, much older than God, that when God came along he destroyed the evil ones, including this huge creature with the enormous skull and long tail. Maybe the whole world was hell until God vanquished hell and all its monsters, such as this one.

Skye marveled. The sacred bones had started feverish speculations in him, things he had never thought about. He could not explain it. Why would giant bones make him so itchy, so unhappy with his paltry store of understanding? He had paused at the bones only a minute or two and yet in that time, his mind had catapulted into realms he had never dreamed of before. Suddenly he knew how Victoria's people must have felt when they first saw the bones; how the bones fevered their minds, fired their imaginations, and soon enough the giant bones were sacred to them, and had to do with their own origins. Skye wondered whether other tribes had found their origins in these bones. And what had they seen? A big bird, like the Crows? He left the shadowed crypt and returned through a peaceful twilight to the camp.

"The man who cared for horses?" Victoria asked, carefully.

"Dead. I can't reach him. He's hung high up."

"The spirit put him there," she said.

It was as good an explanation as any. "Did you put the broken tooth back?" he asked.

She stared blankly, then shook her head, and that was answer enough. He found Mary starting a campfire. "Did you put the broken tooth back in the skull? The one Mercer chopped out?"

She stood, and slowly shook her head.

"Someone's been here and did it," he said.

But they saw no evidence of anyone.

"Very strange," he muttered. He thought maybe one of the Sarsi had done it before they all left.

Their task was to move Mercer from the riverbank to the lodge. Skye brought a robe, and he and Victoria slid the man onto it. The explorer groaned and uttered one long wail.

"Is it all right with you if we shelter him?"

Victoria eyed him coldly. "I would not want it any other way. We will take care of him. Those who are mad must receive the greatest respect."

"Filomena, will you ever forgive me?" Mercer said. "I could not help myself."

They waited but the explorer made no more mention of Filomena.

Victoria slipped into twilight, toward a slough filled with chokecherry brush, and there harvested the last of the cherries as well as more of the bark and roots. She mashed the roots and set them to steeping in water that Mary had heated in a leather bag, using hot rocks. This decoction she slowly fed to Mercer, who sipped, gasped, sipped again, and gradually swallowed much of what she was giving to him using a horn spoon.

It was an old Crow remedy to quiet a person and settle an upset stomach. Skye thought it would have to do; there was little else growing there.

"Who are you?" Mercer asked.

"I am Victoria."

"Where am I?"

"You are in the lodge of Mister Skye."

"Who is that?"

Mercer didn't wait for a response but closed his eyes and slipped into quietness. Victoria stood, her work done. Mary covered the explorer with a buffalo robe and they all crawled into their beds. It had been a brutal day.

Skye slept restlessly, something nagging him about camping so close to the great bones. If Mercer was able, they would leave for Fort Benton in the morning.

Some time in the night, Jawbone screeched. Skye awakened, and in one swift move lifted his Hawken and slipped into the night, the quarter moon his lantern. The horse was untouched and standing calmly. None of the other horses had been stolen or hurt. It was not uncommon for a horse to startle in the night but Skye ached to leave this place of the bones.

"Nothing," he whispered to his women.

"The spirit," Victoria said. "Jawbone saw the spirit."

They slept fitfully the rest of the night except for Mercer, who seemed to sleep the sleep of the dead, never stirring. But when dawn's first light began to collect in the smoke hole, Skye discovered Mercer sitting up and staring. His arms were still grossly swollen but dropped to his sides now.

"Where am I?"

"On the Missouri River."

"How did I get here?"

"We brought you here."

"Who are you?"

"I am Mister Skye. These are my wives, Victoria and Mary Skye."

"Why did you bring me here?"

Skye hesitated. "You asked to be brought here, to see some large fossilized bones."

Mercer stared. "Why would I do that?"

It was plain to Skye and his wives that the explorer had no memory of recent events. He wasn't incoherent, just blank.

"We lost Mister Winding, sir," Skye said.

"Who is that?"

"Earlier, we lost Mister Corporal. Floyd Corporal."

"Sorry, the name's not known to me. Should I know it?"

Skye scarcely knew how to reply. "Have we met, sir?"

"Graves Duplessis Mercer at your service, Mister Skye. But I am a little hazy about how I ended up here. Am I a prisoner?"

"No, not that."

Up to a point, Mercer seemed himself, but that was only if he spoke of events long past. It became clear that his ordeal on the cliff had blanked his memory. Engaging Skye and his entourage, the trip, the prairie fire, and the long trek to the bones before returning to England simply eluded Mercer.

"This is an odd place to camp, Mister Skye, down in this gloomy trench."

"We came here because you wanted to see the bones, sir."

"That's very strange. Now tell me, why do my arms torture me? They're swollen. My shoulders are unbearable. My fingers thick as sausages."

Skye hardly knew how to proceed. "The Sarsi Indians here took offense, sir."

"Took offense? But why?"

Skye decided that moment to hold off. "Let's get ready for travel, Mister Mercer, if you're up to it. We'll head for Fort Benton and they can put you on a flatboat going down the river."

"Why would I do that?"

"It was what you had in mind, before . . . this."

Mercer struggled to his feet, and stepped out into the hush of predawn.

"It's all very odd," he said. "I seem to have lost some time somewhere. What is Fort Benton?"

"We'll talk about it on the way, sir," Skye said.

## forty-two

S kye and his women thought Mercer would be able to travel at least a little while. It would be good to get him out of the gloomy canyon where sunlight didn't arrive until midmorning and departed midafternoon.

It was Victoria who saw what to do next. She began packing Mercer's robe and then realized it contained memories. She found Mercer sitting patiently, awaiting whatever would occur next, and quietly laid out the robe before him. Skye and Mary swiftly caught on, and joined her.

There, before the explorer, was a pictograph chronicle of events since the prairie fire had destroyed his journal, done in his own hand. Most of the marks scraped into the hide with umber greasepaint could be deciphered only by Mercer but some were plain to anyone. His sketches of the skull, his measurements, his drawings of bones. His record of daily passage through the high plains was more obscure, yet plainly intended to trigger memories.

Mercer gazed blandly at the robe, set hair-down before him on the ground.

"What is this, pray tell?"

"It's your journal, sir. After the prairie fire destroyed your journal, you kept a log of events here."

"How quaint. I'm no artist, Skye."

"No, no artist. Neither am I. But each of these little drawings has meaning for you. These mountains here, those are the Snowies, shown from the east. I daresay this is the Musselshell. These figures here are Indians on horseback, wouldn't you say?"

"Why would I do this?"

"You are an explorer and a journalist. I believe you intend to write up your experiences when you return to London."

"Well, that's an entertaining little twist, eh?"

"Look at each of these, and tell us what it means."

Mercer suddenly smiled, that famous toothy grin. "That's a good game, but not today, Skye."

"We'll bring out this robe again, then."

Victoria rolled it carefully. Somehow, the robe would be the key to Mercer's recollections.

"One last question, Mister Mercer. You're in North America looking for material to write about, correct?"

"Quite correct."

"You came out the Oregon Trail and left it accompanied by some Shoshones, correct?"

"Perfectly correct."

"You planned to write about Mormon polygamy, correct?"

"I believe so, but one learns to follow one's instincts."

"You were present at the moment Mary's family gave her to me as my second wife?"

"Was I?"

"You were curious about it."

"Who wouldn't be, sir? There's a fine little yarn to be told in it."

Skye continued to grill the explorer. It was plain that he hadn't lost much; mainly the period from the time his wagon burned to the present. Yet he could not remember either Winding or Corporal.

That was enough for one session. They helped Mercer up; his arms and shoulders hurt so much he gasped, but his legs were all right. Victoria would lead his horse. Mercer could not rein it.

Skye started them up the precipitous trail to the open country south of the river, and felt relief when they escaped that gloomy, mysterious valley of the bones. He preferred the great open vistas where he could see as far as tomorrow, where he could follow a cloud's passage for a hundred miles, where a man was not hemmed by anything.

Mercer began to howl. It sent shivers through Skye. The man bayed like a wolf, the voice eerie and lost. Skye kept his party going, thinking that Mercer's howling would subside, but it didn't.

The explorer was plainly in distress, and Skye began hunting for a campsite. North, the ancient trench of the Missouri sliced through the high plains as if the foundations of the earth had been ripped apart. He descended a giant coulee to a small flat where a spring purled out of a crack in the underlying sandstone and fed thick brush and cottonwoods for half a mile below it before the runoff vanished. It would do.

They lifted Mercer down. The man was fevered, his face ruddy, his breathing coarse. Victoria and Mary silently began making camp though it was only midafternoon. Skye knew he needed to hunt; they were down to pemmican and jerky. There was spoor from antelope and mule deer here, and a calling card from a black bear. He hoped to surprise a deer.

They settled Mercer on his robe. Mary began collecting

wood for a fire. Victoria would soon decoct one or another of her herbal remedies and let him sip.

"Skye, why do my arms hurt?"

"Because they were tied to a pole across your back, straight out, with rawhide that shrank in the sun as it dried. It stopped the blood."

"Did you do that?"

"Some Sarsi Indians did."

"But why, Skye?"

Skye's gaze lifted to the ridges. "You had offended their beliefs, sir."

"How could I do that?"

"The tooth, sir."

"I have all my teeth but one."

Skye laughed. "The monster's tooth, sir."

Mercer exploded. "You'd bloody well not make jokes. I hurt so much I can't even think. My shoulders! If you had my shoulders right now, the pain in them, you'd be lying on this clay weeping. I keep a stiff upper lip, and I don't need jokes."

"As you wish, sir."

"Monster's tooth! You low-bred dog! You off-scouring of London's alleys! You damned deserter! You barbarian, fleeing all that's right and proper! You degenerate! You seditionist! Skye, you should have been shipped to Australia long ago!"

"It's Mister Skye, sir."

"Mister! Mister! You? Mister Skye, is it?" Mercer cackled.

The explorer's manner brooked no further talk, so Skye set about his camp chores. He watered and picketed the horses and inspected their hooves and pasterns. He slid the packs off the pack animals. He dragged the lodgepoles to a level spot where Victoria and Mary would raise the lodge. He unsaddled Jawbone, slapped him on his rump, and Jawbone screeched

285

and bared yellow teeth, and then headed for the spring water and the thick brown grasses nearby, scattering his wild mares just for the joy of it.

"What was that?" Victoria asked.

"He hurts."

"Sonofabitch, so what?"

"His memory is returning. He knows who I am."

Victoria stopped wrestling the lodge cover, slipped close to Skye, and touched his lips. "So do I," she said softly.

Skye plucked up his Hawken, checked his possibles, and walked down the endless coulee. He felt like walking. He would hunt and he wanted to sort things out. But there was nothing to sort out. Whether from pain or fear or something else, Mercer had turned on him and the trip to Fort Benton would not be pleasant. Skye would do his duty, take the man to safety, and endure whatever the man pitched at him or his women. It would soon be over. Skye's responsibility ended at Fort Benton, and then he and his wives could drift south to Victoria's country, his own country now, along the Yellowstone.

It was a quiet afternoon, without a breeze, the sort of breathless weather that comes just ahead of fall. The afternoons were plenty hot, but the long eves and nights made this September time pleasantly cool. He struck a brushy spot not fifty yards from camp and found himself staring at a sleeping grizzly, a brown giant with unkempt hair, sprawled in a bed she had scraped clear under some protective deadfall from cottonwoods. He froze. He studied the trees, looking for one he could climb but there was nothing.

She awakened, sniffed the air, and turned her massive head. He studied the area and found the cub twenty yards off, its head up, watching Skye.

He hurried back to camp. It would not do to camp so close to a grizzly sow.

"What?" asked Victoria.

"Big brown sow down there a bit. Cub with her. Taking a nap. Woke up, sniffed, and didn't like us here."

"You going to kill it?"

"Ten men with ten rifles couldn't kill it, and my gun is the only one in camp. I don't like having horses around here."

Mary was already undoing the lodge cover and letting it slide back down.

"What are you doing, Skye?" Mercer asked.

Skye's temper was a match for Mercer's. "It's Mister Skye, and we're getting away as fast as we can. There's bear."

"Wave your arms and chase him away."

"It's a sow grizzly, not a black. And she's protecting a cub."

"Well, I'm not moving."

Skye ignored that, saddled Jawbone, loaded the packs on the ponies, saddled Victoria's and Mary's horses, and helped the women load.

It came time to load Mercer.

"I'm not going," he said. "I hurt too much."

"Then we'll have to leave you."

"I'm in command here, Skye, and I say we stay. If we leave that bear alone, it'll leave us alone."

"That's probably true. But I'll not take the chance."

The explorer didn't resist when Skye, Victoria, and Mary all helped him up.

"I don't tolerate insubordination, Skye, especially from a degenerate hiding from the civilized world."

"We'll leave you here if you want. You and your robe and your horses."

"I am dependent on you, and loathing every minute of it. Get me to Fort Benton," Mercer said. "Then I can be rid of you and your unwashed wives."

Victoria stared.

Skye led his party up the coulee to the trail. The grasses shimmered in the breeze, and as far as he could see was virgin land. But this little party was no longer harmonious. One man had turned bitter. It was like a great cloud bank obscuring the sun.

## forty-three

Skye led his party upriver on a well-formed trail over high ground. The world was silent. Barely any breeze sifted through his shirt. He watched distant ravens circle and a hawk soar by, looking for dinner.

Mercer rode sullenly, radiating a heat that kept the rest at a distance. They passed from grassland to hills covered with jack pine, resinous in the midday sun.

He kept a furtive eye on Mercer, whose swollen arms and shoulders were tormenting him with every bounce in the saddle. The man rode alone. The women hung back, and Skye kept well forward. No one wanted to be near the explorer.

Mercer stood it for a while, and then kicked his pony forward.

"How far to Fort Benton?"

"I don't know. Maybe fifty miles. Seventy miles."

"How many days?"

"That depends on you, sir."

"I want a direct answer, Skye."

"How many miles do you plan to go each day?"

"Damn you, Skye, what kind of guide are you? Have you ever been here?"

"Yes."

"Then you should know."

Skye put heels to Jawbone until his horse pulled ahead a bit. It was better not to respond to a man itching to pick a fight.

"Find a campsite, Skye," Mercer yelled at Skye's back.

Skye nodded. Mercer was fevered and hurting. This was dry country, with desolate shoals of pine collected on slopes and no sign of a spring or river. They would need water for Mercer. Victoria's decoctions were all that made it possible for Mercer to be moved. She had that splendid knowledge of nature's own pharmacopoeia and was making liberal use of it to treat him.

"I want to rest!"

Skye halted. Mercer tumbled off his horse, unable to use his hands or arms dismounting, and headed into some brush.

Skye turned to Victoria. "Any water nearby?"

"River."

When Mercer returned, he glared at the three of them. "Well?"

"We'll follow the next coulee to the river," Skye said.

"Help me up."

Skye and Victoria lifted Mercer. It was not easy. His arms were useless. They handed him the reins, knowing he could barely hold them, and started off once again, Skye leading his company.

A while later they hit a giant canyon running toward the river and Skye turned into it. This was white-rock country, with crenellated bluffs along the skyline.

They reached a flat with a fine cold spring bubbling out of

a white cliff, and plenty of brush and trees below it. Skye stopped there. This was as close to paradise as a camper could get and there was the promise of game.

"Go on, go on," Mercer said.

Skye reached up. "Time for you to get some rest. I'll hand you down."

"Go on, go on, damn your cowardly hide."

Whatever Skye did, Mercer contradicted. Find a campsite. Don't find a campsite. Stop here. Don't stop here. Keep going. Don't keep going. Skye ignored it all.

This was a good place. Skye rode Jawbone around the meadow, finding thick grass for the domestic and wild horses. He checked the brush, finding no bears or other trouble. He returned to the others just in time to hear Mercer berating Mary.

"Keep your greasy hands off me," he snarled.

Mary, who was helping him down, paused.

"Get me off this nag, Skye," Mercer snapped.

Skye stared.

"You do it, Skye. Your women are full of vermin. I don't want them touching me."

Victoria and Mary stopped cold.

"That got your attention, didn't it, Skye?"

Mercer decided he could dismount himself and almost managed. But he lost hold and tumbled into the clay.

"Help me up, Skye."

"I think you can stay right there, sir."

"East London scum. Deserter. Louse-ridden squaws. Degenerate. I thought you were an Englishman. How did I get tied up with this lot?"

Skye resisted the rage welling up in him and nodded to the women. They turned away, collected deadwood, and soon had a fire going.

It was a temptation to leave the man and his horse to fend for himself, but Skye knew he would not. There are obligations and duties and one of them is to get a feverish man to safety, and another is to fulfill a contract. He had promised to deliver this man to Fort Benton and so he would.

They rolled the cursing Mercer onto his robe and dragged him into the shade of a giant willow tree.

Stonily, Victoria began preparing her medicinal tea for the explorer. She had one bark to calm him and a root to mitigate his pain. Skye wished she had one that would heal his distemper.

Mary heated stones she had collected and placed next to the crackling fire. These would be lowered in a small well-greased leather sack containing Victoria's herbs and water. The stones would bring the water to boil and Victoria would have her tea. They had lost their metal pots in the great fire, and the women were resorting to ancient methods.

It was a splendid day but for the sourness emanating from Mercer. Skye studied the horizons, where puffball clouds rose and marched across the heavens and slid out of sight. The weather would change soon. There were mare's tails high in the sky, a forerunner of change. It would turn cold and cloudy, and maybe rain some. Maybe they would have to put up the lodge if the weather turned. Skye checked the site to make sure it was well above any flash flood watercourse. It was well placed, ten feet above the gully that might carry water in a deluge. He had chosen a good place. That was his business. His skill. His way of life. His communion with the whole natural world had meant survival and safety for all the while he had been in North America.

Mercer's distemper spread like a miasma and Skye and his women steered clear of him, keeping out of shouting range. But in time Victoria had her tea, so she filled a horn with it and carried it to the shade of the willow, where Mercer glared up at her. He sat up, and she held it to his lips because he couldn't use his arms.

"This is an abomination!" Mercer yelled.

Skye heard Victoria responding quietly. She was telling him her tea would comfort him and reduce his pain and swelling.

"Filthy squaw!"

He heard disorder over there and hastened to the willow tree. Mercer's robe was soaked. The horn lay on the earth, empty. Victoria's leather skirt was splattered.

"Get this wahine slut away from me!"

Victoria bolted. Skye stood, staring at the explorer, whose face reflected triumph. The man was enjoying every moment of this.

"Afraid of me, aren't you, Skye. You won't even defend the virtue of your women. I insult them and you don't even respond. I insult you, and you just let it pass. That's because you're a degenerate."

The bright light of day filtered through the willow leaves, giving the shade a dappled, friendly light. But it was not a friendly place.

Skye patiently considered this fevered man's transgressions. "If I respond softly or say nothing, and take whatever guff you dish out, you'll enjoy it. That would mean I'm your servant. If I say anything at all about your conduct, you'll take it as proof that you're a well-born Englishman dealing with an insolent underling. If I don't seem to mind the offenses to my wives, that means I'm a degenerate, as you put it." Then he offered his own mysterious response. "Address me as Mister Skye, sir."

"Mister! Mister! What fun you are, Skye."

"Victoria will try again to give you some tea. It helps. I've sipped it time after time when I needed help. It's an anodyne for pain. It quiets your distemper. You can knock the horn away again or drink up and feel better."

"Don't let that pile of filth in here, Skye."

Skye plucked up his hat and retreated into the clean sun and sweet air. It was as if he had the Black Plague in his own camp, lurking there, impossible, cruel, rude, and full of white men's conceits.

"Don't go over there, Victoria."

She laughed, suddenly and unexpectedly. "White men are such savages," she said.

"I will try to help him," Mary said.

"You'll be abused."

She shrugged.

Mary dipped the hollow horn into the steaming tea and then carried Victoria's potion to the tree sheltering Mercer, and knelt beside him. There was some muffled talk at first.

Skye waited, ready to do whatever was required. It didn't take long. He heard hard male laughter, a surprised feminine response, and she stormed away. The stain of the tea was spreading across her skirts. She was straightening them as she fled.

She stood in the sunlight, tears welling in her eyes, her small fists clenched.

Skye hurried to her and took her in his arms. "You did what you could," he said.

"That ain't it," Victoria said, obviously annoyed at Skye.

"What do you mean?"

"Don't be so blind," Victoria retorted. "He insulted her."

Skye felt Mary collapse into him, cling to him, and felt her tears soak his shirt. Skye held her for a long while but she seemed taut.

Finally, when Mary had calmed, Skye slipped over to Mercer and found him flat on his back on his buffalo robe, his eyes fevered and merry.

"If you touch my women or insult them, I'll kill you," Skye said.

"But why, Skye?" Mercer asked, his eyes bright. "What don't the three of you do each night?"

# forty-four

s that day waned, so did summer. Skye watched a gray mass rise on the north-western horizon, and knew the seasons were changing. This land often received an equinox storm and this would be it. Whippets of cold air snaked through the coulee.

The women wordlessly undid the lodgepoles and erected them on the flat, well above the dry watercourse, but they stayed as far from Mercer as they could go. Gusts of air made it hard to raise the lodge cover. Skye wanted to help, but they had always chased him off. They soon tugged the heavy cover upward and pinned it together with willow sticks. Victoria, squinting into the rising wind, began collecting the heaviest rock she could carry and pinned down the lodge. Mary collected armloads of deadwood and stored most of it within the small lodge.

Skye looked to the horses, checked their pickets, released Jawbone to discipline his wild bunch, and headed for Mercer. The explorer had wrapped his robe tightly about him under the willow, and stared malevolently up at Skye.

"Maybe you'll have to drag me into the lodge if it rains, Skye. Then I'd ruin your sport," Mercer said.

Skye wheeled away. He had no intention of sharing his lodge with Mercer if he could help it. But an icy rain would change matters. He would do what he had to do. He would shelter the fevered man even if that man was as loathsome as any Skye had ever met. Not many days past, Skye mused, he had liked the man.

He walked away from the willow to the sound of Mercer's cruel laughter resonating behind him.

There wasn't much to eat. They were down to a little pemmican. Skye knew that the eve of a storm was a very good time to hunt so he pulled his old Hawken from its sheath, checked it, and headed down the coulee hoping to scare up some meat. Jawbone trotted behind, an uninvited guest, but Skye let him come. The horse might be handy to drag a carcass to camp.

The farther he got from Mercer, the better he felt. He worried not so much about Victoria, who was tough, but Mary, who was open and vulnerable to Mercer's cruel taunts. Tonight in the darkness of the lodge he would gather his younger wife to him and simply hold her, and let his embrace tell her all that there was in him to say to her.

He saw the yearling buck frozen across the dry watercourse, its two spikes all the antler it could manage at that age. He lifted his Hawken, aimed at the heart, and squeezed the trigger. The old Hawken barked, its voice lost in the whirling wind, and the young mule deer crumpled where it stood.

"I am sorry," Skye said. "You will give us meat and life."

It was the Indian way to apologize to an animal just killed, and Skye had gotten into the habit of it. It was good, and was a reminder to spare life, take only what was necessary for food.

Jawbone trotted beside Skye across the rocky dry wash and up the grassy slope beyond, where the deer lay. It was dead. Skye's shot had gone two or three inches below where he had sighted, a fault of that particular weapon, but it had killed cleanly.

The young buck was too heavy to lift or drag but Skye was not three hundred yards from camp, so he returned, saddled Jawbone, collected some woven elk-skin rope, and returned to his meat.

It took Jawbone no time to drag the deer, by its hind legs, back to the camp. Skye looked for a place to hang the carcass, wanting any spot other than the willow tree where Mercer lay. He finally settled on a cottonwood near the cold spring. With the help of the women he raised the buck and began work. There was little time before full dark and maybe rain. He gutted the deer, scraped out the cavity, and then butchered a rib roast. It was cold and bloody work and the deepening dark made it dangerous too. But both of the women were with him, peeling away hide, sawing into tender meat, and soon, just before utter blackness overwhelmed them, they collected some venison steaks and ribs, and carried them to the lodge.

Skye raised the carcass several feet higher, and hoped that would discourage uninvited guests. But he doubted that he could lift the carcass out of bear range. It had grown so dark he could scarcely make out the lodge, and he hastened that way, aware that the temperature had dropped in minutes. Just before, it had been a mild summer's eve. Now it was wintry, not much above freezing.

Maybe it would cool off Mercer's fever.

The rising wind made it impossible to start a fire outside the lodge, though that would have been preferable for cooking meat. The sparks from their flint and steel flared and died without igniting any tinder. Victoria, muttering, gave up and headed into the deep dark of the lodge, heaped some tinder under the smoke hole of the shuddering lodge, and nursed the tinder into flame.

The women fed tiny sticks into the fire while Skye marveled at the bright warmth. One moment the world was dark and alien; now a tentative blaze was blooming in the lodge, casting friendly bouncing light everywhere.

They would need to cook the meat by suspending it over the flame on green sticks. Victoria sliced the bloody meat into thin strips, jabbed sticks into them, and set them beside the small fire. It would take a long time.

Looming out there in the night was the presence of the explorer, the ghost under the willow tree. Skye hoped the rain would hold off. He hoped this night not to suffer Mercer in close quarters. But he knew, somehow, it was a futile hope. There was rain-smell in the breeze and before long the rattle of rain would be heard on the lodge cover. He hoped the old lodge given them by the Atsina would turn the water and had been kept well greased.

It was odd. There in the sweet warm intimacy of their lodge, the world was good. Just outside, not eighty yards distant, lay a man who exuded evil: whose eyes and tongue were evil, whose sweat and spit and urine were evil, whose foul breath was evil. Mercer had not always been that way, but now he was a man unloosed from all restraint.

The rain hit as suddenly as a thunderclap. One moment the wind was eddying; the next, a roar thundered down on the lodge, spitting water through the smoke hole, each drop hissing in the fire.

Skye arose, wrapped a robe around him, and plunged into the night. He could scarcely get his bearings. He headed toward the willow tree, found it, found Mercer sitting against the trunk, wrapped tightly in the robe.

"Come," Skye yelled over the roar.

"Ah, the degenerate Skye is going to let me live!"

Skye whirled at him. "You will keep your silence. If you offend my women, I will put you out. Your fate is yours. Live or die."

Mercer laughed. Even in that darkness, Skye could see those even white teeth all in a row.

Skye helped the man up and then plunged into the driving cold rain. Mercer followed.

"Bloody cold," he yelled.

Skye didn't answer. He was done talking to Mercer. The next words he would say to the man would be, *Get out*. They made the lodge and stumbled into its warmth. The rain was driving at enough of a slant so that little was entering the smoke hole. Victoria had adjusted the wind flaps well, as always.

It had been eighty yards, but Skye's and Mercer's robes were drenched. Mercer stumbled in and Skye pointed to a place at the door, on the right, the place of least honor. This guest in Skye's lodge would not be given the place of honor next to him, at the rear.

"Bloody wet evening," Mercer said. He slid to the ground and cast aside his robe, its pictographs suddenly visible in the wavering light. Then he had the sense to stay quiet.

Victoria fed deadwood into the fire. It flared, and the meat roasting on sticks next to it bled juices. Skye settled back in his damp robe. He was thinking of a fine chill fall, with air crisp and clean, the sun warm on his back, heading toward Victoria's people after depositing this man in Fort Benton. He was thinking of his newfound wealth, a hundred pounds, money to buy a new rifle, some blankets for his women, maybe some spectacles if one of the posts had some ready-mades. His eyesight was changing. It was harder to read and harder to see things at great distances. A hundred pounds would buy him a fine pair of cheaters.

The women busied themselves in deep silence. Neither they nor Skye could escape the presence of that man lying there next to the door of the lodge. Now and then the lodge shuddered under the impact of a gale wind, and always the staccato roar of rain drowned out everything but the thoughts in one's head. The lodge began to drip in a few places, single beads of water slowly collecting, trembling, and then falling to earth. Skye rose, cut some white fat off the meat, let it soften in the heat, and then began rubbing the leaking spots. It did no good. This rain would drive through a pinhole.

The meat finally was brown and hot, and its savory fragrance filled the lodge. Victoria silently pulled a stick free, its slice of meat pendant on it, and handed it to Mercer, who accepted it with clumsy hands. It fell to the ground. He stabbed it and lifted it up.

He cleared his throat. "Mister Skye, Madame Skye, and Madame Skye," he said. "I apologize to you for offensive remarks and equally offensive conduct. Thank you for letting me stay in this lodge."

That was as startling as an earthquake.

"I am very sorry," Mercer concluded.

No one spoke.

Time had frozen.

"Well, eat up," said Skye. "Plenty of meat here, killed a buck, enough meat to fetch us to Fort Benton."

Mercer bowed his head. "We thank thee, Lord, for these thy gifts."

Skye paused. The women stared.

They ate in silence.

Which person residing in that body was Graves Mercer?

*forty-five*

The Missouri River is a tough stream to ford, even at low water. Skye had to get his party across it to reach Fort Benton. He didn't know which ford to use so he followed the trail most heavily worn, and found it winding into an ancient bed of the river and then around a bend to the actual channel where the river sparkled. The adobe fort loomed across the water on a broad flat, its bastions guarding its walls. Lodges were scattered around it.

This trail took Skye and his party upriver a mile and then it dropped straight toward the water's edge close to the smaller opposition post, Fort Campbell. The river ran low now but that was a lot of river between the south bank and the north, and the water wasn't moving slowly, either. It was hurrying here, sucking at anything in its way.

Skye turned to Mercer. "I'm going to have Victoria lead your horse."

Mercer nodded. He had been subdued ever since that night of the storm. His hands were all but useless, and Skye didn't want him trying to rein a horse, especially if the ford involved a drop-off and the horses had to swim a channel. It would be all Mercer could manage just to stay in the saddle.

Victoria took Mercer's reins. Behind them, Mary was herding the packhorses and the wild bunch trailed along at its own pace. They were all on the bank, staring at the icy water, which showed not a ripple that might suggest a ledge or a ford.

"Let me sound it out," Skye said, steering Jawbone toward the cold water. The horse hated cold, laid back his ears until they were flat on his skull, and then minced in, high light steps that splashed water everywhere. The ford descended quickly until water was pushing at Jawbone's belly, and Skye was keeping his feet high and forward. The flow threatened to push Jawbone off balance but the determined young animal bulled ahead and then suddenly the bottom rose. They could traverse the river there without swimming.

Jawbone clambered up the north bank and shook himself so violently he almost tossed Skye to the ground. Skye watched the others plunge in, start a hundred-fifty-yard passage. It went smoothly. Mercer kept his balance even when his horse began sidestepping under the pressure of the flow. Victoria made it, but her moccasins and lower skirts were soaked. Mary had a hard time dragging the packhorses into the river, and in the middle, when the current was wetting their bellies, two of them bolted forward, the packs rocking on their backs, the lodgepoles and lodge careening behind them. The wild bunch simply swam. Then, suddenly, they were on the north side, water rolling off them, thoroughly chilled. The sun had lost its summer's potency and now was a wan and subdued friend.

The American Fur Company post stood downriver, its flag flapping quietly. Skye had worked for the company back in the beaver days. Now its business was buffalo hides and peltries of all sorts.

There it was. Civilization of a sort. It basked in the bright light, snugged under yellow bluffs. It had been erected maybe fifty yards back from the riverbank.

Every hour of every day the clear cold water of the Missouri, fed by mountains upstream, hurried past on its way to the Gulf of Mexico. For Yanks, it was passage home. For Skye and Mary and Victoria, it was just another big stream.

This was a sleepy afternoon hour. Skye saw no one moving through the scatter of lodges around the post, or anyone entering the massive, and wide open, front gate. He rejoiced. His long hard journey was done. He would soon have Mercer settled there, awaiting transport downriver. Then Skye and his wives would stock up. Five hundred dollars was a lot of money. It would buy rifles and blankets and tools and kettles and horse tack. It would fix his family's fortunes for a year or two.

He had done it: taken the London explorer where he wanted to go, shown him what he wanted to see, saved him from fire and other disasters, nursed his health, shared stories. Skye had faithfully done what he was hired to do and had done it well. Now would be the harvesttime, a farewell to the adventurer. They would outfit and head south. Who knows where? Victoria's people, maybe. Fort Laramie, maybe. There was work to be found at Laramie, on the Oregon Trail. People wanted guides with them.

But all that could wait. He watched Victoria wring out her skirts, Mary smooth the doeskin and let its water drip away. He watched Mercer, who sat quietly, eyeing the fur post a mile distant.

It was time to move. Skye led them along the riverbank,

past the opposition post, over level meadow worn by the passage of countless horses. They reached the scatter of sagging buffalo-hide lodges that dotted the plain. Then Victoria urged her pony forward until she was alongside Skye.

"Sarsi!" she said.

He studied the lodges, not certain of it. "You sure?"

"The same ones!"

Skye was suddenly grateful they were in the powerful reach of the post. He slowed until Mercer caught up.

"Victoria says those are Sarsi lodges and likely the same bunch. It makes sense; come south to visit the bones, come here to trade before going back to British possessions."

"You don't say! Will they . . ."

Mercer's sudden fear was palpable.

"Posts are safe ground. They won't touch you."

"But, Skye. Sarsi? Protect me! What if . . ."

"Mister Mercer, sit up. We'll ride in there and you have nothing to worry about."

But as they approached and were recognized, they had plenty to worry about. Sarsi swiftly congregated around them, their gaze on Mercer, following along with every step of the horses, even as Skye's party pierced the great gate and entered the post's yard, a small rectangle girt by high adobe walls, the warehouse, and other rooms.

They were the same band of Sarsi, all right. There was the headman, he who had a secret name, and there were the others. Mercer began chattering and shivering. He seemed half wild. A few of the post's engaged men materialized from various rooms, their dress drab compared to the brightly clad young Sarsi.

Skye looked for trouble and saw none. The Sarsi stood in deep silence, their gaze riveted upon the one back from the dead. Skye spotted a man who might be in charge.

"Can anyone talk the Sarsi tongue?" he asked.

"Yes. And you?"

"Skye, sir. Mister Skye."

"Ah! I should have known. I'm Ezekiel Lamar. Let me fetch the trader."

"Good!"

Skye hoped it might be Alexander Culbertson, who had governed this post for a generation but had retired to Peoria, Illinois, with his Blackfoot wife Natawista. Culbertson had come upriver frequently since then, sometimes bringing the annuities the Yank government gave to the Blackfeet, sometimes bringing the post its resupply from the American Fur Company. Officially, he was still the post's factor even though he was largely an absentee one and in charge of all the upper Missouri posts for American Fur.

But it was no man Skye knew: a beefy Scot, Andrew Dawson.

Skye dismounted and shook hands.

"What brings these Sarsi in here? Why do they stare at that man? Who's this fellow?" Dawson asked.

Skye made the introductions. "Mister Mercer is the explorer, here from London, collecting stories."

"Fine, fine, but why are these Sarsi staring at him?"

They were indeed staring, their gazes riveted on Mercer, who shrank under them, rubbing his arms, and looking about ready to leap off his horse and flee.

"Long story, Mister Dawson. But would you do the honors?"

The trader nodded.

"Tell their headman, whose medicine is to reveal no name, that Mister Mercer lives. See what the man says."

Dawson conducted a considerable conversation with the headman, using no hand-sign that Skye could follow.

"It seems that his people sacrificed Mercer to the spirit of the big bones but here he is. That can only mean that Mercer has powerful medicine. They have gathered here to see the medicine man, dead and now alive, bearing the bruises of his death. This makes not a bit of sense to me, Skye."

"I would be most grateful if you called me Mister Skye, sir."

"Yes, yes, your reputation precedes you. But here they are. There's Mercer. And now he's the object of their veneration, it seems."

Mercer began laughing wildly. "Bloody savages, almost murdered me, left me to die, killed my teamster too. And now they think I'm bloody immortal. Hang the whole lot, I say, string every one up, send them all to hell."

Skye started to object but Dawson suddenly loomed large, standing close to Mercer and his horse. "Mister Mercer, they're in awe of you. They have their own beliefs about life and death. They are friends of us all. There will be no more of that talk. They trade here. Friendly people, friends of the Piegans and Bloods. Do not make trouble for yourself."

"Make trouble for myself! My God, man, they made trouble for me! They tied me up and left me to perish! Hang the lot!"

Dawson was not pleased. He turned to the headman and spoke at length and listened at length. Then he turned to Mercer.

"You are absolutely safe among them."

Mercer nodded curtly, dismissing the Sarsi. "When can I get transportation downriver?"

Skye stared. Mercer had turned abrupt and demanding again, his gaze imperious, his manner imperious, his posture lordly. He was addressing underlings and servants and rabble.

"No one is traveling that I know of, sir. Not until spring."

"Then find me a boat! I'll go myself!"

Dawson smiled. "Mister Mercer, dismount, I pray. Come join us for a supper. We've much to discuss."

"I will not abandon this horse until these vermin are driven out of this place."

Dawson saw how it was with Mercer.

"They wish to place gifts at your feet. They wish to be touched by the man with medicine. They wish to bestow a name, He Who Has Come from the Bones."

Skye helped Victoria and Mary off their ponies and began putting his horses into the pen with the help of Lamar. Out in the yard, Mercer sat his horse, gazed imperiously at the young Sarsi quietly collected around him, and the minutes ticked by without any change at all.

# forty-six

Sundown resolved the impasse. Always at that hour the gates of Fort Benton were closed, and Lamar or another of the engaged men invited any tribesmen within the post to leave.

"Sundown, sundown," the man bawled, and wordlessly the Sarsi retreated into the quiet flat surrounding the post. Mercer watched imperiously, and when the last Indian walked through the massive gate the explorer stepped down, handed his horse to the nearest employee, and headed toward the chief trader's handsome house, which snuggled against one wall of the fort.

Dawson was sitting on its veranda, smoking his pipe, keeping an eye on events. Skye had settled his wives in a small room reserved for women. He would stay in the company barracks along with the engaged men and now sat beside the chief trader. A peace descended on the post along with a sharp chill.

"I shall want a room, sir," Mercer said.

The tone instantly troubled Skye. The man had slipped back into his imperious ways.

"I will be pleased to accommodate ye, Mister Mercer," Dawson said. "The gentlemen bunk just over there."

"A room, Mister Dawson, a room."

"I wish we had one, Mister Mercer."

"You do. Your dwelling here has several rooms."

"This is a private home, sir. It houses either the factor or the chief trader." Dawson suddenly relented. "Ye may have one, if ye wish."

Mercer smiled, a row of white teeth again. "You are a gentleman, sir, welcoming me in this manner."

Dawson rose from his hand-hewn chair, went inside, and a moment later a handsome young Indian woman materialized.

"Letitia will show ye the way, Mister Mercer," Dawson said.

"Good. Just the ticket. What time is dinner, Dawson?"

Mercer scarcely noticed the woman, who picked up the parfleche containing the small sum of Mercer's possessions. But Skye knew intuitively what Dawson's household arrangement was. She was a tall, striking Blackfoot.

Dawson considered it a moment. "We will put food on the table whenever ye are ready, sir. Shall we say an hour?"

"I shall want some duds, Mister Dawson. I shall write you a draft. Let us proceed to the trading room, eh?"

"Can it wait until morning, sir? The room is closed and the day's accounts are in the ledger."

"Surely you can accommodate a man in need of a few items of clothing. I haven't a shirt to my name."

Dawson stirred unhappily. "Very well," he said.

He knocked the dottle from his pipe, left it at his chair, and headed across the yard to the trading room, which was on the river side of the post next to the great gate. He turned to Skye:

"Long as we're about it, is there anything you need?"

"Yes, sir, if you'll accept Mister Mercer's draft."

Mercer hurried up. "What's all this? A draft?"

Skye nodded. "I'll get it."

Mercer laughed oddly.

Skye headed toward his gear, stored in a heap beside his bunk, found the robe with Mercer's debt instrument painted on it, and headed for the trading room. Dawson had lit an oil lamp, which cast yellow light into the far corners. This was a pungent, pleasant place, with thick blankets stacked on shelves, bolts of gingham, trays of cutlery and arrow points, sacks of sugar and flour, barrels of hard candy, a rack of new and used rifles, strings of bright beads, plugs of tobacco, and a hundred other items that Indians bought in exchange for the furs and pelts they heaped on the trading counter each day.

The explorer had already heaped clothing on the hand-sawn counter when Skye pushed in, carrying his heavy buffalo robe.

"A dollar for a ready-made shirt? This is madness! I won't pay it," Mercer was saying. He had a blue chambray shirt in hand, waving it so that the sleeves danced.

"They come a long way, Mister Mercer. At great risk. The company loses ten or fifteen percent of everything in transit, every year. We've had entire boatloads vanish in the river."

"Bosh. I've heard that before. What you do is charge the most you can get away with, and offer the least."

Dawson took it easily. "Yes, and the Opposition upriver does just the same. And if they charge a bit less than we do, or pay a bit more for pelts, we feel it here."

Skye waited quietly while Mercer complained about most of his merchandise. The courteous Dawson nodded and absorbed it. Then the chief trader dipped a steel nib pen into an inkpot and scratched out a bill of sale. Then he pulled a pad of preprinted debt instruments.

"It comes to eighty-seven and forty-two cents, Mister Mercer. I've filled out this instrument. What we need is your signature and the name of your bank, and your endorsement of the clause that says there will be collection fees."

"It's Barclay's Bank," Mercer said. "All right." He signed, initialed the proviso.

Dawson, finished with Mercer, turned to Skye. "What may I do for you, my friend?"

Skye hoisted the robe to the counter, fleshed side up, and showed Dawson the carefully worded instrument painted there. A hundred pounds on account, and signed by Mercer.

Dawson studied it. "A rather unusual draft, wouldn't ye say, Mister Skye?"

"There was no paper."

"Come hither, Mister Mercer. Here's a draft for a hundred pounds on the back of this robe, and it carries your signature. I can cut this out of the robe and ship it to St. Louis, and the company can forward it to London for collection. But I should like your guarantee."

"What's this! What on earth is this?" Mercer glanced at the robe, over which he had spent so much time. "A damned forgery, sir."

Skye felt his blood rise. Suddenly he knew, he *knew* what was coming. "You guaranteed it," he said tautly.

"Guaranteed what? What did I get? You almost got me killed. I got nothing out of the whole trip. You were so incompetent you got me into a fire, failed to protect me from savages, and bungled everything so badly you're lucky I even talk to you."

Skye choked back his mounting rage. "Did we agree on a hundred pounds and did I bring you here safely?"

"We agreed on nothing! I had my own men. I didn't need a bloody guide or some lice-ridden sluts. You claptrap bunch of parasites hung on like leeches, wanting handouts, charity. I couldn't find any way to get rid of you."

Skye tried hard to stay calm. "It's owed me, sir. You were taken where you wished to go."

Mercer grinned. "My gawd, a confidence man of the wilds!" He snatched the inkpot and carefully poured a black puddle over his painfully wrought signature on the leather.

Skye sadly watched the ink spread and sink in.

Dawson looked solemn. "The company asks two-bits a sheet for paper, but I'll donate a sheet. Here, Mister Mercer. Draft a payment for Mister Skye."

"This bloody impostor? This bloody degenerate? For what? Tell me, for what?"

Skye thought to count the ways. For saving Mercer's life just a few days earlier. For showing him strange things, introducing him to strange people worth writing about. For keeping a prairie fire at bay. For putting food before him. For showing him how to survive without white men's tools. For sheltering him from weather. For nursing him through grave illness. For translating among the Indians. For his knowledge of the American West.

But the man was leering at him, triumph in his eyes, enjoying every moment of it. Here was the man, his soul naked.

Dawson intervened. "Mercer. I don't think I'll let ye out of here until ye pay the man."

Mercer's smile was dangerous. "Oh, is that how it is, eh? I'm going to enjoy this. Came along, Dawson. Let's have dinner. Just you and I, eh?"

"I have invited Mister Skye and his wives."

"Squaws? That reprobate at my table?"

"My table, Mister Mercer."

Dawson herded them out of the trading room and locked it with a heavy iron key. He spotted one of his men in the yard and beckoned.

"Mister Mercer will sleep in the yard, or wherever he wishes, and I want you to extract his things from my bedroom."

"Yassum," the man said, hurrying to the house.

"Mister Skye, bring your ladies to dinner."

Skye nodded. The chief trader was the absolute master of this small world and Mercer was finding that out. "We are pleased to join you, Mister Dawson."

"What? What?" yelled Mercer.

"Ye have chosen not to enjoy our company, Mister Mercer. Ye may bed where ye choose. The manger, in the horse pen, makes a good bed, I'm told, if ye pitch in some hay first."

"Oh, Mister Dawson, you think you're god out here, lord of your own world. How little you know."

Dawson ignored the threat. Skye nodded, knowing that no dinner with the chief trader could ever assuage the loss he was undergoing, the demolition of dreams, the brutal discarding of ordinary justice.

Dawson clapped Skye on the back. "A little of Scotland's finest will work a little warmth into ye."

Skye was in no mood for a little warmth. But the darkness evaporated as he fetched his wives from their room. They met him at the door, refreshed, beautiful, and glowing in the evening light.

"We'll be dining with the chief trader," Skye said.

"Something's wrong," Victoria said.

"I'll tell you later."

They were swiftly welcomed into Dawson's home. Mary had never seen a furnished home, every shining piece of furniture in it brought upriver. There were oil portraits of Dawson's ancestors on the wall. She marveled. Victoria had seen such things but that didn't allay her curiosity.

"Where's the explorer?" she asked Skye.

Dawson replied. "He chose not to join us. He chose to bed down out in the horse pen, madam. Welcome. Now, madames, and Mister Skye, shall we have a wee drink, just to whet the appetites?"

They had more than a small drink. They had more than they should have and the next day they didn't remember much.

And the next day they heard that Mercer had been forcibly booted out of Fort Benton at dawn.

# forty-seven

one. Skye learned about it the next day. Graves
Duplessis Mercer had hied himself to the Opposition post, Fort Campbell, discovered that an ex-
press was leaving for St. Louis within the hour, traded his
nags for passage, and hopped aboard a large voyageur's canoe paddled by an engaged man and floated down the river.

If all went well, Mercer would be in St. Louis within a
month and reach London in November. Skye absorbed that
numbly. Now there was nothing in his purse and nothing to
show for hard and dangerous service to the explorer.

He found his women loading the packhorses.

"He's gone," Skye said.

Victoria nodded stonily. "We should not have taken him to
the bones. The spirit has repaid us."

Skye plucked up his robe and headed for the trading
room, and waited patiently while Dawson completed a trade
with a Blackfoot woman, a robe for some hanks of beads.

"I owe you putting up the horses," he said. "Would this
robe do?"

Dawson shook his craggy head. "It would not do, and put it away, man. The bastard skipped, did he? It is a bad thing. I'll send word down the river and maybe something'll come of it."

"We're going to head south," Skye said.

"Not for a little bit."

Skye waited grimly. The chief trader would ask for some labor to pay for horse feed.

"A man gets stiffed, and it's like an arrow through my own heart," Dawson said. "I can lend you a little bit. Pick what you need."

"How'll I pay you?"

"Some robes at any American Fur post. Or one month as an engaged man. After that it's nothing but a bit of bookkeeping."

"I'll do it. Thank you, Mister Dawson."

"Ah, ye'd do the same, would ye not?"

Something unspoken passed between them that made them brothers of the wild.

Skye needed powder and shot, a few tools, an axe handle, and then he indulged in four-point blankets for the three of them, and a bit of foofaraw for the ladies, particularly some bright blue beads they cherished.

Dawson smiled. "It comes to nineteen and a quarter, and ye needn't be in a hurry about it."

"I'm always in a hurry to pay debt."

"That bastard," Dawson said. "He'd better not show his face in any post run by American Fur."

The women had his small caravan readied in the yard and even had saddled Jawbone, ignoring the laid-back ears and snarls emanating from the young stallion.

He handed them their four-point blankets and blue beads.

Mary ran her hand over the smooth nap of the wool, her eyes shining. Hers was cream with blue bands at the ends; Victoria's red with black bands.

"Dammit all to hell, Skye," she said. "Dammit all."

They forded the Missouri and rode into a golden autumnal day, with the air crisp and sweet. The cottonwood leaves were starting to turn. The sun's light sparked off the river. The land seemed clean without Mercer in it.

Leisurely, they drifted south toward the land of Victoria's people, enjoying the rhythms of the horses under them, the cold nights and bright days. Nature was bountiful. Skye shot a buffalo cow and they spent a few days jerking meat and making pemmican, employing chokecherries growing abundantly everywhere. They feasted on hump rib and tongue, watched Jawbone's wild ones fatten, fleshed and tanned the buffalo hide, repaired the old lodge, but always kept a wary eye out for marauding war parties or hunters.

They found the Kicked-in-the-Bellies band of Victoria's people on the Yellowstone, enjoying a fall hunt when the hair was thick and the animals were fat. They wintered that year north of the Yellowstone beneath the Birdsong Mountains, peaks sacred to the Absarokas, a range that stood apart and north of the main chain of the Rockies. Lewis and Clark had called this place Rivers Across because streams debouched into the Yellowstone from north and south there.

It was a good winter, with many guests filling their lodge. Skye and his wives had no trouble preparing a dozen buffalo robes, which would more than pay his debt to the fur company. The cold sometimes enveloped them, and they were forced to bury themselves under a heap of robes in their lodge. The women braved frostbite to collect deadwood to keep the lodge warm. There was never enough wood to keep the north wind at bay. Between the hard work, the elders told stories and passed along the story of the Absaroka people to the next generation. Sometimes they talked about the mysterious bones. Young men prepared themselves for manhood, learned the arts of war, made their vision quests, so they might receive the spirit helper who would guide their lives henceforth.

Skye worked all winter at subduing the wild horses, and eventually he succeeded. These he gave to Victoria's family; they would return the favor if Skye was ever in need of horse-flesh.

When spring was just around the corner and the ground was still frozen so passage was not difficult, Skye packed up his goods and his lodge, and began the long trip south to Fort Laramie on the Oregon Trail. Times were changing and Skye knew it would not be long before this life, lived so amiably by the Crows, would come to an end. Not far away was the time when these people would be placed on reservations. He wanted not only to prepare his women for that but to make a living. The idyll would not last. The time when he could take his rifle out upon the plains and feed and clothe himself with it, and care for his women with it, was drawing to a close.

He knew a certain sutler at Fort Laramie, a Colonel Bullock, who often arranged matters for wayfarers who needed a guide or a responsible party to escort them west. Skye could do that. Many an old trapper was doing it. The Sublettes, Jim Bridger, Broken-Hand Fitzpatrick. It was a living.

So Victoria hugged her family, Mary hugged them too, and they started toward the army post far away on the North Platte River. He knew it well. It had been a fur post for decades before the army bought it and turned it into a supply base and entrepot on the Oregon Trail.

They worked their way around the Big Horn Mountains,

up and down giant shoulders of land, ever southward. They were a solitary family on the move across an endless and hollow land. But one day they struck the Platte and turned east along its well-worn trail, the very trail that had carried thousands of Yanks to the Oregon country, a flood of them each summer. But now there was not a soul on that worn trail. In the mornings the trail was ice-bound and hard; by afternoons soft and exhausting.

Then one afternoon they reached rough country and found themselves in the military reservation of Fort Laramie, crammed into a jaw of land between the Platte and the Laramie Rivers. Mary and Victoria saw the soldiers, cavalrymen in blue, details collecting firewood to feed those hungry stoves or working the cavalry mounts in close drill, or constructing outbuildings.

"They're all the same damn blue!" Victoria said. "Can't tell one from another."

"Army likes it that way," Skye replied.

Victoria grunted. How could a warrior fight if he was the same as every other warrior?

Other groups were receiving instructions in firearms and the tactic of volleying from drill sergeants. A great many of the blue-bellies were caring for horses. A farrier corporal was operating a smithy where horses were being shoed for spring campaigns.

They progressed toward the old adobe and log post, entered a yard, and Skye suddenly headed toward a log structure with a great verandah at its front.

He watched Mary and Victoria absorb all of this. They had little experience with the Yank army, and most of it bitter. Both of his wives were suddenly subdued, aware of power, aware of some sort of medicine in the flapping flag and guidons.

A hitch rail had been planted before the post's store, and there Skye dismounted, tied the other horses, but let Jawbone stand. That horse would not submit to tying, but neither would he roam.

The sheer ugliness of the beast drew the gazes of some of the cavalrymen, who flocked close.

"Better not get too close," Skye said.

"Does he kick?" asked one.

"No, he kills."

The trooper laughed uneasily.

A door clapped, and a black-suited, silver-haired gent boiled out on the verandah. "Well, bless my eyes, sah, it's Mister Skye and his ladies!"

It was Colonel Bullock, the Virginia-born sutler, retired from active service but still in the West because he liked it.

He invited the Skyes to his bailiwick, and they walked past burdened shelves and bags of goods that would put any trading post to shame, back to Bullock's cramped office, where he hastened to supply chairs for his guests.

"Well, Mister Skye, sah, you have magnified and amplified my day. It is good to see you! Now, introduce me to your lovelies."

Skye did. "This, sir, is my dear Victoria and here is my beloved Mary. They both speak excellent English and in that I am most fortunate."

"Worthy wives for a worthy gentleman," Bullock said. "Mister Skye, sah, your reputation abounds. You honor us by your presence. There's not an officer here who doesn't know of you. There are stories told of Mister Skye around every campfire, in each barracks, among all the guests and travelers who drift through this post."

Skye nodded, embarrassed. What had he done that was different from what hundreds of others had done?

Mister Bullock slid his monocle into his eye, much to the alarm of Skye's ladies. "In fact, sah, I have a bundle that arrived by army courier just a week ago. Addressed to Mister Skye, Fort Laramie. It's from the American Fur Company agent in London, I believe. Monsieur Borchgrave. The company does a heap of business there, you know, all through Borchgrave. Well, sah, he sent the bundle here, confident that it would wend its way to you before the year was out. Let me get it."

Bullock dug into a pile of materials behind his desk, and extracted a well-worn package wrapped tightly in butcher paper, its surface begrimed by months of slow passage from England to this far corner of the known world.

Skye reluctantly cut the twine, fearing bad news from his family. But when at last he popped the wrapping off, he discovered a number of newspapers. The *London Times, Manchester Guardian,* and several others. Nothing more. Intuitively, Skye knew what he would find within each one, and he wasn't sure he wanted to read any of them.

# forty-eight

Skye leafed through the yellowed papers. Those around him sat solemnly, awaiting what was to come. These were dated from late November, 1857, to early December. These were about five months old. Mercer had found swift passage to London.

He tried to read but his eyes had changed. He could barely read the print, even at arm's length.

"Do you have some ready-made spectacles, Colonel?"

"A tray of them, Mister Skye."

Colonel Bullock swiftly produced a tray of wire-rimmed eyeglasses, which Skye sampled one by one, and finally settled on one that fit his right eye perfectly and his left eye less sharply. He jabbed the wire around his ears, and found himself able to read. He would buy these as soon as he could.

"This is the *London Times*. It says its correspondent, Graves Duplessis Mercer, is freshly returned from North America, where he spent a season beyond the borders of the Republic, observing strange native cults, odd natural phenomena, and things unknown to the civilized world."

Victoria was frowning. Mary looked rapt, marveling that Mister Skye could examine the marks on this paper and turn them into words and ideas.

" 'In late summer, I witnessed an extraordinary event: a renegade Briton, a deserter from the Royal Navy named Skye, lives like a lord of the wilds beyond the borders. He took it upon himself to acquire a second wife, though his first is perfectly serviceable. Of course I use the term wife loosely, this being a purely whimsical transaction involving female slavery.

" 'The brief transaction proceeded as follows: Skye, a shaggy, degenerate sort who fashions himself a Beau Brummell of the wilderness, adorned with a battered top hat that he believes grants him status, transacted an arrangement with the girl's father, a Shoshone savage with several such daughters to spare. I wasn't able to ascertain the exact purchase price, but young wives go for a pony or two, or maybe a blanket, or a hank of beads. At any rate, the arrangement complete, our wilderness Brummell, with no evidence of so much as a trim of his tangled gray hair, collected this second wife, and hied his way to his ill-kempt lodge, a conical tent made of skins.

" 'Now, here is the mystery: what are the arrangements among wives and this rustic Lothario? The odd cult of the polygamous Mormons, currently settling around the great lake of salty water, is clear enough: each lady has her own household and the master of these domestic nests visits each in turn. But here, hundreds of miles from civilization and law, matters are somewhat different. This master of two wives has but one lodge and was not seen evicting either wife at any hour.

" 'Now, among savages it is a matter of prestige for a headman or chief to acquire several of these willing wives. It is quite common to find an important man possessing half a dozen wives, and these fill his lodge along with his numerous offspring. When the lodge is too small, his wives build him a larger one, so that some lodges house a veritable crowd of all ages, including a few parents and grandparents as well as squalling infants.

" 'The wives prefer it because it lightens the burdens of maintaining the lodge. It falls to women in these rude societies to do the heavy labor. They collect firewood, slaughter game brought to them by their hunter-mates, flesh and tan hides, fashion clothing out of them, produce not only the daily meals, but also the preserved food, dried meat known as jerky, or a mixture of berries, shredded meat, and fat called pemmican. What's more, the senior wife in these savage societies gets to sit beside the master of this odd household, and is called the sits-beside-him wife. She is the boss; the junior wives, often her sisters, are at her absolute mercy. So just what advantage this wretched Shoshone woman gained by being sold into this carnal servitude is not easily fathomed. Nonetheless, on this occasion she was all aglow, having been sold by her father for a fancy bride price and handed over to the degenerate who bid for her.

" 'Skye himself, though once an Englishman—he claims to be born in London but I could not detect it in his voice—has now given himself over to the wild lands and wild practices to be found out beyond the rim of the known world. . . .' "

"Liar," said Victoria.

"You must tell me what those things mean," Mary said.

Colonel Bullock was caught between two impulses, the first to gaze politely on Skye, and the second to guffaw. Skye saw the colonel subside into cautious politeness.

"Let us not pursue this any further," Bullock said, stiffly.

"Do you make me to be a degenerate, Colonel?" Skye asked.

"Of the very worst sort, Mister Skye."

"And am I a rude Beau Brummell?"

"Unsurpassed, sir."

"I note that Mercer alludes to our private arrangements but dodges the matter."

"Censorship, Mister Skye. He could not very well discourse in a public newspaper on the subject without incurring the wrath of the crown's censors. It might even get him in trouble with the church, or the sedition laws, or the blasphemy rules."

"Yes, you have it, Colonel."

"What the hell is this stuff?" Victoria demanded.

Skye turned to her. "Mercer is aching to tell his readers in London that he thinks I . . . ah . . . take my pleasure of both of you, but he can't quite manage to say it."

Mary sat straight in her chair. "Ah, Skye! I wish you would!"

She began to howl happily. Skye was amazed. He thought such a sentiment might rise from Victoria but in Mary it was an astonishment.

Skye suddenly felt the need to steer the conversation elsewhere. That was all too intimate for Colonel Bullock's ears, no matter that the post sutler was an old friend.

"Ah, I shall see about the rest, here," Skye said, rattling papers to restore decorum. "Let me see. There's a piece or two about the prairie fire. It seems he and his teamsters might have survived it without loss if the renegade Skye had not insisted on staying put rather than outrunning the flames."

Victoria looked grim.

"Find the story of the bones," Mary said.

Skye opened several more, and finally found one that might be about bones.

"A Savage Shrine on the Missouri River" was its heading. Skye delved into it, and soon found absorbing material:

"'When the wretch Skye, who was always angling for a small tip with which to buy whiskey, suggested he could take my party to a place on the Missouri River that was sacred to the savages in the area and a great mystery, I immediately was all ears. This was a place of fossil bones buried in sandstone, and known but to a few tribesmen, it having been hidden for aeons from others. He would probably demand a shilling for it, but I succumbed, always on the search for new discoveries.

"'What sort of religion?' I asked, fearful that we would be invading someone's Westminster Abbey.

"'Why, lord love a duck, matey, it's just a heap of bloomin' bones and they have invented mighty stories to explain them," says this rude philosopher of the wilds.

"'With that we proceeded across uncharted country, the oaf getting us lost time after time. I had to straighten him out by employing a compass. But it due course we did strike that mighty trench, after crossing a vast country never before seen by Europeans. Once we hit the river valley, he sobered up enough to know where to go, and in due course we ended in a sinister little flat, shadowed from the world by huge bluffs, and there, under a protective ledge shielding the bones, were the remains of an ancient beast, protruding slightly from the stone.

"'I measured these extraordinary remains, a task which alarmed the older of Skye's squaws, who thought I was some-how violating the spirit whose bones these were. With some sharp questioning, I ascertained that her people believed the bones were those of a monster bird, and out of the beak of this bird her people had come to populate the world. So she considered the bones to be those of her grandfather. Other tribes, it seemed, had similar explanations.

" 'Indeed, these bones were unusual. The skull measured more than six feet in length from snout to the back of the tiny cranial sheath. There were monster femurs and tibia, and the remains of a long tail. One three-toed foot was visible. I took detailed measurements, employing a buffalo hide for a ledger because my journals were destroyed by fire. In due course, having studied the bones, I discerned that they were of a lizard nature. Not a new species, but a sport, a singular anomaly of nature, in which a creature becomes something other than what it was intended by God to be. And so this ordinary lizard simply grew to truly gargantuan proportion and it was easy to see how the superstitious savages could turn the bones into the remains of their gods.

" 'Now about this time, a party of Sarsi, a small band living in crown possessions to the north, came to visit the bones, and this brought peril to me, as they considered my scientific observations to violate some savage taboo of their own. If that lout of a translator, Skye, had been more accurate I might have been spared the ordeal to come, but in fact he was in his cups and botched the whole business and I soon found myself a captive . . .' "

"I have heard enough," Victoria said.

Skye had his fill too, and folded up the papers. "I'll read these some other day. Perhaps you would keep them for me, Colonel."

"May I read them?"

"Just don't believe them."

"How could I possibly believe them? Were you paid?"

"Not a cent."

"Were you tagging along looking for a handout?"

Skye stood. "They all have their stories, don't they? We invent stories to explain everything. Even the way we cheat others."

"If I find clients for you to guide, the first thing I'll do is make sure you'll be paid."

"That would be helpful."

Skye knew the colonel would devour the British papers and during the next days would brim with questions, and maybe some sly humor too. That was all right. Mercer was writing more about himself and his reputation as a great explorer than about the world he had come to explore, and Bullock would understand that.

Skye wondered whether this bundle of half-truths and untruths would hurt him, and decided they would. Truth sometimes hurts, but all lies eventually hurt someone or something. There were people in England who might still remember him, and what would they think now? Mercer had not only cheated him, but had wounded him. But it was not something to brood upon. Mercer was far away.

"I shall entertain myself with these," Bullock said. "Are these to be kept secret?"

"No. They're published."

Bullock considered a moment. "The temptation is to make a fool of Mercer. All I have to do is show these pieces to a few people. But when I reflect on it, Mister Skye, I think I will say nothing. For your sake, and for the sake of your ladies."

"You are a friend, Colonel."

"I mean to be, sah. You are a man of reputation, and I mean to honor it."

# forty-nine

They erected their lodge in a quiet place up the river a bit from the post, out of sight of the fort and its blue-shirts and its gossip. He was at peace. That night, in the sweet dark, he and his wives lay on their backs looking at the stars parading across the smoke hole.

"Mister Skye," said Mary, "I have something to tell you."

"Yes, Mary?"

"We have made a child."

"Made a child? You'll bear a child?" he asked, full of wonder.

"Our child," she said. "Yours and mine. And Victoria's too."

"You lucky bastard," said Victoria.

Skye thought that was as good a verdict as any.

# Author's Note

Graves Duplessis Mercer is based on the real Sir Richard Burton, British explorer, ethnographer, translator, and journalist. In 1860 Burton visited North America, focusing on the polygamous life of the Mormons in Salt Lake City. Burton eventually published forty-three volumes dealing with his explorations, provided thirty volumes of translation, and was fluent in many languages. He was fascinated by the mating practices, rituals, and cults of various tribes and peoples in the Near East, Africa, and Asia, and recorded these in his diaries and journals for many years. He so affronted Victorian sensibilities that he was forced to live the last decades of his life away from England. When he died in 1890, his wife burned the journals.

# DISCARD

6-08

F       Wheeler, Richard S.
            The canyon of bones.